Praise for Ronna Wineberg's Previous Books

Nine Facts That Can Change Your Life

"Wineberg doesn't write the end of the marriage—she ends with the realization as a turning point. The author doesn't resolve anything too cleanly or neatly, which is something she does quite well throughout this collection. It gives the stories more weight and makes them feel more real, and it also makes the tension between old and new lives more acute. There's still more to each story after the author is finished with her characters, and that's what makes this collection so satisfying."—*Kirkus Reviews*

"*Nine Facts That Can Change Your Life* features fifteen vignettes about emotional mutability and the small, silent decisions that precipitate big changes—like the moment when one character, in the midst of an urgent, harried visit to an emergency room, decides she has to leave her husband, the true end before the divorce that follows."—*The Village Voice*

"…the fifteen stories comprising Ronna Wineberg's *Nine Facts That Can Change Your Life* are true literary gems by a writer with a genuine flair for deftly crafting truly memorable characters."—*Midwest Book Review*

"Wineberg plays with our phony sense of certainty and entices us instead to live in a probabilistic cloud of opportunity and possibility—far more promising and self-actualizing. Characters in her collection leave behind the variables that have defined their lives—marriages, religion, community—and befriend strangers in hopes of making new connections and finding new joy. Some are successful and some are not; that's just how probability works."—*Bloom*

On Bittersweet Place

"Wineberg's quintessential American story of belonging, family life, heritage, and pursuing the American dream will resonate with listeners."—*Library Journal* (audiobook review)

"*On Bittersweet Place* is as much the coming-of-age story of the Midwest as a diverse and thriving urban center as it is Lena's."—*The Millions*

Second Language

"While chronicling the ends of relationships, Wineberg is actually planting the beginnings of new life for her characters...These stories possess full, beating hearts that capture our attention and our sympathy. We are immensely attached to the characters. We yearn for understanding in the same way they do."—*Other Voices*

Artifacts
and Other Stories

Ronna Wineberg

 SERVING
HOUSE
BOOKS

Artifacts and Other Stories

© 2022 by Ronna Wineberg

Published by Serving House Books
South Orange, New Jersey

www.servinghousebooks.com

ISBN: 978-1-947175-56-3

Library of Congress Control Number: 2021942564

Member of The Independent Book Publishers Association

First Serving House Books Edition 2022

Cover: Zach Dodson

Author Photo: Whitney Lawson

Serving House Books Logo: Barry Lereng Wilmont

Also by Ronna Wineberg

Second Language
On Bittersweet Place
Nine Facts That Can Change Your Life

To Daniel, Genia, and Simone,
and also to the memory of my mother and father

Acknowledgements

The following stories in this collection have been previously published in somewhat different form.

"Hurricane" appeared in *Eureka Literary Magazine*.

"Dislocation" appeared in *Colorado Review*.

"Second Wife" appeared in *Confrontation*.

"Double Helix" appeared in *North Dakota Quarterly*.

"The Feather Pillow" appeared in *Crone's Nest*, and won Third Prize in the Denver Woman's Press Club Short Story Contest.

"Sleuth" appeared in *Valparaiso Fiction Review*.

"Kaleidoscope" appeared in *Evening Street Review*.

The guess is that there is always a kinship between souls.
Souls are either close to one another or far from one another.
—Isaac Bashevis Singer

The eye never has enough of seeing, nor the ear of hearing.
—Ecclesiastes

Contents

1

Framing the Picture

WHEN MY MOTHER-IN-LAW DECIDED to have open-heart surgery, I noticed a change in my husband, Lew. His mother lived in Boston but often traveled to Manhattan for her medical care; she was certain the best doctors practiced here. Earlier this summer, she had complained of pains zigzagging down her legs. I winced to hear her wheezing when we spoke on the telephone. Now she'd decided to take action.

Rita was the sort of woman who wasn't afraid to speak her mind. With her stylish clothes, her soft dyed blonde hair and pale green eyes, her toned arms glittering with gold jewelry, she was still beautiful. From the first, she had embraced me like a daughter. She bought me gifts, made a point to talk to me. She taught me to soften the color of my hair and buy fine fabrics, not the inexpensive ones my mother had favored.

My mother had been more distant. There were strict rules in our house, a right and wrong. I cleaned up after myself, refrained from cursing and listening to loud music. But when I was a teenager, I stopped going to church, stayed out all night, and finally moved to California for college. I worked as a waitress a few nights a week, drank too much, dabbled in drugs, and drenched myself in imitation Chanel N°5. Weekends, I sketched and snapped photographs by the ocean. I met Lew at a Grateful Dead concert. He was in graduate school, a smart, handsome Jewish boy from the East Coast. I was a confused young woman from Evanston, Illinois, with bleached blonde hair and taut currents of sexuality ricocheting through me.

Rita telephoned to tell us about the surgery. "My doctor up here says I need it." She coughed and paused to take a breath. "I'm coming to New York for a second opinion. If they think my heart is bad, they'll do surgery right away."

Lew and I were each on an extension of the landline.

"This sounds serious, Ma," he said.

"Triple, quadruple bypass. They don't know," she said. "They may

15

need to replace valves. Then recuperation. Cy will come to New York with me. We'd like to stay at your apartment."

Rita had left Lew's father years ago. She hadn't remarried, but had become involved with a number of men over the years. Cy Zucker seemed to be her companion for good.

"Ginny and I will take care of you," Lew said. "You'll stay with us for as long as you like."

"Rita," I said, suddenly breathless. "We'll help you all we can."

I felt odd, after all these years, still calling her Rita, as if there should be a special name for a mother-in-law, an endearment. I could never bring myself to call her "Mom." I needed a word, like the Russian one for grandmother, *babushka,* or the Yiddish word Lew used to describe those in his family, the almost-related, not by blood but bound by circumstance. *Mishpachah.* A grand, warm family, like the one I had longed for as a child.

Rita's mother once told me that forty days before a child is born, the child's groom or bride is determined in heaven. I loved her stories. She was a gnarled old woman with a gummy smile. She spoke as if she were God's own messenger.

But I wondered whether those in heaven also decided the exact moment when two people who believed they were meant for each other suddenly realized they were not. Was it predetermined that some would find happiness, while others would never discover their intended? Did God also decide who would have open-heart surgery and survive? I wanted to ask Lew's grandmother this, or my mother, but both of them were dead. My father had left us when I was a child. All I had was my mother-in-law, and I could hardly ask her.

I tried not to think about how these losses had affected my life. I often felt as if I wandered in a perpetual rainstorm, without protection. There was Lew, but the protection of a parent or grandparent was different from what a spouse could give. My mother—may her soul be kissed, cared for, and all the other blessings one hopes for a spirit—had never lost her God-like power to try to protect and defend; she retained an omnipotence and wisdom even after she'd died.

There was so much to worry about after we finished our

conversation with Rita. I pulled back my wavy brown hair and twisted it into a ponytail. Would she be okay if she had surgery? What would it be like to have Rita and Cy—a relative stranger—living with us for who knew how long?

It was July and hot in the apartment, even though our window air conditioners were turned up high. I sank into the living room sofa and stared at the dust balls that gathered on the bookshelves. I worried about the world, too. The stock market had lost 200 points in an afternoon. Would there be enough money to retire? Would we even be alive to retire? I owned a framing business and worked in our apartment. A young woman I had done framing for had gone mountain climbing in the west and when she returned, she felt fatigued. The doctor found melanoma. She died, just like that, six weeks later. Another customer, a friend, had died of leukemia. He'd had a heart transplant, and he'd contracted leukemia from the donor. His wife had died in the World Trade Center. Their two children were orphans. It was almost too much to bear.

Here today, gone tomorrow, honey, my mother always said, the sweet scent of her lilac perfume swirling around her. Now Rita might have serious surgery.

I shared all this with Lew that night in bed.

"The more people you know," he said, "the more you hear about tragedy."

"I suppose." I slid close to him, encircling his large, bony hand with mine. I marveled at his practical view of loss and death. "Don't you ever become overwhelmed by emotion and just break down? Even inside yourself?" I said. "Like with your mother. The possibilities. She's really sick, honey."

He was silent, then sighed. "Of course, I feel bad about *things*. I feel terrible about her surgery." Then he smiled. "Maybe my tear ducts are stuck."

But Lew wasn't joking the next morning. "This is not a small thing, Ginny," he said gravely as he poured cornflakes into a blue porcelain bowl. "She's seventy-nine." His dark bushy brows squeezed together and his jaw tightened, just as it did when he sat bent over our finances, calculating assets, liabilities, or investment losses.

That expression of Lew's, the one he reserved for upsetting situations, alarmed me. I imagined his blood pressure rising, anxiety pumping in his chest. And I was alarmed, too, because I knew that having Rita and Cy here for an extended period would put enormous stress on Lew and me.

"If the operation has to happen, then so be it," Lew said, resigned. After breakfast, he collected his keys and wallet from our oak dresser, ready to go to work. He wore a white shirt and khaki pants, no tie. He slipped on a blue blazer. His body was solid and muscular; he bicycled and jogged to keep in shape. He was partially bald, and his gray hair created a neat line across his scalp. "If she needs surgery, we'll do it."

"The nurses and doctors do it," I said.

He smiled. "I mean, we'll take care of her. We'll go to the hospital. Every day. The horror stories I've heard. Missed medications, the wrong surgery done. I'm going to protect my mother."

I'd never seen this instinct so fiercely in Lew before, not even with our two children. He was a man's man, and distant; long ago I had begun to think he was too distant. We'd had our share of problems. Nine years ago, he'd had an affair with an old girlfriend. I'd discovered condoms and a hotel receipt in his pocket when I dropped off his jacket at the cleaners. I was devastated. But I loved Lew and didn't want to lose him. Our children were still at home. I didn't want them raised by single parents. I worried about money. I didn't want to lose the warmth of Lew's family either. And I remembered how lonely my mother had been without my father.

Lew had ended his affair, and I'd gotten past it; I'd forgiven him. We had worked on our relationship. I didn't like to dwell on problems. We looked to the future, and, for a while, we were closer.

But I realized as he left for work now that our closeness had slipped away; he had changed, even before his mother became ill. He had become short-tempered and preoccupied. Both of us were at fault, I knew, each involved in our work. But I couldn't lie to myself. I was concerned about our marriage. What if Lew had another affair? And I had begun to understand that practicality was his passion. Not emotion or art or intimacy. I hadn't noticed this when we first married, but now I did. When life flowed smoothly, he seemed happy. When it didn't, his irritation rose to the surface like a lightning storm.

Lew was a neurobiologist at City College and studied the eyes in zebra fish. When we had lived in California, we used to sit by the ocean, and I would draw while he collected rocks and specimens of seawater. He loved to study zebra fish, he told me, because they were transparent. You could watch their development without a microscope and see what was inside them. Lew wanted to travel to Uganda and the Amazon, study species of fish there and compare them to zebra fish. Our son and daughter were in college. Our son had struggled with ADHD, and together, Lew and I had guided him, found tutors and medicines. Now our son was doing well, and I was grateful for that. But I was right in the middle of my life. I didn't want to go to Africa or the Amazon. I longed to stay in one place, spend more time with Lew, retire my mats and frames and start to paint, as I had been doing when he and I had met.

Rita and Cy arrived three days later. Cy had been a lawyer and, before that, a pilot in the Air Force during World War II. He had thin white hair, a long nose, and the bulky shape of a football player.

He didn't really intimidate me, but I didn't know what to say to him.

"Say anything," Lew said. We stood in our bedroom. "He's just a person."

"But he's here, in the apartment." I shook my head. "I don't really know him. I can't leave him alone. I can't work while he's here. He's our guest. An elderly man. Someone has to take care of him."

"My mother will."

"No, she won't," I said tartly. "We're taking care of *her*."

Rita and Cy were staying in the spare bedroom. My framing studio stood in an adjoining room. All I needed sat there: a computer, mats and frames, a long wooden table cluttered with customers' orders, rulers, and X-Acto knives.

"She can't take care of anyone. She's having surgery," I said.

"We don't know that for sure. The doctors have to decide."

"You see how she breathes and limps," I said, impatient with Lew's denial. "Look at reality; they're going to put her in the hospital and cut into her."

His long, handsome face turned pale. "I hate when you talk like that. Cut into her. This is serious. Have some empathy. Be kind to Cy." He frowned and yanked a wisp of gray hair behind his ear. "You only think about yourself. I hate your fucking neuroses."

"And I hate it when you talk to me like that." I walked out of the room. Perhaps it was better to have a companion, I thought suddenly, like Rita did.

Rita's illness tapped something dark and ugly in me. In Lew, too. As if unhappiness was seeping into our lives. It was August now, hot and muggy. She and Cy had been in our apartment for two weeks. Lew was grouchy, parceling out his time between his mother and the zebra fish. I wished everyone would go away. My framing projects languished.

Two young women worked with me part-time, and the business was doing well. The overhead at home was low, better than a city rental. I specialized in museum-quality preparations, but we framed everything. Kimonos in big boxes. Beer bottles. Paintings. Photographs. In the spring, I had even framed Michael Fox's toilet paper; a house painter had grabbed a few pieces when he had worked at the celebrity's apartment. I'd learned that everything depended on how you looked at things, framed them. The celebrity's toilet paper looked like art now, encircled by a beige linen mat and mahogany frame. People longed to trap life, preserve it in the act of living it, infuse a moment with immortality.

I did this, too. I took photographs, framed them, and hung them in the hallway of the apartment. Lew and I in front of the Fillmore Auditorium, his beard dark and full, my hair so blonde it looked as if I'd poured on bottles of bleach. Lew, my mother, and my childhood friend Wendy at our wedding in the yard at Rita's house. Wendy and I were still friends now. She lived in Boulder. Her father-in-law lived in Manhattan, and every few years or so she visited him here.

There were photos of Lew and me as happy young parents; our son and daughter as babies. Graduations. I realized there were no photographs from the last few years.

In ten years, I hoped to retire. I loved my work, but I wanted the problems and disgruntled emails to stop: *The frame doesn't match the walls. You'll have to do it over. A hundred dollars for that?* And I wanted to get back to my painting and drawing, the still lifes and portraits. Colored pencils lay on my desk unused. My drawing pad sat unopened.

The first week Rita and Cy had stayed with us, I had appointments to keep and deadlines. I delayed other projects, the gluing and sawing, the carpentry of frames, which I loved to do. It seemed indulgent to construct frames while Rita endured tests and evaluations. She returned to the apartment each day exhausted. Lew accompanied her to appointments. Cy sat aimlessly in our living room.

On my calendar, I penciled *Hospital Duty* for the next four weeks. The doctor had told Rita she needed to have the surgery, but he wanted her to take more tests first and consult with more doctors. Every morning Cy waited at the kitchen table for his breakfast. I prepared his oatmeal and bananas, a slice of unbuttered whole wheat toast, and his coffee with two packets of Sweet'N Low. He ate in silence.

My mother had prepared breakfast for my father every day of their married life. "How stupid," I once told her when I was a teenager. "What were you, his slave? Cooking, and then he leaves you."

"You'll see when you grow up, honey," she'd said. "Husband and children. You'll be good to them. You'll be laughing all the way to the kitchen."

My mother was from Chattanooga. She pronounced the word as if it were a sultry endearment. *Noooga*. As if she were making love to the sounds. "Don't ever forget, I'm from Chatta*nooga*, honey. That makes you half southern. That's the soft, sensual, alive part of you."

She was an outsider in Evanston, with her soft drawl, layers of makeup, and the straw hats she wore in the summer. She had moved there with my father. Now I felt like an outsider in New York. A Midwesterner. Lew and I had moved from Chicago for his work seven years ago. Though I had wanted to come here, I had never gotten used to this city. The sharp staccato voices, the shrill horns and traffic. Lew had *shpilkes* like the city did. He was always busy, never stopped. When we met, I had admired this.

Now he and I rarely spent time together. Lew worked long hours on his experiments. I hadn't noticed so much when I was involved with framing, friends, and the children.

"You could go to the doctor with Rita," I said to Cy after breakfast one morning. "Keep her company."

He glanced up from his paperback Nero Wolfe mystery. He was sitting in the armchair in the living room. He shook his head. "I'd be in the way." *The New York Times* lay on his lap.

"You and I could go to a museum," I suggested, trying to think of ways to entertain him.

"Thank you. I'm happy right where I am," he said.

While he read or paced in the living room, his bulky body clothed in gray pants, a neat white shirt with gold cuff links, and a blue tie, I decided to clean the apartment. I sponged the inside of the kitchen cabinets and organized the spices. I pulled items from beneath the sink in the bathroom that the children had used: hair dryers, bent tubes of toothpaste, the old red hot-water bottle with the patched rip. I dusted the night table in Lew's and my bedroom, sponged off the flashlight I kept there for emergencies. I inserted a new battery.

I couldn't concentrate with Cy rustling the newspaper or pacing, and Lew grumpy, Rita limping to her appointments. Cleaning took my mind off things. After I hauled out the trash bags of useless, neglected items, I returned to my room and worked.

Each day, I tackled a different area of the apartment, as if I were readying myself. For the hospital visits in the next weeks, I supposed. For my conversations with Cy.

"You sure clean a lot," he said one day. He had a deep, gravelly voice.

I laughed. "It's a hobby of mine."

"Doesn't give you much time for anything else."

"Keeping busy keeps the devil away." I smoothed a wrinkle on my jeans. "My mother always said that."

He shrugged. "My wife used to clean like that. All day while I was away. I was so busy. The law was my mistress. One case after another, all the phone calls."

I set my sponge on the round table with the blue marble top.

"If you keep busy enough, you don't notice life around you," he went on. "When my wife died I hadn't even realized anything was wrong with her."

"You can't blame yourself," I said, trying to be positive, though I didn't know what had happened to his wife.

"But you can pay attention. Well, I don't want to distract you." He heaved in a breath and brought his book close to his face, so that it almost touched his long nose, then moved the book farther away. "Forgot my damn reading glasses."

That afternoon, I went to Metro Drugs and bought him a pair.

"Are you staying in the apartment because you're afraid?" I asked when I gave him the black-framed reading glasses. "Of the crowds here? The traffic?"

"Why would I be afraid? Boston is a city, you know. I'm completely happy right here. There's no place I want to go."

He slid the reading glasses halfway down his nose. He squinted, as if to see me more clearly. "I think you're trying to tell me something. Are *you* afraid in the city?"

"Of course not. You have to cross the street to get where you need to go."

"I completely agree. If you're afraid, you won't go anywhere."

"But I hate living on an island," I said suddenly, more fiercely than I'd intended. "I mean the city. That you can be trapped here. In an emergency."

He stared at me with slitted eyes. "No more trapped than in any other place."

I didn't tell Cy this—I hadn't even told Lew—but since we'd moved to New York, I had felt a slow hardening inside. Like a disease, arteriosclerosis. I tried to hide this. But I looked away from the homeless. The man with craters of wrinkles on his face and a bum leg who stood near our building and begged. The deliverymen. I didn't talk to cab drivers except to inform them where I needed to go.

Over time, I'd noticed this tension growing inside me, as if my heart had closed into a tiny ball, like a fist, so tight no one could pry it open, as if I were protecting myself.

In the dark of early morning on the day of her surgery, I helped Rita dress. She felt frail, her body like a bag of bones. I grasped her arm to steady her as she stepped into her red dress, then I zipped up the back.

"How nice of you to get up, Ginny," she said weakly. Her hair was perfectly combed, and her nails were polished a pale pink. But her fingers trembled. "Please look after Cy."

It was five in the morning.

I nodded, slipped my arm through hers, and escorted her to the front door of the apartment. I heard Lew's footsteps behind us.

"I'm scared, Lew," Rita said to him. "I don't want to be late."

"For surgery, Ma? They'll wait for you. It's not a train that's going to leave without you."

She frowned. "That kind of ride, I can do without."

At the front door, I hugged her. An odd feeling surged through me, like the sensation that bubbled inside me on the giant roller coaster I had ridden with my father at the amusement park in Chicago, a flutter of fear and something else. I realized the feeling was love.

I brushed my hand against Rita's wide fingers and thought of my own mother. She had died suddenly, alone, a heart attack five years ago. My brother hadn't been able to reach her for days. He'd called the police. They had found her on the bedroom floor in her house. I didn't even have the chance to say goodbye. I hated to think about it. I remembered her long slender fingers and the way she used to play piano, her fire-engine red nails trimmed short so she wouldn't hear the click-click of her fingers against the keys. Red because the color made her feel alive, she said. She loved to sing, too, Édith Piaf songs or Jacques Brel. Melancholy melodies about love and broken hearts.

I pressed my arms around Rita. "Good luck. I love you," I whispered.

I waited for her to say "I love you" back.

"I know you do," she said.

There was no shade on the sidewalk where I stood later, flagging a taxi to go to the hospital. I had sent Cy there earlier so I could finish an order for work. It seemed my life was littered with half-finished projects—framing to be done, even boxes to unpack of items that belonged to my mother. I'd lugged some of them from Chicago to New York. She had given me these before she died. I had never opened them. I hadn't been able to bear it. They sat piled in a storage area in our building's basement.

I waved in vain for a taxi and thought about Lew. We hadn't made love in weeks. Between Rita's increasingly frequent phone calls about not feeling well, and now with her and Cy in the apartment, Lew and I had been preoccupied. I loved sex, sex with him, and this felt like a great absence, like the lack of shade on this hot day. I remembered the romantic trysts he and I had had in the afternoons when we first met or even a few years ago.

Cars whizzed past, but no taxis. The city was a nervous, manic creature with the blare of horns and crowds so dense that when I walked, I bumped into an arm, a leg, a backpack.

Finally, a cab stopped. "Take me to Mount Sinai Hospital, please," I told the driver. I gave him the address.

His reflection filled the rearview mirror. He was a grizzled old man with greasy gray hair. *Abraham Davidowitz*, the license posted in the cab read.

He gazed at me in the mirror and said, his voice like a bark, "Hospital? What's the matter with you? You don't look sick."

"My mother-in-law is there."

"Stay away from those places. Whatever she has is contagious."

"I don't think so," I said.

At the hospital, we waited while Rita was in surgery. Cy sat reading another Nero Wolfe. Lew worked on a grant. I thumbed through magazines, finally left the waiting area, and went to the hospital cafeteria.

I bought two Styrofoam cups of coffee, one for Lew and me, one for Cy. A woman hurried past me clutching a tray of food. I stared at her dark curls, the upturned nose, suddenly sure it was my childhood friend Wendy. We hadn't seen each other for years.

She sat at a table alone and eyed me. Then she waved.

I rushed over to her. "Wendy?"

"Ginny," she gushed. "What are you doing here?"

"My mother-in-law. Open-heart surgery. What about you?"

"I can't believe you're here." Then her expression became serious. "My father-in-law. Cancer. In the brain. Sit down. Bob and I came to see him."

"Cancer? Oh no. I'm sorry." I sat next to her. "You didn't tell me you'd be in the city."

"This happened so fast. There wasn't time. And your mother-in-law. I'm sorry, too." She paused. "We must have been meant to meet here. Coincidences are orchestrated in heaven."

Bob was upstairs, she told me. Lew is, too, I said. We smiled at each other. I wondered if she noticed my wrinkles, the way my eyelids drooped, the stress I was sure had settled on my face. Lines were etched on her skin, but the bright black eyes belonged to my friend from Evanston, Illinois, with the infectious laugh. The math wizard.

We had been to one another's houses when we were growing up, and we knew each other's families, the classes we attended, the boys the other had slept with. Our talk was like a warm breeze in this stale, sterile hospital. Then she began to complain about her husband. "Bob hangs his shirts to dry on the clothesline outside because he insists clothing lasts longer that way," she said. "Isn't that silly? I think it's miserly. He even hates to wash his clothes."

We laughed until tears swam in our eyes. What were we laughing about? The whole, absurd trajectory of our lives. I realized Lew and I didn't laugh like this anymore.

"Lew won't give away his aunt's old couch even though we don't have room for it," I said.

She laughed again. "Do you remember the Spanish dialogue? *El desfile fue estupendo, verdad?*"

I chimed in, "*Yo no creo, pero que gentío.*"

The parade is stupendous, isn't it?

I can't believe all the people who are here.

She went on in Spanish, but lost me. I didn't remember more, only the smells of cakes baking in Wendy's childhood kitchen, my mother's body swaying as she played piano. Mrs. O'Malley, our Spanish teacher, the stale smell of her classroom, like a hospital. Her blood-red lips and nails, her sullen swagger, the index cards on which she wrote a check mark if you failed to recite correctly. Our gangly teenage bodies pumped up with hormones and hope. We mouthed the Spanish words with exaggeration then, hoping to please the teacher. Hoping to please.

Wendy and I had been close then. Despite the time apart, we were still close. The resurrection of intimacy, I thought. She had always been more forthcoming than I was.

I didn't like to talk about my problems. Still, it was hard to keep things inside. I had told her before about my marriage, Lew's affair. Wendy seemed to free something in me.

She gazed at me now. "I have a relationship," she whispered.

"What do you mean?" I asked, confused.

"A boyfriend," she said, so softly I could hardly hear. She grasped her fork and pushed a pile of limp green beans to one side of her plate. "Sexual." Her face flushed with pleasure.

I didn't know what to say.

"This is a weird place to tell you." She shook her head. "But we're here. Why not? It's not the best thing, this scenario. I mean, I was raised to want happily ever after. But it helps. Then I'm not so annoyed that Bob hates when I put his shirts in the dryer. He makes a big deal about things. It doesn't bother me so much."

"It sounds like it bothers you a lot," I said. I felt my eyes growing wider. "How do you arrange it? The boyfriend."

"We meet in hotels." She leaned toward me. "I'm so free with him, Ginny. It's like he's tapped another part of me. I love the sex. Oral, everything." Her face glowed; she looked beautiful. "But it's hard to have secrets. I can't go into details, not here." She rested her hand on mine. "Lew, is he any easier to get along with?"

"He's okay. People don't change."

"That's a fact, like death and taxes." She glanced at her watch. "Damn, I'd better get upstairs. I told Bob I'd relieve him."

Then we laughed again, as if there was no tomorrow. We hugged; I hated to let go. My mother's voice hummed in my head: *You live as if there's no tomorrow, Ginny.* As if, as if.

I had told Wendy years ago that Lew and I were like oil and water. I hadn't understood this when I met him, when we married, when I was awed by his intelligence and all I wanted was to get my hands on him and make love.

For example, I was accustomed to someone saying "Good morning" in a cheerful voice.

Mornings he often said, "This place needs to be cleaned up. The apartment is a mess." I might be lounging in bed on a weekend, and he had been up for hours. He didn't sleep much. No kiss, no smile that said, "I'm happy to see you. I'm happy you're the woman in my bed."

I was used to my mother's voice, a visceral expectation, the habits of childhood. "Good morning, honey," she always said, like a song. She would stand at the side of my bed, smiling. The full lips, no lipstick yet, too early, the slightly yellowed teeth. Too many cigarettes. She bent toward me, her face close to mine; her lilac scent shimmered on her skin. "Honey, how did you sleep? Did an angel come visit you last night?"

My mother and I never really talked, not like Rita and I used to, or Wendy and I did. My mother never took me aside and had a heart-to-heart discussion, mother to daughter. She rarely mentioned sex. Never said the word. She spelled it aloud. *S-E-X.*

My father lived in Florida. When I was a child, I visited him. He lived in what's now called Boca Raton. Mouth of the rat. It wasn't even a development at the time. I'd seen my father during the summer. He liked flamboyant ties, pinks and reds, and he had lady friends. I always felt in the way. My brother and I would visit him, one at a time. He couldn't handle two kids at once, my mother said. That's why he left.

Right before Lew and I got married, my mother and I had a talk.

"Honey," she said to me a week before the wedding. Her blue eyes looked dreamy. "I am so happy you're marrying a Jewish man."

I wasn't expecting this. "You are?" I was sure she disapproved; the thought of her great disapproval intensified my pleasure in marrying Lew. I was sure she didn't want me to marry a man from a different faith.

"Absolutely."

"Why?" I asked.

"Lew is generous, kind. If he cheats, he'll feel guilty. Not like your father." Her mouth puckered as if she might spit. "When Lew cheats, he'll buy you all sorts of beautiful gifts."

"Oh," I said. "Why do you think he'll be unfaithful?" I waited for her to say more. But there was no more.

Even if my mother were alive, I wouldn't tell her about the problems between Lew and me. She was part of a generation that believed in bearing troubles with a stiff upper lip. No whining. No complaints. I once told her that things weren't perfect between us. He had a temper.

She said, "Ginny, men are like trolley cars."

"What do you mean?"

"As soon as one leaves, there's another behind it that comes along."

I had wanted to ask her, "What about the children, all the years you spend with a man? What if you love him? And what about Daddy? When he left, who came along, and stayed for good? Just tell me: who?"

She might have smiled her soft, lazy smile, the one that masked all real emotion. She might have said, "Oh, honey. Trolley cars never stay. They have places to go, people to meet. You can't rely on a man for that, to stay for good."

But instead I remained silent.

"All you can expect from a man is intimacy," she went on as we talked a week before my wedding. "Physical intimacy. S-E-X. Nothing more. Don't forget that either." She flashed her smile, put on her black straw hat, and went to sit in the sun.

I watched her go outside, caught in the swirl of her perfume.

What about emotional intimacy? Intimacy of presence?

That was a conversation we never had.

Cy was pacing in the waiting area when I returned from the hospital cafeteria. Lew sat working on a manuscript about zebra fish. Rita was still in surgery.

"Are you hungry?" I asked Cy. He had a listless, lost expression on his face. The coffee I'd bought for him was cold now. "Let's get something to eat." I felt responsible for him. "Then after Rita's surgery is over, I'll go home and make dinner."

Cy lumbered next to me as I made my way back to the cafeteria. We sat at the same table where Wendy and I had been. He settled into his chair, his big bulk hunched over hot coffee, a grilled cheese sandwich, and French fries.

"I needed a break and food," he said. "You could see that. Thank you." He gulped his coffee and took a few bites of his grilled cheese.

I nodded.

"This is why I don't like to leave the apartment. At least, right now. Why I'm happy there. You leave, and you end up in a place like this."

"You mean a hospital?"

"Yes, a hospital. Life almost always ends here."

"You have to be optimistic," I said, as if convincing both Cy and myself. "The doctors think they can help Rita. You need to have hope."

"Hope. Yes. But there's a beginning and end to everything. You'll see that more as you get older. We all have our illusions. Everything ends, though. Relationships. Life."

I thought of my mother and father. My mother alone in her house at the end, gone. My father gone, too. How foolish, I thought, to try to give Cy advice.

"The thing is," he said, "whatever you do, enjoy the beginning. Make peace with the end. That sounds like a cliché. A damn Hallmark card. But I don't care. It's true. People say, 'Follow your bliss.' That's a bunch of shit. Appreciate what you have. That's what I've learned."

"So that's the secret to life?" I teased, trying to lift the mood of our conversation.

"Just ask me." He laughed lightly and slid the plate of French fries toward me, offering me some. "I know all the secrets."

After the surgery, we visited Rita in recovery. She was sleeping, pale, like a corpse, tubes snaking from her face and arms. The nurse said the first hours were the worst. Lew, Cy, and I took turns going into the recovery room. Finally, I said we should go home.

"No, I want to stay," Lew said. "But if you want, you should go now. Cy and I will meet you later."

On my way home, I thought about my conversation with Cy. It had lightened my mood, just as being with Wendy had. I felt more relaxed with him now, and I realized I liked taking care of him. I had loved taking care of the children when they were young and of Lew when he and I were closer. I hadn't been able to take care of my mother or father at the end of their lives. If I helped Cy and Rita now, maybe I could somehow right that wrong.

At the apartment, I sliced cucumbers for a salad. I'd order a pizza when Lew and Cy came home. I needed to telephone the children and tell them that the operation was over. But I decided to clean the bathroom drawers first and then work on a framing order while I had the time. The conversation with Wendy spun in my mind. She was creative in how she lived. Perhaps I should have been like her, had a lover. Tapped into another part of myself. Then what Lew did or didn't do wouldn't have bothered me so much.

I placed a rag and a bottle of Windex on the white Formica vanity in the bathroom and lifted paraphernalia from my drawer. I discovered there was no dental floss. This seemed a matter of great urgency suddenly, and I frantically searched all my drawers and the medicine cabinet. Then I pulled open Lew's drawers and rummaged through them for floss. If he had none, I would rush to Metro Drugs to buy some, just as I had rushed to get Cy's reading glasses. Why were these minor annoyances so aggravating now?

I pulled out objects, but no floss. I yanked out another handful and was about to dump everything back into the drawer when I slowed down and began to take note. Band-Aids, soaps, razors, business cards. And three flat plastic packets with sharp edges. Blue and white. I picked them up. Lew and I hadn't used condoms since the children were young.

I stared at the plastic squares as if they were a dead mouse, and sucked in a breath. My heart beat wildly. Years ago, I had discovered the condoms in Lew's jacket, but we had overcome that. Don't jump to conclusions, I told myself. Why weren't we like those zebra fish—transparent? Why weren't our hearts, needs, and desires transparent, too?

I cupped the packets in my palm and breathed in the stale bathroom air. Then I imagined the future, traveling the world with Lew while I struggled to keep an eye on him. What was the cost of safety? The safety of this apartment, our family, this life with him? What was the cost of life without him? Without his family? I hurled the condoms in the drawer and slammed it shut.

"Did you ever frame Michael Fox's toilet paper?" Lew asked later that night after Cy had gone to bed.

"Months ago," I said. "In April."

He sat on the bed and untied his shoes. "I was thinking about that at the hospital. You've been great with my mother. You haven't been able to do your work; I've hardly been able to do mine." His tone was softer than it had been for months. "We just have to get through the next days to be sure she's okay."

"Lew." I stood on the other side of the bed. "When I came home from the hospital, I was cleaning out drawers and realized I had run out of dental floss. I went to yours, and I found…" I hesitated. "Condoms," I said. It sounded absurd even to me. I felt guilty, as if I had been spying.

Lew didn't blink. "Those things?" he said calmly. "They've been there for years. It's nothing to worry about."

I could fling open the drawer and check the expiration date. But I didn't want an investigation or debate or even to catch him in a lie.

"I wanted you to know," I said.

He was silent, and so was I. We eyed each other. Helplessly. I wished I could see inside him.

He hurried to me and hugged me.

"Okay," I said and stepped back.

Then he began to empty his pockets: wallet, keys, change, setting them on the dresser next to his briefcase. Preparing his possessions for tomorrow.

He looked at me closely. "I told you, they're old and left over; I just never threw them away. What are you going to do? Follow me around wherever I go? Search my drawers, my pockets, my wallet?"

"I found them by accident. You're a grown man."

"It's just like you to bring up a topic like this when my mother is so ill."

"A topic? This is our future."

"What do you mean?"

"I think it's over between us," I said suddenly. "Yes, I think that's so."

"Because of that?" He stared at me. "We used to use them."

I was silent. Then I said, "Not since the children were young."

"Do what you want." He sounded weary, sad. He went into the bathroom and slammed the door. I heard the whoosh of water. Then the sharp flush of the toilet, like thunder.

He emerged from the bathroom in his pajamas, slid into bed, beneath the quilt. "You're exhausted, and so am I. Let me know if you'll be at the hospital tomorrow."

"The hospital, yes," I said. "Lew, I won't change my mind."

He lay on his back, his hands resting on his ribs. He shut his eyes. "Can you turn off the light?"

"Is that all you have to say? It's not the condoms, Lew. Can't you see what's happened to us? To our marriage? To you?" I stopped. "To me?"

He didn't reply.

I jerked the curtains shut and switched off the light. The room was dark and still; I felt as if I'd walked into midnight. I dropped my clothing on the floor. My jeans made a soft swish as they fell. Then I slipped on my white silk nightgown. I lay in bed next to Lew, my muscles tense. If I'd been smart, like Wendy, I'd have had a lover waiting in the wings. But I didn't. All I had was whatever existed between Lew and me, or what didn't.

The space between us on the bed seemed like a huge chasm. It seemed to grow larger and deeper as we lay there. I waited for Lew to repair this, to speak with emotion, to pull me close. I waited for the resurrection of intimacy. Hoping for it. For him to kiss me like he used to.

He didn't move. Neither did I.

When I realized I would not be able to sleep and heard the steady grumble of Lew's breathing, I slid from bed, threw my robe over my nightgown, and lifted the flashlight I kept for emergencies from the night table. I tiptoed out and followed the thin beam of light. When all else fails, milk calms the nerves, my mother always said.

I plodded through the hallway, past the gallery of photographs, as if I were a sleepwalker who had just awakened and realized where she was. I used to imagine when I was in college, before I met Lew, that one day I would lie down in bed and just stay there; this was the best way to have a nervous breakdown. I thought of it as a *brake down*. After all, what would bubble inside you then would be something like that—a yearning to stop the rush of time, to put the brakes on what was happening or not in your life. But how could I do that now? I had an ill mother-in-law, a houseguest, and a troubled marriage.

I trudged toward the kitchen. And what became of all those other relationships, forged over time, with love? Mother-in-law, daughter-in-law, friend? Dissolved into some kind of oblivion, too?

Maybe I was more like Lew now than I'd imagined, I thought suddenly. Maybe I was just as guilty of an emotional coolness as he was. I shivered involuntarily.

At the end of the hallway, a light flickered. Cy stood in the kitchen, his big bulk wrapped in a red cotton robe, yellow and white striped pajamas peeking through. He filled the narrow space between the counters. His back faced me. I thought perhaps he had come to have a glass of milk, too, to seek some comfort.

"Can I help you?" I asked.

He turned to me, startled. "Oh, it's you. Can't sleep either?"

"No." I willed myself not to display any emotion.

"Well." He studied me. "So you have troubles, too."

"Yes," I said.

We eyed each other, and then he began to hum, a Jacques Brel song, one of the ones my mother used to sing. Cy's voice was melodic and sweet. I knew the words by heart. *One day you won't even remember his name...*

I thought about Lew. "I doubt that." I sounded sour, bitter. I vowed to change my tone.

"You have troubles that befit your age," he said gently.

"I suppose." I felt transparent. "Though I don't feel very young."

"You may not, but you are. I was eighty-seven last month," he said. "I have troubles that befit my age. My wife, she had gallbladder surgery seven years ago. But there was a complication. She was home already. I told her to wait to see if the pain would go away. Give it time, I said. Don't be impatient. I finally took her to the doctor the next week. I never imagined something would happen. She died that day."

"That must have been awful," I said.

He shrugged his broad shoulders. "You wonder what the story of your life will be. At each step. Then something happens, and you know the next chapter, but you've got to wait for the next. She can be a lot of trouble, Rita. But she's what I have. I love her. I never thought I would love a woman again. After fifty years of marriage. But I do." His voice was tender. "I can't bear to lose someone again."

"No," I said.

His eyes exploded into tears. I placed my arms around his wide back. His old skin felt warm against mine, and I tried to still his emotion. "Rita will be okay," I said, more like a prayer than a statement.

"Damn. I'm sorry." He wiped a hand against his eyes and stepped back. "I don't know what's the matter with me. I was a litigator, a fucking football player in college."

"It's the unknown," I said. "Surgery. It's emotional."

He nodded. "Everything is. Life is emotional."

I suddenly envied him. That feeling, the spark in his voice when he spoke of Rita. This made me think of all that I longed for: to have my mother back, to have lived with my father, for Lew and me to love each other like we used to.

A whirlwind of feeling churned inside me, and I bit my lip to stop all that grief. But I couldn't. Cy put his arms around me, and I wept. I imagined that if I had been close to my father, I might be standing here with him, like this. Or with my mother, if she were alive. Or with Lew—if he and I could just find a way back to each other. I wanted us to find a way. The thought soothed me, and I loosened my hand, away from Cy's back, but he continued to embrace me. I realized he was comforting me. My body felt limp, but something seemed to open inside me, like petals of a thousand flowers, delicate and tender, and I felt something give way right in the center of my heart.

Hurricane

FOR WEEKS, ALICE AND HER HUSBAND follow the paths of the hurricanes Ivan, Frances, and Jeanne. Every night, they sit side by side on the sofa in the den, a foot apart, and watch the television news, marveling at the wild, destructive powers of wind and weather. Now that Mara, their daughter and only child, has gone to college, she is not the main topic of conversation.

Will the storm touch Palm Beach or Fort Myers or Miami? Douglas wonders aloud. His mother used to live in Florida; they often visited there. How much damage will residual effects cause on the east coast or in New York City where they live? Alice nods, but she is not concerned with facts. Only with the photographs. Tears gather in her eyes when she sees footage of the newly homeless, smashed trailers, the guillotined trees. How can people live? Douglas talks about the force of the water, the longitudes and latitudes. He describes the historic nature of three storms emerging one after the other. She and Douglas are so skilled at discussing facts and probabilities about everything, Alice thinks, except themselves.

She doesn't blame Douglas. Not completely. They live with silence, and she allows it. She doesn't tell him this: her dissatisfactions with their marriage—though she has told him in the past—or about her lover, or her feeling, like a whirl of panic inside, that she is slipping farther and farther away, not just from Douglas, but from others, too. As if she has been shaken by uncontrollable forces—not unlike wind and weather—and although she is still intact, her insides feel hollow.

Ann Arbor, Michigan, where Alice grew up in the 1950s and '60s, was a hotbed of strict morality. There were steadfast rules about how a girl should comport herself. When a boy and a girl are together, both the boy and girl should each have both feet on the floor. In a skirt, keep your thighs glued together. Wear blouses with Peter Pan collars buttoned securely. Alice silently reviews this litany as she sits next to

Douglas. She had her short, sandy hair dyed this week, brushed with soft blonde highlights. She is slim and wears a low-cut black J. Crew sweater and jeans. Douglas stares at the television and doesn't seem to notice her. Alice won medals in high school for diving and swimming. A way to control her bubbling teenage hormones, she thinks. She can still hear her mother's voice: Never reveal cleavage or acknowledge you are endowed with breasts. Never display emotions, particularly desire.

"The world is falling apart," Douglas says. "Terrorists. Iraq. Hurricanes. What next?"

He doesn't seem to want an answer, and Alice nods again distractedly. She likes to imagine that her relationship with a man other than her husband is a mistake, as having happened against her will, as if she'd been dragged down to Hades by a force as strong as wind and fierce weather, to a den of iniquity and sexual pleasure.

Douglas enjoys traveling. He loves trips to obscure destinations and will never go on a tour. He teaches medieval history at a university, supervises graduate students, and writes scholarly papers; sometimes his travels are arranged for his work. He and Alice have visited ruins in all parts of the world. Machu Picchu, Sacsayhuaman, the Western Wall, Mesa Verde. Archeology was her favorite subject in college; it was Douglas's, too. She is drawn to the fortitude of the ruins. She envies the stone. The strength, the silence, the absolute stability.

"Things were built solidly in ancient times," Douglas said last year on a trip to Mexico. He likes to lecture and rattled off dates and dynasties. From the first, Alice loved his intellect and practicality, his ability to repair cars and electronics, to garden, jog, kayak. She didn't realize how different they were: his efficiency and her delight in luxuriating in the world. His need to collect experiences as if they were treasured objects, and her need to talk to him about whatever thoughts or feelings flitted through their minds.

"You learn about a culture from their ruins," he said as they walked past a stone pyramid. "About the way people live. What's close to their hearts. Their souls."

Alice listened carefully. Douglas usually didn't talk about the soul.

"I love these ruins, too," she said.

"I can tell you're thinking that I never talk about spiritual things," he said and brushed a hand through his gray beard and mustache.

"You're right. I like it when you do."

"I do *feel*," he said defensively. "I just don't show it."

It's Monday, and during the workday, Alice listens to the radio to stay abreast of the news and follow the hurricanes' paths. She checks her email for updates or messages from Mara. *Hi, Mom. Doing fine. Where do I order contacts from again? College is GREAT.* She misses Mara more than she anticipated.

Alice is a writer. She wasn't always. She was a social worker first, and still is, a part-time social worker and part-time writer. This gives her the best of both worlds, she thinks, though she knows there are better ways to earn money. Three days a week at the Samuel Goldman YMCA on Fourteenth Street, she consults with private clients and runs groups for mothers of adolescent girls. She used to run groups for new mothers there, but she has decided that the challenges of a new mother, while they may seem profound at the time, are nothing like the angst of parenting an adolescent. A daughter's constant critique and rejection can be deadly for one's ego. This is what Alice tries to work on with her patients. Strengthening the mother's ego. This is what you need in life, she believes, coping skills to guide you and others through whatever life brings.

Two days a week, she writes articles for a parenting magazine. "Articles" is an exaggeration; if she can write one piece or interview a few people, she is doing well. The writing, that process—the hammering out word by word, a sentence, a thought—takes longer than she ever imagined. But she had always wanted to be a writer when she was a girl in Ann Arbor, swimming laps and struggling to cope with that strict moral code.

She would never announce to the world that she is a writer. This seems too bold, too self-important; it is an adjunct to her work. Just as her lover is an adjunct to her life.

Writing complements her social work. She knows that with an adolescent, a mother needs to be direct, firm, and empathetic. No matter how difficult a daughter's behavior. Just as one should be when writing or when talking with a spouse, though this is easier for Alice to do with her daughter than with Douglas.

Now that Mara is in college, Alice worries about sex and protection, emotional involvement and date rape, AIDS and STDs. On occasion, Mara has allowed her mother to discuss this. She has promised to insist a boy use a condom. To delay sleeping with someone until she is sure of emotional commitment, though Alice knows what a great request this can be.

Before Mara left for college last month, they talked about this.

"Even though we've discussed it, I need to tell you again," Alice said then.

"What?" Mara, tall and willowy, wore a gleaming gold stud in her nose. She tangled a long strand of her shiny brown hair around her finger.

Alice sat across from her daughter in the den and recited the litany. Like her mother had done when Alice was young. Delay sleeping with a boy until you are almost ready to marry. Alice stopped. "At least, until a relationship is serious," she went on. Her mother had said until *after* you marry. She had referred to "relations," not sex. And be faithful. Always.

Mara rolled her eyes. "Oh, Mom."

Alice felt herself blush and inhaled a gulp of air. Did the scent of her lover still cling to her? Could Mara smell him? She smiled weakly at her daughter. Everything she has counseled Mara not to do, she does herself.

The relationship with Todd began in fantasy. Alice has high moral standards and a religious sensibility. She goes to synagogue because she enjoys the melodies, the feeling of being apart from the world, diving deep into herself and reflecting on God and prayer, gratitude and forgiveness. Douglas has no interest in this and works on Saturdays. He doesn't believe in God. He says that synagogue and prayers are mumbo jumbo.

Todd attends synagogue, too. She noticed him four years ago and had imagined then how it might feel to make love to him. She was

attracted to his wavy dark hair, his blue eyes and long lashes, wise
eyes, she was sure, his trim body, the way he swayed in concentration
in prayer. On some Saturdays, when both their spouses are otherwise
occupied because neither spouse has a spiritual life, Todd and Alice
meet at a hotel. They have done more things sexual together than
she knew existed: top, bottom, side, anal, oral. A liberating litany of
positions.

It is an odd ritual, Alice knows, after worshipping and imploring
God for blessings, to then break a commandment. She no longer
thinks of the commandments as carved in stone, though, of course, at
one time they were. She thinks of them as floating commandments:
if you are very good at following a few, perhaps it is not so terrible to
break one. The truth floats, too. She is astounded by her ability to lie, to
say she is going to synagogue when she is really meeting Todd. When
she reads about adultery in the newspaper, the stoning of women or
an article about a woman in Afghanistan imprisoned and sentenced
to death for adultery, Alice feels both deeply ashamed of herself and
thankful she was born a Jew. Douglas showed her an article last week
and shook his head. "Not only do fanatics want to take over the world;
they want to bring us to the moral dark ages. Not that adultery is to be
condoned. But death?" Then he glanced at the green granite kitchen
counter. "Can't you throw out those newspapers? Go through the
mail? Put away the groceries? The kitchen is a fucking wreck."

"Cluttered," she said. "Not a wreck. You don't have to swear. It's
not the end of the world."

Alice knows words are important. She has written about this in
her articles. If a parent says to a daughter, "You make me sick when
you stay out late," the *you make me sick* lingers in the girl's mind. Let's
say they are discussing curfew. The conversation becomes heated. The
mother loses her temper. *You make me sick.* Those four words may be
the only ones that remain in the daughter's consciousness.

Words have become a problem for Douglas. "You are disorganized,"
he says if Alice leaves dishes in the sink. "You can't function," he yells if
she loses her keys. A social work friend once told her that at fifty-five,
men become mean. That's what happened with Douglas. It happened
when he was younger.

Alice considers her time in the hotel with Todd an extension of her spiritual life. She has begun to view sex as spiritual. Because she feels so alive with him.

From the first, Alice noticed how Todd used words. The precision. He is a furrier and works in a small family business. Recently he has become interested in spiritual matters and studying Kabbalah. He was an English major in college, reads poetry and novels. He's had thoughts about learning to become a healer. If it is possible for one person to heal another, he said. He was sure that phenomena existed in this world that one could not explain. "Take this, the two of us, sitting here." They were at a restaurant.

She noticed how he spoke about fur, the gradations, the quality, the nap, cut of fabric. How he spoke about his family. His wife and two children, all of whom he loved. "I want to be clear from the start. I love them all." He spoke about noticing Alice in the synagogue and the green of her eyes, he said, which were flecked with delicate gold.

On Saturday, in two days, Alice will meet Todd in a hotel. They always split the cost. He finds the place, using Priceline.com so they can get a deal. They have made love in large rooms with views of bridges, and rooms so small there is hardly space for a bed.

She became involved with him at the time Douglas's father became ill. Douglas is an only child. His father moved in with them three years ago, six months before he died. Alice had underestimated the needs of the sick. She had been close to her father-in-law. The first week at their house, Harry developed violent diarrhea. He looked pale and thin. One morning at breakfast, he fell asleep at the table and began to lean to the left, almost slipping off the chair, and Alice ran to him. The man began to twitch as if his body were plugged into an electric socket. She yelled his name over and over until he finally replied weakly.

Alice prayed for God to give her the strength to handle the situation. That week she went to bed with Todd.

On Thursday night, the week of Hurricane Jeanne's fury, Douglas walks out of the bathroom naked. Not without clothing, but without his beard and mustache. He has had these since Alice met him. She stares at him. He looks like a stranger. Even his smile is different. Wider. Unfamiliar.

"Do you like it?" he asks.

"I don't know." His chin is bare, without a cleft that she had imagined. The space between his nose and lips is smaller than she thought, his lips narrower. His mustache and beard were pepper-colored and set off his skin nicely. Now he looks sallow. Still, more youthful. But a stranger.

"Why did you do it?" she asks.

"I had gotten so gray. White even. I looked like an old man."

"I didn't think so. You should have asked me."

"I didn't think to." He rubbed a hand against his bare chin. "Do you like it?" he repeats.

"We should talk about things. But yes, I like it."

"Good. I was hoping you would. Just in time to surprise Mara."

The next day, Mara comes home from college, her first visit, to see her parents and some friends. Alice is struck by the glint of joy in Mara's eyes as she sweeps into the apartment and plops down a duffel bag bulging with dirty laundry. She talks excitedly, nonstop, about the dorm, her roommate, classes. Douglas comes home early, and Mara tells them about her favorite course, "The Uses of Enchantment," named after a book by Bruno Bettelheim, she announces. "Do you know the difference between a myth and fairy tale?" she asks her mother.

Alice guesses. "Fairy tales tell stories, and myths have greater insights?" They sit side by side on the sofa, Alice's arm around Mara.

Douglas looks on, sitting across from them.

"Close, but no cigar," laughs Mara. "A myth is pessimistic, a fairy tale optimistic."

"Like Persephone," says Alice. "That's a pessimistic story."

"Yes," agrees Mara. "Or Oedipus. It's about fate. You can't escape your fate in myths. The gods exact punishment. Myth is about superego."

"To be Freudian," says Douglas.

"Absolutely Freudian," Alice says.

Mara chatters on. "Think of any fairy tale, like Hansel and Gretel. They got what they wanted. They escaped. And the names are generic, Little Red Riding Hood, the dwarfs, no character development."

Like the husband, the wife, the lover, Alice thinks.

Douglas goes back to reading *The New Yorker*.

"Interesting," says Alice. "That's true. In fairy tales, you don't know the characters like you know the gods. But novels really define character. Like Henry James's novels. Virginia Woolf's."

"We aren't reading them, Mom. That's a class for next semester." She stares at Douglas. "Dad, you shaved your beard and mustache. It looks good."

He glances up from *The New Yorker* and smiles.

Before dinner, Douglas and Mara watch the news. Alice goes to her computer in the small room behind the kitchen while the lasagna bakes. Restlessness rises inside her just as it did when she began with Todd. Now she types: *How to be a caretaker.* She is writing an article about this. She thinks of all those for whom she has cared: her parents, her husband, daughter, father-in-law, her patients. And she would like to care for Todd. But he won't let her. He has a wife. She types: *You hold your breath when you begin a project because you could be interrupted any time.* This small room has a high ceiling, its only asset, and one large window opens to a courtyard, but the window is painted shut. Alice stares outside. There is so much white, white like a dream, a cloud, a mist that obscures all vision. She hides here, waiting for tomorrow. She remembers the sounds of the bell when her father-in-law was too weak to speak; he shook a small glass bell to let her know he needed help.

She daydreams of Todd. He sings sometimes when they have walked along the East River, "*Non, je ne regrette rien,*" or the Beatles, "Yesterday, all my troubles seemed so far away." He has brought the A-O volume of the *Compact Edition of the Oxford English Dictionary* to the hotel, and they have looked up words and discussed definitions and origins. She has dived into the muddy waters of emotion with him, has told him things she has never told anyone. He has confided in her. And he loves to garden. He has a small yard and a large townhouse, but would rather have a large yard and small house.

On Saturday, Alice goes to the service at the synagogue and afterward, in drizzle and dampness, to a hotel. Mara has made plans to spend the day with friends, and Douglas is working.

In bed, Alice traces Todd's face with her hand. She loves his humanness, that the space between his nose and lips is not symmetrical, that his skin is creased by his smile, his body muscular, except when he stands and zips his jeans. The flesh is pliable by his waist.

"I love it when I see you," she says.

"See me?"

"You know what I mean." She laughs. "Like this." She sweeps her hand across his chest and gazes at all the places she was taught not to look: chest, waist, genitals, the smooth curve of the thigh, and into his eyes. How much joy are you entitled to in life? she wonders. "When I see you, like this," she says, "and then when you're gone, I miss you all over again."

"I miss you. That's the nature of this kind of arrangement."

She hates when he mentions an arrangement. It makes what they do together seem transactional, without connection. Without feeling.

"I have less time than I thought today," he says. "I'm sorry. My in-laws…" His voice trails, and she kisses him, muffling his words.

"I love you," she says after they make love. She pulls the blanket over them to be sure he is warm.

He stares at the ceiling. He doesn't need to speak. Alice can see the words forming in his thoughts. He loves the sex.

"Don't say that," he says. "I am very, very—"

She presses her hand to his lips. "Shh. Don't say anything. It will ruin this." They lie in silence, and after a few minutes, she slips out of bed and puts on her clothes. He watches, as he watched her undress. She doesn't bother to shower. His salty scent clings to her like glue.

"You're leaving?" he says. "Don't. I still have time. I'll leave just a little earlier than usual. Don't go."

He has told her this before. But she wants to leave first. It is too

difficult when he is gone, and she is in a room alone. She blows him a
kiss and smiles as she opens the door. "I'll see you next time."

Outside, the sky has darkened. Alice wanders from the hotel as
the rain begins to trickle down. She thinks of all the ruins she and
Douglas have visited. Ruined lives, hopes, plans. How the stones still
stand despite wear and weather and neglect. She has always wanted
to live happily ever after with Douglas. Now she doesn't know how to
live happily anymore.

She thinks of the phrase Todd mouthed once when she told
him about her moral standards from childhood and that this made
it difficult for her to have an affair. But not impossible. Hebrew
words: *Gam ze ya'avor.* This too will pass, he said. She thinks of her
expectations of him, her great need for him, of Todd's lesser need for
her. She remembers the ancient Hebrew prayer that people centuries
ago wore in amulets around their neck: *May the Lord bless you and
keep you; may the Lord cause His face to shine upon you and be gracious
unto you; may the Lord lift up his countenance upon you and grant you
peace.* And of the light in Mara's eyes, her whole life ahead of her.

Guidance. Everyone is asking for guidance among the ruins.

Alice is not far from the Museum of Natural History and she
pops open her umbrella and hurries there in the dampness for shelter,
past the dinosaurs that rise like bony giants to the gift shop. She buys
rocks, all sizes, shapes, and colors, and pays with a credit card.

"These are heavy," the saleslady says.

"I'll put them in here." Alice holds up the black canvas bag she
got for free from Bloomingdale's, shaped like one of the fancy French
Longchamp bags Mara likes so much. "I'm not going far."

Outside, the wind has picked up, and water lashes against her
raincoat. The hurricane has trickled here, she thinks. She hops on a
crosstown bus, and on Second Avenue, she manages to find a cab.
She asks the driver to take her home, but then she changes her mind
and asks to go to Eighty-Third Street, near the East River, near her
favorite place on the promenade where she used to stroll with Mara
when Mara was a child, where Alice first kissed Todd.

She imagines the stones she and Douglas have seen, how she

admired them because of their sturdy silence. What have they witnessed? The weight of life. Births, deaths, misunderstandings. Wars and betrayals. They have survived them all. She remembers the thin white mist at Machu Picchu, on their honeymoon, mist so fine and delicate like a bride's veil.

She has read books, stories, and clinical material about what it feels like to be the "other woman" and has discussed this with patients on occasion, but right now she would say this: the phrase describes the feeling completely. *Other*. Outcast. Pariah. Standing on the edge of a community. A hope. A shared life.

At the promenade, she walks in the rain. Not many people brave the elements, though she notices a few people yards away. She walks, bag of rocks in one hand, black umbrella in the other. The wind by the river is strong. Her sturdy umbrella has not been blown inside out yet.

She passes the spot where she and Todd first kissed, in the daylight, in the sunshine, kissed recklessly—what if someone they knew saw them? She didn't care then. Todd liked the danger, and all she wanted was to touch his lips with hers, touch him, skin to skin. The most essential need that day by the river. She didn't care what destruction this would bring. She would have given everything to touch him then, and she realizes that, in a way, she has. This is his cost to her. She has given up her peace of mind, integrity, her belief in goodness and morals, right and wrong. In all she was taught in Ann Arbor, Michigan. All she has tried to teach Mara. She has traded it for this: shades of gray. Ambiguity. Isolation. Patients who look to her for answers. A husband who reads instead of talking to her. A lover who has only small slices of time to give her. She has willed herself not to care about the contradictions in her life, but she is not stone.

She strolls past others who brave the weather. A heavy, sullen teenaged boy who wears a drenched white shirt; a red-and-blue baseball cap sits on his head backward. An old, bent woman with gray hair, who hobbles with a cane and wears a long brown raincoat and black orthopedic shoes, clumsy as boats. They are everywhere in New York, Alice thinks, people like this, the lost, the misplaced, the oddities, the forgotten, and although she knows she does not appear this way, with her pretend French bag and her chic khaki raincoat, an Eddie Bauer umbrella opened gracefully above her, inside she feels the same as she imagines these people must feel.

At her favorite spot along the East River, Alice stops. The wind blows fiercely and rain pours down. The residuals from the hurricane. If Douglas were here, he might comment on the speed of the wind, the amount of rain that falls per minute, and insist they seek shelter. These details are superfluous. It is simply not fit weather for man or beast. But she gladly lets the wind race through her hair.

The metal railing is slippery but she grasps hold of it, then, on a whim, climbs up onto the low cement wall. The rocks feel heavy in her bag. She wonders if someone will stop her, but this is New York. No one does. She stares at the horizon, far away, the expanse of Queens hazy in the rain, and she feels an odd liberation, so drenched she may never warm up.

She thinks about when Douglas's father was dying with the chemo, and of her own mother in Ann Arbor, and all those beliefs her mother passed on like edicts. Then Alice imagines that she jumps, like she used to leap into the water as a child, falling down, down, unafraid—as if she is a character in a fairy tale or the puppet of a god in a myth, light and lithe as a girl, or as if she is Virginia Woolf herself—splashing into the murky, unforgiving water, shoes tumbling off, going to a place deep inside herself, leaving her confusion behind.

The wind whips against her. She blinks, gulps a breath. She throws a stone into the water, and another. Then she carefully climbs down the cement wall and stands in the fierce weather. She will give Mara these stones, artifacts of the earth's history. She will give Douglas some, too, she decides, a gift, a kind of offering. She has nothing to really offer him, to offer herself. What can she give? Wavering affection, but affection nonetheless. Alice wishes she were made of stone, but she knows she is not. She turns away from the river. She imagines Mara and Douglas waiting for her, and she begins her journey home.

We Worry about the Wrong Things

"YOUR PARENTS ARE OLD NOW," the doctor said. "They shouldn't be on their own. They need to be living in a protected environment."

Sophie nodded, although the doctor couldn't see her. They were talking on the telephone. He was in Chicago; she was in New York. Everyone needed to live in a protected environment, she thought. She needed protection, too.

She'd met the doctor last year when she was visiting Chicago. She had driven her mother to an appointment with him.

"Your mother isn't eating enough," he went on. He didn't pause or vary his flat inflection. "We need a solution. I'd like to help her."

"Is there something I should be doing?"

"I'm seeing her again on Friday. I'll let you know what I find."

Sophie mumbled, "Thank you," and hung up. But she found she didn't feel one bit grateful. *He* should be doing something to help her mother. She wanted a magician, she supposed, not a doctor. She drummed her fingers on the kitchen table, then opened her laptop and booked a flight to Chicago. Even now, at fifty-three, she thought of Chicago as home, although she'd lived many other places, was in the middle of a divorce, and had two sons who were in college. She taught in the legal clinic at a law school. She was a bona fide grown-up, though if you looked inside her, you'd never know it, she thought.

The front door to the apartment swung open as her boyfriend, Dennis, walked in. He closed the door and threw his battered brown leather briefcase onto the couch.

"Hi," she said. "I'm going to Chicago."

He bent and brushed his lips against hers. "What happened? Did something happen to your mother?"

She told him what the doctor had said.

"It's good you'll be there." Dennis sat beside her. "It's hard, Sophie. Maybe she doesn't want to eat. It's possible. You can't eat for someone else."

"I'll encourage her," she said as brightly as she could. "She just needs encouragement. Tell me about your day."

Dennis was tall and a little bulky, with thinning, wavy gray hair and a wide smile. He wasn't smiling now. "My day doesn't matter. You know, I've had my losses, and I can tell you that a relationship continues inside you. It might sound stupid, but I still feel my brother's presence, my mother's. I talk to them every day."

She nodded.

"Not out loud, of course."

"No." Sophie smiled at his attempt at a joke, then went on seriously, "But I don't want to lose my mother, not yet. Not before our relationship is resolved. It's not resolved."

"Nothing is ever completely resolved."

"If you want to know the truth," she whispered, "I'm afraid."

"I know," Dennis said. "Life is scary and then it's over."

"Oh, Dennis." She held his hand. "If I lose her—when I do—I'm afraid I won't remember her."

"You'll remember." He lifted her hand to his lips and kissed her fingers. "You remember everything."

This was the summer the future was arriving, Sophie thought. Her mother was failing. Her divorce was proceeding. She was finalizing the financial papers, which she found an overwhelming task. Everything seemed to be failing her this summer, especially her logic and math skills, which were mediocre at the best of times. She made mistakes calculating expenses for groceries, for clothing, dental bills, and subway rides. She used a calculator but still made mistakes. The German paralegal, a stately woman in her mid-sixties, had little patience for Sophie's errors and state of mind. Sophie's lawyer warned her: This is the most important document you will ever have. A divorce decree will affect the rest of your life.

But everything affected the rest of your life, Sophie thought as she stood in the slowly snaking security line at the airport, in the white metal detecting machine. And nothing moved fast enough for her, not this line, not the divorce, nor coming to terms with the end of her marriage. The only things that moved quickly—at a breathtakingly too-rapid pace—were her mother's decline and her relationship with Dennis.

Her mother was eighty-three and had survived pancreatic cancer, nine years so far. Almost no one survived the disease; Harriet was in the smallest of percentages. But statistics were statistics. Real life was real life. She had survived but struggled with a host of new health problems that sprang from the cure.

Sophie had been seeing Dennis—a euphemism; she was sleeping with him—for a year and a half. They'd become involved when she still harbored a glimmer of hope that she and her husband, Bill, might reconcile. At the beginning, Dennis was a distraction. He had gone to the same high school as Sophie, a year behind her. At first, she remembered just a little about him. She knew he'd been a football player and swimmer. His auburn hair had turned gray; he was a little overweight though still athletic, and he had a bright smile and buoyant manner. He had endured a bitter divorce, lived in a house he owned with his brother in Memphis, and had been passing through New York when he called her. His sister, a friend of Sophie's, had encouraged him to call. When he and Sophie met, he said, "Divorce is hell, and it can take so goddamn long. It's good to do everything when you're young. That way, you have more time left: to fall in love, have kids, get divorced." He had laughed, a little sadly.

Sophie had slept with him because she was attracted to him and she was feeling sorry for herself. Then she found herself falling in love with him. He remembered when her wavy brown hair had been long and cascaded to the middle of her back and that she had worked in the school store, selling pencils and black marble-patterned composition books. This helped her to remember herself, but also to remember him: how he'd won the swim meet for the school, how eloquent he'd been in an English class, and how he'd orchestrated a student uprising when a substitute was giving a test. The students ripped up the exam.

Dennis liked to say: every important thing that happens in life depends on who comes along. He had grown up in the small suburb next to hers, almost identical to it, where modest houses sat crowded one next to the other, like relatives. The flat Midwestern landscape seemed to unspool forever. Humid summer nights created a web of heat, and fireflies darted fitfully through the air. In winter, the ground was covered with ice and snow, the sky with intractable clouds. Fathers were postal workers or factory managers or salesmen, like her father. He had sold blouses for Ship'n Shore. When Sophie was growing up, she couldn't wait to leave, but now, sometimes, as she navigated the streets of New York, she craved the quiet predictability of her first home.

Her soon-to-be-ex-husband's father had been a surgeon in New York, a very important surgeon, Bill always said, as if to be a regular person with a regular job meant nothing.

Dennis was a pediatrician and worked locum tenens, substituting for doctors who were away. This month he'd be in Memphis for a week, then Allentown, Pennsylvania. Sophie thought: how can I have a relationship with someone who is in and out of my life? But she could, and she did. Still, she hadn't made a commitment to him. She couldn't bear to, not after the end of her marriage. She couldn't bear to depend on anyone in that way again. And she was unsure. She had been unsure about Bill at first and now she felt this about Dennis.

This vacillation was a flaw, along with her other flaws: a general disorder about financial matters, a tendency to be late except to work, a desire to enjoy herself rather than to tackle any unpleasant task.

She and Dennis had taken a road trip in his old Volvo to Memphis the month before. They strolled in the southern summer heat on the banks of the Mississippi, ate meals at a Cracker Barrel, and watched the ducks waddle down the red carpet at the Peabody Hotel. It was one of the happiest times of her life.

Bill was also a doctor, a surgeon like his father, and he was rigid and exacting, critical. She had loved him, but though she'd tried, she hadn't been able to please him. He had broken her heart. They had been married for twenty-five years. Now they never spoke.

Sophie hadn't told her mother about Dennis or much about the divorce. Harriet was irascible and opinionated; Sophie had stopped confiding when she was a teenager. The habit had stuck.

The block where her parents' beige brick house sat looked neglected. They had lived in the house for fifty years. Her mother had been an impeccable housekeeper, but now paint was chipping, leaving large rusted bald patches on the blue window trim. The windowpanes were smudged and needed to be washed. The house next door was empty—the couple had divorced, moved out, and been unable to sell. The lights were off, curtains drawn, the house abandoned. The neighbors on the other side were from Bulgaria. Every summer they went back there for months, leaving that house empty, too.

Across the street stood a compact two-story contemporary, a Frank Lloyd Wright wannabe, designed by an architect who had lived there; the house was once the jewel of the neighborhood. Now it was a rental. Sophie's father had told her he couldn't quite remember who was living there. The grass in that yard was too tall and needed to be cut. Weeds jutted out among the patches of hostas and roses. Two pickup trucks crowded the driveway, and two muscular middle-aged men in T-shirts and shorts, with webs of tattoos imprinted on their arms and legs, leaned against a white truck, drinking beer and smoking what Sophie presumed to be pot.

The air was hot and humid. Sophie hurried to her parents' house, pulling her suitcase behind her, then throwing her arms around her father after he opened the door. Seymour was eighty-eight and shorter than Sophie now, his thinning hair completely white. In the kitchen, she squatted and hugged her mother, who sat bent by the table and didn't rise from the chair. Harriet was terribly thin, as the doctor had said, her chest flat, her nose too large for her narrow face now, the freckled skin on her arms and hands stretched like dough, the bones sharp beneath her skin. Her eyes were still a lovely green-blue. Her breath and body smelled stale.

"How nice to see you, darling," Harriet said, her voice a low whisper. She fluttered her fingers toward Sophie. "You look beautiful as ever."

"My bluebird is back," Seymour laughed.

"Put your things away," Harriet said. "I can't help you with that now. I wish I could."

Sophie sat with them for a few minutes, then carried her suitcase to her old room, still furnished with two oak dressers, a desk, and two beds, the room where she and her younger sister, Patty, had fought, slept, and grown up. She remembered once peeking out of this room at her parents, her mother with shiny brown curls and dressed in a blue satin suit and sparkling costume earrings, ready to go out with Sophie's father. Sophie had been in awe of her mother at that moment. Her parents were affectionate with one another, held hands. That evening Harriet had kissed the top of Sophie's head, taken her hand, squeezed it.

"We'll see you later, Bluebird," Seymour had said, tall and smiling in his dark suit. He started singing: "When the red red robin comes…" then stopped and shrugged at Harriet's frown. "Off key," he said. "I'll try again tomorrow."

He had grasped Harriet's hand and the two of them were off.

Oh, sure: Sophie's parents had bickered. She and her sister had from time to time overheard their parents' fights and intimacies. Even so, Sophie had envied them. They were a couple.

She unpacked and returned to the kitchen where she found her parents sitting side by side, dozing, her father's hand resting on her mother's. Sophie tiptoed in. They were still a couple, she thought, with companionship in old age. She felt a little envious of them. Then she stopped herself. She had the pleasure of Dennis's company, at least for now. Every morning when she woke up beside him, she kissed him and said, "I love you, I love you."

"Come live with me," he'd said last month.

"I'm living with you now, in this bed."

"Let's really live together."

She had smiled but said nothing.

Sophie wandered around the house as if it were a museum. Her mother napped off and on, sitting in the living room, and her father read the newspaper, an activity that became a nap as well, his sleeping face tilted toward the pages. Then he trudged to his desk in the basement, where he worked on paying bills.

The house *was* a kind of museum, Sophie thought. Her high school diploma sat in her old bedroom, in a dresser drawer, the stiff paper pristine in its red leather case. Dusty high school yearbooks were piled on the night table. A full set of Shakespeare's plays in small blue volumes lined a bookshelf.

Her father loved to read. Her mother had been a school counselor. Harriet's counseling books sat on shelves in the spare bedroom, now turned into a small, dusty den: *Living Past Loss; Separation and Individuation; Depression;* and others, books Sophie once thought were grim and unpleasant. Harriet had had literary aspirations at one time but settled for a gossip column. Folders stood stacked on the small desk there, filled with columns she had written long ago for the local newspaper, gossip columns: "Listening In" by Harriet Latkowski.

Sophie didn't look through the books or the newspaper columns or yearbooks. Instead, she went back to the living room and stared at her mother's wasted body, the slow laborious shuffle as Harriet rose and made her way to the kitchen to get a glass of water, the movements like an old, scratched 45 rpm record playing on the wrong speed.

"Have something to eat," Sophie said, pulling open the refrigerator. "Here, an apple, cheese. Peanut butter. I can make you scrambled eggs. I'll cook for you. Aren't you hungry? You look like you're starving."

Harriet shook her head. "I don't feel so hot. Where's Daddy?"

"In the basement."

"I wish he were here. He would tell me what to do."

"I'll get him," Sophie said.

"Leave him alone. Age has treated your father well, but treats others unfairly. Brutally." She eyed the room. "If we move from here, this house, I don't want any of this crap." She pointed to the kitchen table, the living room. "I want only pictures. Pictures all over the wall. I want everyone there with me. Oh, honey, talk to me. I'm lonely."

"But I'm right here, Mom."

Harriet smiled sadly. "It's never enough. Your visit. A life. There is never enough time."

"I suppose not," Sophie said, trying to make sense of her mother's sudden dip into the philosophical.

"You suppose not? Of course, there's never enough time. I need to rest again a little, honey. You go rest, too. You've had a long trip."

Her mother trudged to the living room and sank into the armchair, shutting her eyes.

Sophie went upstairs and sat on her old bed. She sucked in a breath. Everybody had something, aging parents or trouble with their kids or work, or cancer, another illness, or a bad marriage. These were the burdens of life, and she'd better get used to them, she thought.

She heard the roar of the trucks from across the street as the engines started. Then she called Dennis on her cell phone.

"Sophie," he said. He wasn't at work today. She smiled. His voice lifted her spirits. "Are you there?" he said.

"Yes, yes. I was thinking," she said.

"Your mother?"

"Not good." She explained: the lack of eating, the difficulty walking, a new refusal to bathe. "She didn't get up to say hello when I arrived. She always stands up and throws her arms around me. I can do a million things for her, and I don't think any of them will change a thing." She sighed. "I don't mean to give you a litany of complaints."

"I asked. You answered. Give her ice cream, anything that puts on calories. And don't argue."

"Argue?"

"If she says she doesn't want to do something, you can try to convince her, but it doesn't pay to argue. She wants some independence. I've heard the appetite is the first to go."

"What's that supposed to mean?"

"What I mean is: Fix what you can. The rest, forget it. Enjoy her company. I know it's tough. Sorry. I didn't intend to give you a litany of quick fixes."

She laughed. "I gave you a litany of complaints. But it's comforting that you listen. Comforting to talk to you."

"For me, too."

"Seymour, where are you?" Harriet called out from the living room, her voice tinged with fear. "Sophie."

"Call you back," she said and hurried downstairs.

"Oh, honey," Harriet said, gathering herself. "You were upstairs? On the telephone?"

"Yes. The cell phone."

"I'm sorry to disturb you. I didn't realize."

"No, I came to visit you. Dad is in the kitchen now, I think."

"I don't know where he is. He hardly hears what I say anymore. Oh, he never liked to hear what he didn't want to. But now he doesn't hear anything. I'm lonely. I'm losing people all the time."

"You have Daddy. Whether he hears or not."

Her mother smiled a half smile; the frown lines softened. "Oh, yes. I know I'm lucky. You're here. Patty comes to see me. I'm lucky she lives in Chicago."

Sophie nodded. She had called Patty from the airport. They'd talked about the doctor's advice to move their parents to a retirement home, a protected environment. "I'll see how things are when I'm with them," Sophie had said. Whenever Sophie was in Chicago, Patty took a break from visiting their parents.

"And that caregiver you arranged," Harriet went on, "comes over every once in a while. She cooks a little, checks up on me." Harriet paused and her voice faltered. "But your father…people think we're a couple. But we're really not anymore. He doesn't hear me. He sleeps." She fluttered her hand toward the kitchen. "Oh, he sleeps because he's old, but even so. Look in there."

Sophie walked to the doorway and peeked in. Her father was sitting at the kitchen table, his eyes closed, his head back. She understood her mother's point. Sophie wanted to talk to her, really talk, to tell her about Dennis, the divorce. Ask about her mother's life. But Sophie didn't know where to begin. She had stopped talking to her mother about important things years before, so it was hard to know what to say now. She thought of her mother sitting here day after day, barely able to walk, reading or staring into the room.

"You see," Harriet said. "I'm on my own."

"You need company," Sophie said.

"It's not company," Harriet said. "I don't want to take any more goddamn pills. I don't want to take that Coumadin. It's poison. People bleed and they never stop."

"Dad," Sophie said loudly. "You're sleeping."

His eyes popped open. He lifted his head. "No. I'm not. I heard every word."

"What did we say, dear?" Harriet called out slyly.

"They bleed and they never stop," Seymour echoed. He lumbered into the living room. "But I didn't hear you saying what you usually say, Harriet. Did you tell Sophie: there must be a better way to get old? Has she said that yet, Bluebird? Did she tell you what I say: If you don't start eating, you'll end up spending the rest of your life in bed? Did she tell you that, too?"

The house and the room were so hot that Sophie slid off her nightgown and climbed into bed. The sheets felt soft and cool. There was something deliciously forbidden about being naked in her childhood bed. She thought of Dennis. She heard her mother's voice, saying loudly, "Can you help me? I don't know if I can go on," and the swish of cotton as her father helped her mother change into a nightgown.

Sophie bit her lip. The trucks across the street grumbled and sped away. She lay in the dark, listening, and when she couldn't sleep, she switched on the lamp, slipped on a robe, and rummaged through the items on the night table. When Bill had left, she had begun reading catalogues to numb her mind, and now she found an old *Home Trends* catalogue, yellowed and creased, on the night table. *Free Shipping!* it proclaimed. She thumbed through the pages. Myriad products promised to make life easier. The Revolving Medicine Center, where you could keep up to twenty-one medicine bottles arranged for easy access. Who took twenty-one medications? Sophie wondered, and who would want to? There was a can of Ozium, which promised to reduce airborne bacteria and sanitize the house. Maybe that would help. The Every Stain Remover swore it removed everything, even the most stubborn stains. But what about the stain of illness? You could repair leather and vinyl, eliminate flying insects. There were gadgets to improve almost every part of your life, except what mattered. No gadgets for real comfort. No gadgets that guaranteed health.

She put the catalogue on the night table, then retrieved her purse from the dresser. She fished inside and pulled out a small black notebook where she wrote lists. Now she wrote on a blank sheet of paper, like a prompt, a series of phrases that had been revolving in her head.

Too weird for words
We worry about the wrong things
Tolerate it
There is no choice

Too weird for words was her conviction that what had transpired with Bill was beyond language. Sophie felt a kind of hatred for him now. She'd understood his limitations when they married, but had made her peace with them, though, she had to admit, she'd considered leaving him. Then after twenty-five years, he had suddenly left her. If every person was given a certain allotment of anger in life, she thought, Bill had more than his share. He had a small soul.

She was determined to put him behind her.

We worry about the wrong things. Her mother had worried about her father for as long as Sophie could remember. Seymour's father had died at forty-seven of a heart attack. "Don't shovel snow, dear," Harriet always admonished Seymour. "You must protect your heart. Stop! Don't carry that heavy package!" Harriet used to rattle off a list of tasks forbidden to Seymour. But last week on the telephone she'd told Sophie, "Oh, I was wrong about your father. All those years I worried about whether his heart was strong, whether he'd die of a heart attack. I worried about the wrong things. Now I'm the one who's sick."

Tolerate it. This was all Sophie could do, tolerate everything slipping away from her.

There is no choice. What choice did anyone have about most things in life? This was Dennis's addition. It was a cliché, but true. He told her this when she complained about dividing possessions with Bill, about money. Dennis told her this when she complained at all.

How to get divorced, Sophie thought in the morning as she went downstairs to find her parents: Sit in the lawyer's office just as she had done last week. Categorize your life, expenses, and habits. When she met with the lawyer and paralegal, she felt sometimes like a child at home with her parents.

The papers had taken Sophie by surprise. She had seen countless causes of action and headings in lawsuits, but reading *William Weston, Plaintiff, v Sophie Weston, Defendant* had made her feel weak.

Ursula, the paralegal, was precise and unrelenting. "Don't round the numbers," she had ordered in her German accent. "This is a pain, isn't it?"

Nodding, Sophie had thought of the German countess in *The Sound of Music*. Sitting in that office, surrounded by papers, a vague future, she wished the hills were alive with something other than the deadening minutia of monthly budgets and future income.

"I had to do this for my own divorce," Ursula said, "and I didn't have an Ursula to help me. It was awful. I'll never marry again." She entered numbers on the calculator. "I'd commit suicide if I had to go through this another time."

"Let's finish up," Sophie had said, eager to get out of there. "Is any information missing?"

"It takes five years to get over a divorce," Ursula persisted. "You're not ready to get involved with anyone, a man, for five years. Divorce is very traumatic." She pursed her lips as if she might spit with disgust. "Mark my words: the women suffer. And men? They get involved with someone else right away, and it never works out."

Sophie was ashamed to think of how she had once judged friends and their checkerboard attachments, the slew of relationships: ex-husband, stepmother, stepfather, former stepmother, half-brother, stepsister. The relationships seemed confusing, and she was astonished to realize this would be the configuration of her own family.

Harriet sat in the living room in the big red armchair, her head leaning on her chest, her arms wrapped around herself, as if holding herself up. Sophie had at first thought her mother didn't care about the state of the house. She understood now that her mother was incapable of taking care of the house or anything else. The doctor had been right. Harriet needed to live in a protected environment. But what he didn't say had become clear to Sophie: maybe her mother didn't want to eat, like Dennis had said. Harriet was starving herself to death.

"Mom." Sophie sat across from Harriet. She took a breath, gathered her resolve, put the divorce out of her mind. "I've talked to your doctor. Patty has, too. She and I have been thinking of making some changes…we want to move you and Dad."

"Where are you taking us?"

"The doctor says we have to do this before it's too late. You have to live someplace where they feed you."

"Where's that?" Harriet said. "A zoo?"

"Don't be ridiculous. We're going to move you and Dad into an assisted living facility."

"Oh, now I see. A facility, no less. I know what those places are like, Sophie. They're filled with old people. Old people who are sick and dying and don't have hope. What am I going to say to those people? I can't even bear to look at them."

"There are plenty of nice places. Don't make a judgment before you know what the place is like."

"And what do you know?" Harriet waved her thin hand in the air. "How are we going to afford one of these nice places? You can't just move someone without their consent. This isn't Cuba or China; the last time I checked we lived in the United States of America. And it's a free country. A democracy. Isn't that right, Seymour, a free country?"

Seymour shifted on the couch and shook the sleep out of his eyes. "Of course, that's what the country is founded on," he mumbled. "Freedom."

"What use is freedom when one of you is starving?" Sophie said.

"No one is starving," Harriet replied.

"I eat well," Seymour said.

"Too well," said Harriet. "You eat for both of us. Honey, why don't you go work on your bills? Sophie and I need to talk."

He stood up with a smile of relief, lumbered out of the room and down the steps to the basement.

"Dad will move," Sophie said. "You're the one who needs convincing."

"You'll never convince me, honey. You take me away from here, and you'll cut out my soul."

"Mom, don't be so goddamned dramatic."

Harriet sighed. "You could use a little drama in your life."

"I've got more than my share."

"Not that I'd know about. You never tell me what's going on in your life." She dropped her hands in her lap. "I'll die and I'll wonder how you're doing, Sophie. Ever since you were a teenager, your lips were sealed."

"That is an exaggeration." But her mother was more right than wrong.

"What do you like to cook, honey? Now that the boys are in college."

"Oh, I hardly cook anymore. I cooked for so many years for Bill and the kids." She knew her mother was changing the subject. "I eat from a salad bar. I love to eat at Whole Foods."

"I don't cook anymore either," Harriet said.

They both laughed.

"The truth is," Harriet said quietly, "the neighbors used to be disgusted with me when I wrote the gossip column. Now I'm disgusted with myself."

"Why?"

"Sometimes I want to throw myself off a bridge. Look what's happened to me. Oh Sophie, if I only had the strength to jump."

She leaned toward her mother. "Don't you remember when I told you about Bill, about the divorce? I said I felt like jumping off a bridge, and you said, 'Sophie, you'll jump off a bridge and then you'll swim. You'll do what the lawyers tell you, and you'll get everything in order.'"

"I said that? I'm a mess, my sweetheart. This leg, it's swollen. The house is a mess. Do you see how I look? My face is a prune." She pressed a hand against her chin.

"Just do what the doctor tells you. You'll get better if you eat. And if you want to know the truth, I'm disgusted with myself, too," Sophie said.

"You should be disgusted with Bill," Harriet said. "I am."

"Oh, I am. I hate him."

"I'm not surprised. Divorce does that. Love turns to hate. Living in such close quarters with someone can do that. It's an old story."

"Except to me," Sophie said.

"Your father and I are too old to divorce. The time for that is past."

"You?" Sophie said with surprise.

"Nothing's perfect," Harriet said. "Life can be full of crap, excuse the expression."

Sophie nodded.

"You know, honey, Bill isn't the kind of man who would have helped you in your old age. You're better off without him." Harriet shook her head with vehemence. "He was far too impressed with himself. He's a surgeon. His father was, too. They think they're very important. We're ordinary people." She paused. "Let's not talk about moving or Bill or anything unpleasant. Tell me something happy. I don't know. News. Like I would have written about in my column."

"Well, I've met someone," Sophie said slowly. "Oh, I know I'm not divorced yet, but…"

"Those old rules don't apply anymore. Those rules I wrote about in the column. They're obsolete. Forget them. Who?"

"Someone I went to high school with. Dennis Gribling."

"The Gribling family." Harriet leaned her head against the chair back. "He must be a little younger than you. Yes, his mother was active in the organizations, the PTA. Oh, she was very effective. Well-liked. I wonder if she's still alive."

"She's not."

"Too bad." Harriet shook her head again. "So many people gone. But I'm happy for you. If you like him, hold onto him."

"I do like him. He's a doctor. He works in—"

"All that doesn't matter, where he works, those details," Harriet interrupted. "If you like each other, that's what matters. Of course, you're a person in your own right, but it's good to have a companion. Don't vacillate, Sophie. Men are fickle. When that caregiver comes to the house with her pert smile, your father's eyes light up to see a pretty face. Thank goodness, she's here just a few hours a week. He thinks I don't notice, but I do. That's how men are."

"Flirting?"

"Oh, yes. Your father loves to flirt. He even smiles at that nurse in my doctor's office. Shameless smiles. What's her name? And she has bad teeth to boot."

They both laughed.

"It keeps Dad happy," Sophie said. "I'll introduce you to Dennis. Soon." She held her mother's hand. "I'll go home in two days like I've planned. We'll figure out where you'll move, then I'll be back here in a few weeks. I know he'll come and help us."

"Oh, I'd like to meet him." Harriet smiled, then shut her eyes. "But I don't know, dear. Let your father flirt. I feel sorry for him. I think I may be dying."

Back in New York, life got insanely busy. The divorce lawyer called and said it was imperative that she finish up the financial calculations. Bill sent an email saying he wanted to discuss finances. Sophie needed to begin preparing her classes for the fall. After doing some research, she spoke to the directors of two senior facilities in Chicago about moving her parents there.

Dennis was the only sweetness in this tangle of obligations, but his work in Memphis had been extended and he wanted to have a serious conversation about living together.

Don't vacillate, her mother had said. Vacillation was a drug, Sophie thought. Indecision seemed to make time stand still.

But it never stood still. Harriet continued to get worse.

"I'm not feeling so well," she told Sophie on the telephone in the middle of the week. "If I get myself together, I'll feel better."

"Is it something new?" Sophie said. "What's the matter?"

"The same, as always. I don't know, maybe not. I can't explain."

"Dad will take you to the doctor," Sophie said. "Or Patty. Let me talk to Dad."

The nurse at the doctor's office couldn't schedule an appointment until the end of the week. "It was the one with the bad teeth," Harriet reported to Sophie later on the telephone. "No appointment today, no matter how your father flirted. So I'll have to wait."

But Harriet never made it to the doctor's office. She was in the hospital by Friday, and Sophie was back in Chicago. Now her mother was in intensive care, on a ventilator.

The doctor at the hospital, a new doctor they'd never met before, said the breathing tube could remain in a patient for seven days. A ventilator was a limited tool. But the many doctors treating Harriet didn't agree on the timing. Harriet had pneumonia, was malnourished, and was struggling with other problems Sophie had trouble remembering. Where her parents would move was now a moot point.

Sophie, her father, and Patty went to the hospital every day. Patty was a real estate agent, and summer was a busy time of year. "I've rearranged my schedule as best I can," she told Sophie. "But I'll be here every day."

"I'll need your help with Dad," Sophie said.

Patty looked from Sophie to their father. "Okay." She sighed. "I'll cancel whatever I can."

They spoke to the nephrologist, the pulmonologist, the infectious disease specialist, a parade of doctors, day nurses, night nurses, the weekend nurses.

Sophie took notes in her small black notebook. She diligently wrote what each doctor said, the prognosis, course of treatment, the fluctuations in her mother's levels as measured by the many machines: Harriet's oxygen saturation, temperature, heart rate, blood pressure, white blood cell count, urine output, as if the information was a test. If Sophie mastered the details, her mother would survive.

"Your mother is doing better," one of the doctors said. And later that day, another informed Sophie, "There is no change. Your mother is profoundly sick." But two days before, the weekend doctor had told them, "I would not give up. There is still hope."

The hardest thing for Sophie wasn't being in the hospital with its sterile empty corridors and waiting rooms, but seeing her mother in the intensive care bed, the blue accordion ventilator tube taped to Harriet's face, snaking into her mouth. And hearing the labored inhale and exhale of Harriet's breathing, a whoosh of breath as the machines whirred in harmony with their lights that sometimes glowed red, warning of an emergency. Other tubes were attached to veins in Harriet's arms and dispensed medicines and nutrition. All this was alarmingly, catastrophically wrong.

Sophie had just been talking to her mother in the living room of the house about jumping off bridges and the need to eat. They had just been engaging in conversation, unsealing lips. Now Harriet was here, helpless, unable to speak or complain as she would have: about the poor hospital service, the crappy room, the lights that glowed day and night. Sophie could imagine Harriet's gravelly voice: how can a person sleep here?

"She's not making a lot of progress," a doctor said to Sophie and Patty in the hallway. "There's fluid in her lungs because of poor nutritional status."

"You mean the not eating," Seymour said.

"Exactly," said the doctor. "Remember, you are the voice of the patient. Would she want to be on a ventilator? Would she want heroic measures?"

Sophie hadn't discussed this yet with her parents. Patty hadn't either. She had always waited for Sophie to take the lead and talk with their parents about difficult subjects.

"How can you sit there?" Patty said. "How can you bear to see Mom like that? It's too hard."

Sophie shrugged and escorted Patty to the ICU exit. "Why don't you take a break for a while? You can go to the cafeteria or the waiting area. I'll stay here with Dad."

Sophie realized she liked to sit with Harriet in the hospital room, watching Harriet breathe. Sophie liked the quiet of the room, even the hum and whir of the machines, the lights blinking on the screen like stars. Every breath meant her mother was alive.

"Do you think she can hear?" Sophie asked the nurse. Harriet lay sleeping, her coarse hair spread out on the pillow. "I don't want her to be lonely here, at night."

"Oh, we check up on her. And they say hearing is the last to go," Lorna, the short, broad Filipino nurse, replied cheerfully.

Seymour sat in the room, too, asleep. He didn't stir, didn't seem to hear anything.

Harriet was dying, though the doctors hadn't said the word. It was clear to Sophie. Her mother had often been right, Sophie thought as she stood by the bedside, although Sophie had never admitted this. She had distanced herself from her mother because she was like her mother, she supposed, and her own aura of politeness was a way to push her mother away. An old, crude coping mechanism, a rebellion. A remnant from being a teenager. Like sealed lips that no longer served a function.

"This is all crap," Sophie said aloud now, on the fifth day. She paced by the bed. "This fucking hospital. Everything." She sounded like her mother. "What should I do with all this fucking crap?" Sophie said loudly. She couldn't help herself. "Tell me, Mom, please." But Harriet didn't move, didn't respond. Seymour slumped in a chair, sleeping. Patty had gone to the hospital cafeteria to get coffee for him.

Elmira, the nurse at the desk just outside of Harriet's room, looked up at Sophie, and then at the computer, as if she had interrupted a moment of family privacy.

Sophie sank into a chair, listening to the whoosh of Harriet's breath. She had missed it with her mother, the chance to really talk to her. She had wasted so much time, as if there had been an endless supply.

She shut her eyes. She had better be careful with Dennis. The conversation about living together would happen sooner or later, whether she was ready or not.

"She can follow commands," Lorna the nurse said later. "She's more alert today. When you were at lunch, she was up. I asked her if she's having pain. She shook her head no. I asked: do you want the breathing tube out? She nodded yes. She tried to pull it out. That tube is a bother to your mother. I asked if she wanted dialysis. No. Twice, I asked this. There." Lorna pointed to the table near the window. "There's an alphabet card you can use. When she's up, ask her questions. She can answer. She can point to the letters and spell words back. Simple things. Like she told me."

Sophie eyed the card. It was the size of a legal pad. "So I can talk with her that way?"

"Oh, yes," the nurse said. "And don't be alarmed. Her skin is weeping. But we are keeping her dry and clean."

"Weeping?"

The nurse smiled kindly. "Her arms, her legs, they're swollen. Liquid is seeping out. That's why I wrap her arms in bandages." She pulled back the sheet to show the white gauze wrapped around Harriet's arms, as if Harriet were a mummy.

"Five days on antibiotics, the white count is better," the doctor said. He wore a white hospital coat over green scrubs. Sophie couldn't remember his specialty. She didn't remember his name. They stood in the hallway outside her mother's room with her father and Patty.

"Her kidney function is no worse than before," the man said. "We're still working on the pneumonia. The infectious disease doctor will talk to you about that. The good news is: we don't think she has cancer."

Sophie jotted notes in her notebook.

"As we told you, there are problems: the bilateral pneumonia, kidney disease, severe protein malnutrition, anemia, septic shock, multi-organ failure."

"All that?" said Seymour.

The doctor nodded gravely. "She will need several months on a feeding tube. This is, of course, after the ventilator is removed."

"Removed?" said Seymour, surprised.

"Yes, sir, yes," the doctor said. "We told you at the outset, the breathing tube is only temporary. So these are the options," he went on, as if reciting from a textbook. "Tracheotomy and feeding tube after extubation; or extubate her and give the patient pain management. The question is: does she want a feeding tube? She's prone to complications. Or you can give her palliative care. People suffer at the end of life with suffocation, anxiety, and pain. We would make her comfortable." He eyed them. "Even with heroic measures, she may not make a meaningful recovery. Have you thought about this? What are your goals of care?"

"Goals?" said Patty. "To make her better, of course."

Sophie stopped writing, unable to jot words fast enough. She would discuss this with Dennis.

Seymour stood speechless, trying to absorb what the doctor was saying. "My girls will explain this to me." He looked from Patty to Sophie. "I don't quite understand."

"On the positive side, she's alert," the doctor said. "We don't know for sure, but her mind seems to be there. Her body is failing. Still, I'd give her the benefit of the doubt and continue with the treatment as it is."

The window in Harriet's room stretched over one wall, facing west. Afternoon sunlight streamed in, creating swaths of light on the pillow, on Harriet's face, brushing her hair with gold, like a halo.

The doctor had left, and Seymour and Patty were in the waiting area, taking a break. Sophie sat vigil in her mother's room alone. She thought of it like this: sitting vigil. Her children were coming tomorrow to see their grandmother. They were upset about Harriet's condition, and Sophie would try to comfort them. Dennis called often. He was coming here tonight. Sophie didn't want her mother to meet Dennis in this state, yet Sophie longed to see him. Still, she knew how vain Harriet was. Harriet would be ashamed. Sophie had all the time in the world to talk to him, if she was lucky. How much time did she have to talk to her mother?

But she didn't know how to talk to her mother. Sophie's lips were unsealed, but everything she could think to say—about her children, about Bill and Dennis, about being part of a couple or not part of one, about growing up, being a daughter, a wife, a mother, a woman, about disappointment, divorce, even about the unbelievable punishing crap of illness—it all seemed trivial. Even Sophie's future seemed trivial. So many things had gone unsaid. The machines hummed around Harriet as if she were a machine herself, colors glowing on the screen beneath the bright hospital room lights. All Sophie could do was stroke Harriet's hand, helpless.

What she wanted to do, she realized, was lie down next to her mother, but there was no chance of that. The bed rails stood high. Harriet's hands were tied to the rails, in restraints so she wouldn't again try to pull out the ventilator tube. The restraints, a heavy quilted cloth, like canvas, the color of skin, encircled her mother's bony wrists.

Did Harriet want the tube out so she could talk or just to get rid of the thing? Sophie imagined if the tube was gone, her mother would sit up and give everyone a piece of her mind: I don't want any goddamn heroic measures. If I don't make it, I don't.

Instead of climbing into the bed, Sophie knelt on the floor at her mother's side and grasped her mother's hand.

Sophie's whole life fell away, reduced to this: the hospital room, the sunlight trickling in. How could she adequately describe to her mother the discussions swirling around her, or the people, like the doctors in the white coats, who had pushed into their lives? What could Sophie say that would make a difference?

Harriet's hand was swollen, puffy and slack, though the fingers were long, as they'd always been. Sophie touched her mother's skin carefully. "Mom? Even though I didn't tell you everything about my life, you knew. I know you did. You said I needed more drama. You were right. You were always right. I was so wrong. I have more drama in my life now than I can cope with. What a story you would have written about this for your column."

Harriet opened her eyes. She smiled a half smile, as much as she could muster with the tubes.

"You're there!" Sophie stood up and bent to kiss her mother's forehead. She smoothed Harriet's hair. "Can you hear me?"

Harriet nodded twice, her eyes fixed on Sophie's.

"Oh, it's wonderful to see you up. What a siege you've had. You were right last week. You didn't feel well. I hope when these crappy tubes come out you'll be able to talk."

Harriet moved her head up and down three times.

Sophie remembered the card on the table. "Wait. Don't go anywhere. I'm going to get something. You'll like it."

Harriet smiled that half smile.

She found the card Lorna had shown her and brought it to the bed. It was heavy cardboard, the alphabet printed on it in big black block letters. "We'll use this. We'll talk." She brought the card close to Harriet's face. "My lips are forever unsealed for you."

Harriet tried to lift her hand, but it was tied to the bed rail.

"Oh." Sophie pulled open the Velcro that fastened the restraints. The beige fabric fell from Harriet's wrists to the floor.

Sophie held the card near her mother's face and began to point slowly, saying each letter as she pointed: "I L-O-V-E Y-O-U. Do you understand? Can you answer? I know it's not really a question. But say something. Can you? Talk to me."

Harriet's fingers fluttered away from Sophie, up, up toward the card. She began to point.

I L-O-V-E Y-O-U!

Sophie smiled, then said, "That thing, that tube. Does it hurt?"

Harriet shook her head no. She pointed again, one letter at a time: B-U-T L-E-T M-E G-O.

Sophie stared at her mother in disbelief. Harriet had always been such a fighter. "We should let you go?" she asked. "Is that what you're saying?" It wasn't what she had wanted to hear. "Are you sure?"

Harriet nodded vigorously.

"But we're doing everything we can. The machines. The medicines. The doctors. You'll get better."

Harriet shook her head no, very slowly.

Tears welled in Sophie's eyes. "But how can we just let you go? How can I?"

Harriet shut her eyes. She opened them. She pointed. S-I-C-K-N-E-S-S I-S A-L-L C-R-A-P, she spelled.

"It is," Sophie agreed. "It is."

Harriet pointed again, with effort. As the message got longer, her energy began to fade. M-Y L-I-F-E W-A-S G-O-O-D. She smiled at Sophie. B-U-T I A-M D-O-N-E. She rested for a moment, looking deep into Sophie's eyes. I H-A-V-E D-E-C-I-D-E-D N-O-W D-E-C-I-D-E Y-O-U-R L-I-F-E B-E H-A-P-P-Y S-O-P-H-I-E M-O-V-E O-N.

Sophie knew life was difficult, and that no one had the answers. Still, even at this late date, she knew she wanted her mother's advice and blessing. "You mean…I shouldn't hesitate? Shouldn't dawdle? That I should…"

Harriet smiled up at her and nodded, once.

"You mean…" The tears welling in Sophie's eyes spilled over. "I love you, Mom," she said. "I wish I'd said it over and over. I wish we could talk and talk. I wish a million things."

Harriet was getting tired. Her eyes closed, and for a minute it seemed this was the end of the conversation. Then she opened her eyes. They were that beautiful green-blue. She looked at Sophie so intently, as if she could leap out of bed, as if her eyes had the power to speak. Harriet pointed, slowly, her finger trembling from the effort. M-E T-O-O! R-E-M-E-M-B-E-R. I L-O-V-E Y-O-U M-O-R-E. She closed her eyes again.

Standing beneath the bright hospital lights, Sophie could hardly catch her breath. She was balanced between two worlds. The past and the future. The old life, with a husband and a mother, was ending, a new one about to begin. But she didn't feel quite ready for the old phase to be over. Things were moving too fast.

She'd have to make a decision about living with Dennis, whatever that would be. She remembered Harriet's thoughts about coupledness. On the inside, people in a couple could be isolated, vulnerable, like her mother was now. Still, it was good to have a companion. The details of the divorce would eventually be resolved, Sophie knew. The force of living would push her into the future. But she didn't know how she'd be able to traverse the world without her mother.

The only thing certain, Sophie thought, was she would move on, however the future unfolded. For now, she held her mother's hand and watched her breathe.

Personal Eloquence

LIBBY LIKES TO PLEASE PEOPLE. She often acts on this desire without calculation, unconsciously, which can get her into trouble.

"What's this?" her husband asks tonight. The living room lamp casts a golden glow. She sits on the couch, reading the arts section of *The New York Times*. Andrew sits next to her. He's tall and slender, with gray-streaked black hair. He slips his round tortoiseshell eyeglasses to the middle of his nose, adjusting the bifocal portion, and lifts a piece of paper. "Bloomingdale's. Jewelry," he says. "Twelve hundred dollars?"

She catches a glimpse of the Visa bill. "For gifts and part for a necklace for me. You know, wedding gifts, your mother, and—"

"Who did you buy for, an army?" Andrew often neglects financial details. They pool their earnings into one account. This allows Libby to withdraw cash and use it for items he might disapprove of. Or spend cash and charge the rest, paying the balance month by month. Jewelry, for example. She adores jewelry. The dazzling gold ring with a translucent amethyst stone. The matching necklace. Or Prada shoes, brown and beige horsehair flats—on sale—but still too expensive. Things she knows they can't afford. Things Andrew wouldn't understand.

"We'll go broke with these damn gifts. In this goddamned economy," he snaps. "Just give people books, nothing else." He throws the bill on the couch and picks up the sports section.

The living room in their Upper East Side apartment feels cozy on this winter night. Why can't this coziness spill into their lives? Libby wonders. In order to please Andrew, she has learned to lie. She isn't proud of this. She prefers to think of her behavior as self-protection. Protecting Andrew from facts he would be unhappy to know. Protecting herself from his anger. An odd contradiction. She easily confronts people in her work as a nurse, advocating for

72

patients, the women she cares for in the breast cancer clinic at the hospital.

This need to please causes her to be deceitful with others. When Libby's mother used to telephone and ask, "Lib, darling, how are you?" Libby answered, "Fine. Everything is fine." One of the boys was ill or Andrew impossibly cranky. Still, Libby said to her mother cheerfully, "Life is fine."

Now she's an orphan. That's how she defines herself, her parents dead and the boys in college and graduate school, deep into their own lives. Orphaned, in a sense, on both sides.

The past assaults Libby. Objects from her childhood home. Her parents' walnut bureau stands in the bedroom, the old mahogany writing desk in the living room. Her mother's paintings with their bright colors and bold shapes hang on the wall, like her companions.

There are photographs of the boys at preschool, their golden curls. Snapshots of her and Andrew with happy, hopeful smiles—just kids themselves—at the Grand Canyon, their honeymoon, when they had slept in cheap hotels or under the stars.

Tonight, Libby fidgets beside Andrew in the king-size bed. They sleep without touching. She listens to him snore, rough spurts of sound like grunts of surprise. I'll leave you someday, she thinks. If her mother were alive, Libby might say to her: life is passing, passing. Is this enough? With him? But perhaps what Libby would really say is, "Fine. Life is fine."

The bedroom is cold. The hiss of the radiator is weak. Rain begins falling; moisture pellets the windows. Forecasters predict a winter storm, first rain, then slush, then snow. The rain obscures the trail of moonlight that sometimes spills into the room.

Libby lies on her side and studies Andrew as he sleeps. The shiny nose, the round face, a lock of dark hair fallen carelessly onto his forehead. He has aged well. But work kidnaps him. He teaches seminars on public speaking in the city and around the world, peddling his courses, coaching actors and actresses and lecturing to doctors, lawyers, and companies. He's transformed this into a thriving business. He has *become* the business. With all the technological gadgetry he uses, he seems to need no one else.

She has started to distrust him. Is this projection? She pulls the quilt to her neck. She knows Andrew should distrust her. About money. About the unsteady nature of her affections. Is he falling out of love with her? He's away so much, presenting seminars. A few months ago, Libby called him late at his hotel, then on his cell phone. He didn't answer. Is he sleeping with other women? She shuts her eyes. Is she falling out of love with him? Does she want to sleep with another man? She did this once years ago. Does doubt grow like cancer in a marriage?

Patients populate Libby's life. She speaks Spanish with many—the language they understand—and she's become skillful, too, as a nurse must, at the language of uncertainty and grief. But she finds that silence and listening are often the most powerful response.

Andrew taught her this. He sometimes sits with her and experiments with phrases, like sound bites. One night, a few days after their conversation about the Visa bill, he says, "What about this, honey? Do you have a minute?"

"Of course." She sits on the couch.

He stands up, clutching a piece of paper. Then he begins to pace as he might at a seminar. "I want to try out new phrases. New ways to talk about old concepts. Like: not just 'know your audience.' But, tailor a presentation to the audience."

She nods. This is how she lives, she realizes. Her father had a temper and yelled indiscriminately. She learned subterfuge to appease him. To keep the peace. "Good," she says to Andrew.

"So if you're talking to accountants, use numbers, be precise. That kind of thing. Second: listening is an emotional experience." He speaks slowly, enunciating. "A subjective experience. If you concentrate and listen, it's emotional."

"I always listen."

"Not you. Don't turn this into a joke."

She laughs. "Okay, no jokes." But they used to joke all the time. They created games, too. Guess who I saw today? Andrew might ask with great enthusiasm. The game would begin. She would ask: Was it a man or a woman? A friend of yours? Our age? And so on. She would try to guess with as few questions as possible. Or she would say to Andrew: Do you know what happened today? And he would begin.

"When you speak," Andrew says now, "it's essential to connect with the audience on an emotional level." He settles into the couch beside her. "And explain things in threes. This could help you in your work, Libby. People retain between three and seven pieces of information at a time. Three. A magic number. Three little pigs; three blind mice. Three's a crowd. And so on. I have three items I want to discuss. You could do that with your patients."

Bad things happen in threes, she thinks. Her mother used to say that. "Good idea," Libby says to Andrew. "Are you going to prepare a list of these?"

"No. I want to talk about this with bold phrases. Like headlines. I may prepare a handout, too." He scribbles on the paper, stands up. "Remember this one: an emotion lasts for three minutes. Really, less than that. Unless you get locked in. Breathe, and the emotion will disappear. I'm going to expand that. I'll discuss how people feel nervous when they do a public speaking gig. Always have faith the emotion will pass. That should be your mantra."

She nods again. Will her uncertainty disappear? This distrust? Her restlessness? She has tried to be a good partner to Andrew. She knows they lead a privileged life; she should be grateful. And she is. But she wants something from him. For him to be freer, lighter with her, playful. Like he acts with his audiences. "Does that stuff really work?" she says.

"Sure. Though most people are WIFM: what's in it for *me*? People aren't waiting to listen; they're waiting to talk."

"What do you do when I'm not with you on one of those *gigs*?" she asks later. She lounges on the bed in her blue silk robe, leaning against the pillows.

Andrew perches on the edge of the mattress, staring at his notes, typed in twenty-two-point bold. He folds the paper in half. That way, when he lectures, the notes are less obtrusive. In fact, if you don't look closely, it seems as if he isn't relying on anything, he once reported proudly. He showed her. He's a kind of magician. Sleight of hand.

"Human beings love surprises," he tells her.

"What do you *do*?" Libby repeats. He didn't answer the question. "When you're off lecturing and the lecture is over?"

"Oh." He looks up at her. "Dinner in the hotel room, read over my notes. Like this." He flashes a smile, glances down, then locks his eyes on hers. "Call home—to you, my sweet, then to bed."

With whom? A random, unsettling thought, but she says nothing.

"I worry about our money. Where is it going? It disappears. For the kids, the credit card bills, and…" He stops. "But mostly, I concentrate on personal eloquence. That's what I'm paid to do. I've identified three types of people in these seminars. Learners, vacationers, and hostages."

"That's the same for patients at the clinic." True of marriage, too, she thinks.

"The vacationers are the best," he replies. "Hostages are angry. Learners are too eager."

She's learned the value of silence from him, and she waits.

"Are you going to turn this into a serious discussion?" he goes on. "Why do you ask? It's not who I'm sleeping with. It's who I'm thinking of."

"Really. And who is that?"

"It's a joke. Of course, you."

She doesn't reply. She wants him to kiss her lustfully, kiss away doubt.

"Everyone has fantasies," he says. "You can't argue with that."

"True." If you're quiet, the other person often talks, to fill up the silence; Andrew once told her this. A spilling out of thoughts.

"I suppose after a long marriage, people have fantasies," he says. "Why are you suspicious? I love you, Libby. I would never hurt you."

"You can hurt a person even when you don't intend to. Sometimes I feel you love your audience more than…" She hesitates. "More than me, than us."

"That's not true."

"Do you want to know how things are at the hospital?"

"Yes, of course." He reaches for her hand. "Tell me."

That weekend, Andrew goes out of town to give a seminar. Libby's friend Pam comes over. She and Libby grew up in Detroit. They both ended up in New York.

Libby prepares peppermint tea. Then she sits on the couch, and Pam curls into an armchair.

"I don't think you can be sure of anyone," Libby says, blowing on her mug of tea to cool it. They begin conversations where they left off, without decorous exchanges. "How do you really know your husband isn't sleeping with someone else?"

"If you're worried about this, talk to Andrew," Pam says.

"This is completely hypothetical."

"Well, how *do* you know? If he's attentive, wants sex with you— he's probably not cheating. There are tons of books about it, as if there's an epidemic of infidelity. I've seen them at Barnes & Noble. Even books about what cheating husbands say to their wives *and* to their mistresses. As if there's a script." She pushes a strand of her shoulder-length red hair behind her ear. "Mistress. An outdated term."

"Paramour? Lover?"

"Friend with benefits. All of the above."

They sound like characters in a television sitcom, Libby thinks. Except they are real. At fourteen, they used to talk on the phone for hours about boys. Which boy would kiss the best? Be the kindest?

Pam left her husband two years ago. She rents a small apartment in the city. When it's her turn to take care of the two girls, still in middle school, she lives in the big apartment she once shared with her ex. When it's his turn, he moves in, and Pam moves out.

"How's the living arrangement working out?" Libby asks.

"It's hard to leave the kids," Pam says. "Even so, on those days, I'm free. I work, but without other responsibilities."

"Sounds nice, I guess. And how's the search for a companion?"

"I've met someone new."

"Good. Where?"

"The motorcycle club. I'm going to get you involved yet. Last weekend, when the weather was still nice, we went upstate. That feeling of freedom, Libby, riding in the wind. Absolute."

"So who did you meet?"

"Mike. He…he's 250 pounds, rides a Harley. He's so sweet." Pam smiles and sips her tea. "He's very tall. Wears his weight well. He teaches kindergarten."

Libby nods. Pam is petite and pretty. She would be swallowed by 250 pounds, tall or not. "Do you wear a helmet? Does he?"

"Of course. Why do you always ask? Do you think I have a death wish?"

Libby shakes her head, though she's not sure. Pam has always been daring and taken chances. "If you like him…"

"Oh, I do. But why the sudden interest in infidelity?"

"Not sudden. I had that fling years ago. It was brief, and I felt guilty."

"That's in the past?"

"Completely. Still, it's something you think about when you've been married a long time. I do. I'm fifty-two years old. I feel like a mortality clock is ticking, out of control. Are we meant to be with the same person our whole lives?"

"Not 'we.' Are you meant to be with Andrew?"

Libby shrugs. "I don't know." She remembers her accidental passion with a colleague. They squeezed out pleasure in a dumpy hotel. A few months later, he moved to Seattle, got divorced.

"I hoped I'd feel a special connection to my ex," Pam says. "He's the father of my kids. But I don't. Maybe I'm deficient."

"There are no rules. Do you remember when your mother used to come to my parents' house? She and my mother would try to 'get up to date.' Sorting through old clothing, as if that helped them get control of their lives."

"I don't think you ever really get up to date with anything."

Libby gulps her tea and then sets the mug on the coffee table. "I'm going to see Andrew lecture. Here, in New York. He's doing a seminar in two weeks."

"He'll be pleased. He loves to be admired. It's nice he invited you."

"He didn't."

"Then why go?"

"To see what he's really like these days." She is completely honest with Pam, no lies. "To spy."

"Like getting up to date," Pam says.

After Pam leaves, Libby sinks into the couch with a second mug of tea. Gray winter gloom invades the apartment. The rain has turned to slush and snow.

The truth is, she isn't happy with Andrew. A free-floating dissatisfaction. The little things. Really, they aren't so compatible. He is high-strung. Moody. Insists on perfection. He's hardest on those he loves, he jokes. That energy he marshals while lecturing, he carries into the house. A rush of agitation. Practicing presentations. Sending voice-activated emails. He sits at her mother's old writing desk with a glass of wine, reciting messages as if he's a pilot swooping in for a landing. He seizes the space. Libby finds herself feeling smaller, shrinking. She becomes invisible in her own home. It is only when she is tending to patients that she has dimension. She wants to please; this works in her profession.

On Sunday, Andrew returns from his business trip, kisses Libby quickly, drops his suitcase in the bedroom, and retreats to the living room. He puts on his headset and speaks loudly into the mouthpiece. "Rosa," he begins cheerfully, "it was a great pleasure. Damn." Libby hears him fiddling with the device. Then in a booming, conversational voice, he begins again. "Dear Rosalie. It was a great pleasure to…"

Libby escapes to the bedroom, shuts the door. She can't imagine life without him, but she can't imagine life with him. How did he transform from a man who was carefree and adventurous, who drove across the country on a whim, to someone who sits talking to his computer all night?

At work, when Libby presses a stethoscope against a woman's chest, she is listening for heart and soul. If only she could help both. Not just answer medical questions. She wants to reach the soul of the person, communicate with personal eloquence, like she wishes she could communicate with Andrew. Wishes he would talk to her in that way.

"Oh, Mrs. Leonard," a patient said yesterday, Nadeene Bender, who has beautiful, dark, sculpted features and a dancer's body, single mastectomy. Her voice like a song. "The doctors, they take away the sickness. But you, Mrs. Leonard, you are a nice, nice person. If there is good news, I will tell you."

And she did. Or Edna Cervantes, mother of six, who left an abusive husband, double mastectomy. "I wonder—will things ever be right again?"

And Libby described it in Spanish, the chemo, the reactions. The patience. *Anda paso a paso.* You walk step by step.

In the clinic she feels most truthful, engaged, most herself.

During the day, she has taken to removing her wedding ring, to see how this feels. A new doctor at the hospital is unusually friendly. As if the ring provides protection and a warning. She imagines if she can become comfortable without her ring, then she can leave Andrew; the jolt of leaving would lessen. She feels the glow of illicitness. Possibility. Every man a potential partner.

She flirts with the college radio supervisor she's just met, who visits the clinic with a group of students to record a program. The man has neatly trimmed gray hair and a lean build. He wears jeans, a blue shirt, and a navy blazer.

"So what do you do here?" he asks her.

She explains about her patients in the city hospital. Many are recent immigrants.

"I was in the Peace Corps," he says.

They both nod, as if this sharing of information seals a common interest, sensibility. He asks if she would like to have a drink sometime.

She gives him her cell phone number, feeling reckless, like Pam.

A pharmaceutical salesman stops by the clinic. He has a mild, wry manner, and is white-haired, like Santa Claus without a beard. But his skin is smooth and boyish, his smile warm. He tells her about his company's products; the conversation drifts to his many travels.

"You travel a lot," she says.

"Some for work. But mostly I travel because of *malakh ha-mavet.* That's Hebrew for the Angel of Death." He laughs with melancholy. "I travel to escape the Angel of Death."

She is surprised by his frankness, but later she considers this. Does she stare at men and imagine other lives to escape *malakh ha-mavet?*

Was the Angel of Death the one who wound her mortality clock? She is Jewish, like the salesman, and she feels a burst of relief to now have a word for her vague anxiety and malaise, as if she is running in a race. Something chases her, stalks her. She will discuss this with Pam.

And whether she wears the ring or not, Libby evaluates men. Thoughts arise when she least expects them. She tries to swat them away, like flies buzzing around her face.

Today is the seminar. She hasn't told Andrew she will be there. She wants a sign. That is the real reason she is going to see him. She should have told Pam, been absolutely truthful. A few years after Libby's father died, as Libby rode the subway one day, she suddenly missed him. She felt a great ache of absence. She stared at the sky through the smudged window. If only there were a sign, she wished then, that her father still existed in some form. As the train roared on, she gazed out and noticed a billboard. Words in big, bold script: SAMUEL. Her father's name. As if he'd answered her. The rest of the wording on the billboard didn't matter, but she remembers it still: SAMUEL SANDLER, Personal Injury Lawyer.

CALL SAMUEL.

Where is a sign now? About what to do in her life? It's silly. She isn't a New Age person. But she believes in signs. In *malakh ha-mavet*. She will hear Andrew speak. Something will happen. She will know absolutely the truth of her life then.

On her way to the seminar, she slips off her wedding ring. Her hand feels naked. Andrew doesn't often give seminars in New York. It's chilly and dreary today. She remembers when he gave her this ring, surprised her, with its small tear-shaped diamonds, as if the jewels themselves had known what was to come. Libby slid it on her finger; the metal felt cold, uncomfortable. She wanted to please Andrew even then. He was earnest. Dashing. She'd met him in a public-speaking class. She had just graduated from college and was interviewing for jobs as a nurse. She felt unconfident and thought the class might help her better communicate with patients and doctors. She had grown up in a small house on the edge of the nicer neighborhood. Her father sold insurance. Her mother worked in a flower store. Libby was always rubbing two pennies together. Pam's father was a surgeon. Libby felt uncomfortably aware of the discrepancy between her life and Pam's then.

Articulate and careless, Andrew lost his keys a lot. He was cerebral. She loved this about him, loved when he recited a Shakespeare sonnet. He quoted poems, sonnets. He was an aspiring actor, working toward his PhD in English. She was recovering from a soured love affair with a medical student. Andrew's voice seduced her.

The seminar—for lawyers—is held in a large hotel in Midtown. A billboard in the lobby lists a series of seminars. Sessions are presented simultaneously. She rides the escalator up and wanders in the vast second-floor lobby with rooms and hallways that snake from it in all directions, like tributaries.

People are milling about; others rush toward hallways and rooms. So many people, and Libby feels as if she is at a train station. Everyone seems to know exactly where he or she is headed. Libby studies the roster of seminars to find the one on personal eloquence.

She walks into the seminar's room and stands at the back. It is a large ballroom, without windows. Rows of chairs with their gold vinyl backs and seats are arranged in semicircles. Andrew must have done this; he has a protocol for everything, how the chairs should be arranged, the lighting in the room, placement of microphones, which side of the bed to sleep on. He is a master at this.

She takes a seat toward the side, behind a tall man, hoping Andrew will not see her. She wants to be anonymous. To judge him, as if seeing him for the first time. The man beside her is tall as well, with a receding hairline, dark curly hair. He wears a black suit and shining white shirt, looks intent and intelligent. The kind of man, she imagines, she could fall in love with, if she let herself.

He nods at her, and she swivels her head to face the front. Andrew walks in. She listens.

He begins speaking in the sound bites he practiced. He is smooth on his feet, like a dancer, in the front of this room, pacing from side to side, closer to and farther from the audience. His eyes lock onto face after face, and he regards each person in the same attentive way he sometimes regards Libby at home, a manner she has associated with intimacy and trust, one she imagined was unique to the two of them.

This was why Libby fell in love with him. She's surprised and hurt that he displays this manner publicly, a manner she thought was private.

"WIFM," he says now. "What's in it for *me*. People aren't waiting to listen; they're waiting to talk."

At the break, two hours later, women swoop up to Andrew like birds of prey. That's how Libby thinks of them, swooping, fluttering. They look up to him, literally—that must reinforce his sense of mastery, of being sought after, the best, that illusion of importance. A petite blonde inches over to him and rests her hand momentarily on his arm—a brief, warm gesture of familiarity. He puts his arm around her back, a gesture of familiarity, too. Seeing this woman, Libby feels an unexpected stab of jealousy. She is already jealous of all these women, although she hates to admit this. Jealous of their youth, their energy, a future he might prefer to her. He is the man she may want to leave. Yet he still evokes these feelings of jealousy in her. She eyes the blonde again, who is laughing and looking at him with admiration.

Libby slips on her coat and grabs her large black patent leather purse—like a briefcase, and as she stands, Andrew's eyes seem to light on her. He nods slowly, arches an eyebrow, then his glance slides back to the pert blonde. Libby feels guilty, caught. As if he now understands. Her great need for him as well as her doubt.

The man seated next to her stands up and approaches her, interrupting her reverie. He smiles. "What is that guy saying? He just told us a person can make speech perfect. He's wrong. There's nothing perfect about speech. You make mistakes. I make mistakes. Everyone does. And what do you do, I mean, work-wise?"

Libby explains, emboldened; her voice takes on speed and confidence. She is here to learn about speaking and communication, like everyone else, she says. She gives lectures to businesses about health. She spins a tale she can't believe she's making up.

"I do something similar. Of course, with lawyers." The man speaks fast, pausing at the wrong places, in the middle of sentences. She realizes she can't quite follow what he is saying, and when he talks, he doesn't glance at her. His eyes dart to the side, above her, behind her, settling on her face for an instant. He tells her that he disagrees with this theory of speech. The man talks on and on. She wishes she understood him.

"I've got to leave," she finally interrupts.

"I don't agree that you lose an emotion after three breaths. Or was it minutes? Whatever he told us. What about you?" the man says. "Do you think that happens?"

"I don't know. It's different with—"

"With each person it's different. I could tell you were intelligent. Very intelligent. You have a beautiful aura. Bet you could teach this seminar."

He is talking on and on, spilling out his thoughts. She walks away. There is something odd about this man, and his oddness mocks her fantasy. Does he have Asperger's? He seems to have a social disorder that prevents him from looking at the other person, really seeing the person. She doesn't want to be rude, but she suddenly wants to get out of here, to leave behind the seminar, her fantasies, this man, escape to the cozy apartment. But he charges toward her, following her as she looks for Andrew. She can't find him.

Save me from this, she thinks, and feels a jolt of unexpected panic. Where did she put her ring? She pats her pocket. Not there. Her purse? Her wallet? She can't remember. She pushes ahead into the crowd of people leaving for the lunch break. She doesn't belong to anyone, not really, she realizes, doesn't allow herself to belong—an odd, disturbing thought.

She presses her hand against the bare finger and feels suddenly woozy, as if she is riding with Pam and her 250-pound sweetie on a Harley, spinning down country roads, 100 miles an hour, so fast. No helmet. Where is the damn helmet? Where is the damn ring? All she sees is danger. Maybe she's the one with the death wish. Her breath explodes in short, frantic spurts. The imagined landscape vibrates and disappears.

She blinks unsteadily. How long does it take for an emotion to dissipate? She can't remember. How long does it take to learn to tell the truth? The man is walking next to her, talking and talking; she is a hostage. She bolts from him, sprints down the hallway, her purse banging against her side. Running from him. He races behind her, speaking with agitation.

"Wait," he says. "You were right about each person being different. I—"

She hurries away from him again. She is looking for Andrew. Women congregate by the bathroom, chatting happily. People pour into the hallway from other conference rooms and seminars.

Libby is wearing the brown and beige horsehair shoes, and for a moment, they seem ridiculous; one of them almost slips off her foot. She remembers: When Andrew's father was ill, Andrew spoke to him every day, patiently visiting in the middle of the night. Andrew at her side when she had pneumonia, when one of the boys broke a leg. The way he grasped her hand when they hiked in Yosemite last year, a small gesture, but she can suddenly feel his warmth. A million memories burst like comets in her mind, and she rushes into the vast lobby, lost, finally eluding the strange man. She wants to find Andrew, tell him she loves him. Tell him about projection. About *malakh ha-mavet*. No more lies. She will be truthful with him. With herself.

She darts into another ballroom, wandering beneath its high ceiling and crystal chandeliers, bathed in the ersatz golden light. Maybe Andrew is here. The room is empty. She sprints back into the vast lobby. She has to find him. She is running without direction. Searching for Andrew. But he's already gone.

Dislocation

WHEN MARK REYNOLDS COMPLAINED that his back had begun bothering him, Laurel immediately became alarmed. Mark rarely talked about his health. He was a tax lawyer, meticulous, the kind of man who didn't let anything get him down. He kept busy days and many nights with sharpened pencils, calculator, file folders, laptop, and forms.

The back pain had appeared suddenly in August, a few months after they'd moved from Boston to Tennessee. They had relocated because of Mark's work. The move had been arduous for them both.

Mark told Laurel he felt a taut sensation in his back, then a tingling and constant sharp cramp. Pain sometimes zigzagged down his leg, he said. He played racquetball, jogged regularly. Nothing like this had happened before. "It was that damn moving of heavy boxes," he said, "rearranging furniture that's caused this whole thing."

For two days over a weekend, Mark stayed in bed on a heating pad and worked on his cases there. Laurel brought him meals and Advil. He telephoned one of his brothers, who was an orthopedist in Florida, and carefully wrote down the advice. He showed the list to Laurel and placed it on his desk at home:

For Back Problems
1. Take hot baths.
2. Do sit-ups when feeling stronger.
3. Sleep with pillows under arm and leg.
4. Don't bend until back is better.
5. Try changing mattress.
6. Consider Xray or MRI as last resort.

Mark consulted a local doctor, too.
Laurel had hurt her back years ago and had placed a board

beneath her mattress then, which had helped. Mark wanted to sleep on a mattress on the floor now, "the hardest surface there is," he said. He found the old double bed they stored in the attic of their new home. If he used a different mattress instead of the regular one, he told Laurel, he could pinpoint the problem, and determine if the bed was the culprit or something else. Laurel dragged the spare mattress from the attic. Mark helped as best he could. They lived in a spacious beige brick ranch house. They had to wind and twist the mattress to fit it down the attic steps and through doorways. It was a solid old mattress from a brass bed they'd slept in when they first married. Laurel vacuumed it since Mark couldn't bend. She spread fresh sheets and a blanket on the mattress. It lay on the floor a few feet from their queen-size bed.

Jimmy, the youngest of their three children, was the first to notice, or at least to comment on the two beds. He was nine and not much slipped past him. "There are two beds in your room," he said one morning at breakfast. "Are you getting divorced? I mean, everybody fights like you guys, I guess. But the beds."

Mark shrugged and looked at his son. "It's my back. Though I suppose these days one never knows." He held up a newspaper article he'd been reading. The headline read *Divorce Creates 'New Poor.'* Mark shook his head. "The statistics are against you."

Jimmy blinked.

"Mark. Don't tease him," Laurel said. She smiled at Jimmy, and then said seriously, "Daddy's back still hurts him. The bed on the floor might help."

"Oh." Jimmy glanced from one to the other, then pushed away his cereal bowl. "Well, I guess I get it."

That first night after they hauled the mattress from the attic, Mark slept alone on the mattress on the floor. Laurel slept on their regular bed. Mark said that sleeping with another person aggravated his back. She worried his pain was a symptom of something more serious. What if Mark had cancer or a tumor? She could hardly sleep and felt as if she were swimming or perhaps drowning in the big bed, as if her body couldn't absorb the extra space, as if the bed were demanding she do something she couldn't do. She stayed awake long after Mark fell asleep and watched him in the dark as he lay on the heating pad, a large pillow beneath his arm. Then she slept fitfully. In the morning, she remembered her dream: Her mother had been lying on the bed on the floor, not Mark. Her mother's face had been worn and pale. She looked at Laurel and said simply, as if discussing the weather, "Tell Mark maybe he'll feel better tomorrow. Maybe not. But as for me, I'm sixty-five and I'm getting frightened."

Laurel's mother was a schoolteacher. All of her children had botanical names: Laurel, Holly, Rose, and Fern. Laurel had wanted a stronger name like Pat or Jane or Ellen, one that sounded as if it belonged to someone who would take a stand.

Laurel's father had abandoned the family. Laurel would say this simply, as if it explained something about her: "My father left when I was three." She would tell people she barely knew, which because of the move, was almost everyone she talked to these days.

When Mark suggested they place the mattress on the floor, he and Laurel had been married for almost fifteen years. Laurel had imagined that at this point in life there would be a great settling, as the earth might rest after an earthquake. The frenzied time of young children was behind her, she had a degree in landscape architecture, had a good job in Boston where they lived, and she was raising the children with Mark, not alone. She had felt lucky, and imagined a safe, calm stretch ahead of her. Instead, they'd moved; she hadn't found a new job yet; Christopher, their fourteen-year-old, had become moody; and Mark was irritable and busier than ever.

Mark had wanted to move. Some tax lawyers worked for large firms and made lots of money, but Mark had preferred a small solo practice in Boston. Laurel had admired him for that. He handled administrative hearings, too, charged low fees for much of his work, and helped out at Legal Aid. He worked as hard on cases that didn't pay as he did on lucrative ones.

He was offered a job with a large company he had done work for, as the in-house lawyer, with a steady income, who would advise on deals, the whole thrust of business, he said. "I'm ready for a new direction," he'd told Laurel. Then he added so quietly she almost didn't hear, "They're moving. We would have to leave, too."

Laurel told him she didn't want to go, but he held her hand and kissed her fingers, told her reasons they should leave. "Now is the time to try something new. Later will be too late." He would be part of something larger, could still work for clients who couldn't afford legal fees, and could build something for the family, too. A new city would be an adventure.

The children were against it. But Mark treated this as if he were building a legal case. He opened two file folders, one labeled *Why We Should Move* and the other *Why We Should Stay*. He listed reasons in each category. "Your work is portable," he told Laurel. As for the children, "This is modern life," he said to her. "They'll learn to be resilient. Besides, what is happiness anyway? You can be happy anywhere."

Laurel had realized then that she and Mark were fundamentally different. What man and woman weren't? Mark viewed his work as a calling. He would do anything for it. The family had been Laurel's calling, and the outside, too, the planting of gardens and flowers.

In the end, Laurel couldn't bring herself to deny Mark this opportunity. Perhaps she put him before herself, before the children. But she could see he wouldn't be happy stuck in his small office alone forever.

Everyone in the family knew Mark wasn't feeling well. They didn't discuss it much, though. They weren't together like they used to be. Jimmy was making new friends and involved in sports after school. Every night he would ask, "Why don't you take medicine so you'll feel better?"

"This happens," Mark told him, "when you get older. Sometimes medicines don't help."

Christopher seemed too preoccupied to notice. He had term papers to write, missed Boston, and liked to be plugged into rock music. Emily was twelve and took skating lessons and joined clubs. Laurel drove her to the lessons and sometimes stayed there as Emily glided across the ice. Watching her daughter skate gracefully, Laurel felt as if Emily had been a bird she once held in her hands and had now set free.

Laurel kept waiting for life to return to normal. Normal meant there would be no bed on the floor; they would be able to get together with old friends, the children would stop missing home, she would find a job, and Mark would feel better. But his back continued to hurt. He consulted a doctor again. The doctor said it wasn't serious. "I've just badly strained a muscle," Mark told Laurel. "Part of it must be age. The doctor said to try physical therapy if I want. I'll see how things go."

The bed stayed on the floor. At first, Laurel slept alone on their regular bed. Sometimes she would go to the bed on the floor, as if visiting Mark, and if he felt well enough they made love. She loved the feel of his body, had missed it. There was a different kind of pleasure then, the excitement of an encounter, almost between strangers.

It wasn't just Mark's back that concerned Laurel. There had been other changes, too. After they moved, he'd gone to the grocery store and come home with supplies—boxes of salt, cereal, cans of tuna, evaporated milk, and beans. He said that now that they were settled in Tennessee, they had to think about the future. What if there were a war or an earthquake? A tornado? Some catastrophe they couldn't imagine? You didn't know what life would bring. He bought large metal garbage cans and stored food and bottles of distilled water there. He bought a copy of the *Physicians' Desk Reference* and consulted his brother about what medicines to gather, too.

Laurel asked Mark, "Do you think something is going to happen here?" He seemed so certain about what he was doing that for a moment, she thought he knew something she did not.

Laurel became upset that while Mark was able to go to work, at home, he only took care of his back. At night, he would lie on the bed on the floor with a heating pad, reading reports and writing business protocols. He still helped the children with homework, but now they gathered around him on his bed.

She decided the best course of action was to wait for this to pass. He had been to the doctor, twice. Laurel had enough to do to organize the house and family after the move. Sometimes she thought Mark had behaved like this all along, preoccupied by whatever concerned him. Not when they'd met, but slowly this was what he'd become.

She hadn't noticed. On the bed alone at night, she imagined friends they'd left in Boston, and the garden at their small blue clapboard house there, the tulips and roses, the brick walkway she had put in piece by piece.

Days, she unpacked, drove the children, and phoned or emailed landscape companies to inquire about positions. She attended to the countless details connected with being in a new place. Once she took a tour with Christopher on "Bus to the Stars," visiting famous country music stars' estates.

On long, gray weekend days of late fall and early winter, when the rain fell steadily without a break, she played Monopoly or Life with the children.

There is an accumulation of new people when you move. You strike up conversations with strangers, in the grocery store, with deliverymen, the neighbors, almost anyone, since there is no one you know. And people approach you. Laurel was a newcomer. She met people who had been born, grown up, and married, had affairs and switched partners, without ever leaving their block.

Nashville felt like a town still stuck in the 1950s, Laurel thought. It had grown like other places, and different cultures had superimposed themselves on the proper, polite, churchgoing one. There was the music business with its women in high heels and short skirts, tight blouses and hair puffed up like balloons, and the men who wore alligator boots or tried to look like Elvis. There were local universities, the insurance business, health care companies, too, and the newcomers who arrived from east and west, like Laurel and Mark, in search of better jobs, better lives.

Many of the houses sat on sprawling plots of land. The yards, no matter what size, were like forests with magnolias, pines, wild roses, boxwoods, and ornamental pear trees. The weeds grew wildly. Rolling hills rose so close to the city that it sometimes seemed to Laurel as if they had moved to the country. In the summer and early fall, before the cold of winter arrived, birds and butterflies darted through the hot, thick air.

At the grocery, the checker wore a nametag: *Hi! I'm Burt, your Kroger helper. Let me know how I can make shopping fun.* Burt commented on Laurel's out-of-state driver's license and asked if she had just moved. "You're lucky, coming here," he said. "If you have to move. I've been here my whole life. I read on the computer last week that 20 percent of people in this country move every two years. Can you imagine? No wonder people feel dislocated."

Laurel decided that was the problem with Mark. He was dislocated. Not just from Boston. From himself. "Maybe the move wasn't the right thing," she told him. "Maybe you're sick because you're unhappy. Maybe you miss having a practice of your own."

"Sure, there's pressure with the job. But what's black is black and white is white," he said. "Don't make a federal case. A bad back is just that, a physical problem."

Their neighbor on one side, elderly Mrs. Pickney, stopped by to inquire how Mark was feeling. She had seen him having trouble bending in the yard. She gave Laurel a package. Inside were two patches of needlework Mrs. Pickney had embroidered. One was of a table and a vase filled with pale blue flowers. The other had the words *Music City Proud* embroidered across the top and *Nashville Cats* on the bottom. In the center, figures of a man and woman, dressed in wildly colored shirts with guitars, embraced. "I didn't know which one would suit you," Mrs. Pickney said. "So I thought I'd give you both."

Laurel thanked the woman and read the card: *I hope you'll feel healthy again and enjoy your new home.*

Where was home? Laurel wondered. When she'd fallen in love with Mark, she had wanted to make a home with him. But she didn't know where home was anymore—was it in Boston, or Ohio where she had grown up, or Wisconsin where she had gone to college and met Mark?

The neighbor on the other side kept Laurel up to date on the happenings of the block. She knew Mark was under the weather. "You're lucky to have a husband," Sally told Laurel, "whatever shape he's in." Her husband had recently moved out, and she was left with three little girls. One morning, Laurel saw Sally when she went outside to get the newspaper. Sally started to talk to Laurel and began to cry so suddenly that Laurel put her arm around her.

"I've been hoping he'll come back, that we can be a happy family again," Sally said, then eased from Laurel's arm. "I'm sorry for you to see me like this." She brushed the moisture from her eyes with her hand. "But in a way, I guess I'm glad he's gone. You can't wait for things to change forever."

Laurel supposed Sally was right. You couldn't wait forever, whatever it was you were waiting for. Everyone waited for something: Mark for his back to get better, the children waiting to grow up. And herself? For years, she had waited for her father to come back. She had given that up long ago. Then she waited to find someone like Mark and to earn her degree, and for each child. Now she was waiting for this disruption with the move to pass.

Laurel lost her train of thought as Sally told her that the girls had begun wetting their beds and her husband had been cheating all along. "It was probably my own fault," Sally whispered. "I let him get away with it for years."

On the night of their fifteenth anniversary, Mark told Laurel he didn't feel like going out. Could they postpone it? They had planned to go to dinner at a restaurant without the children. Mark was sitting in the bed on the floor, pillows propped behind his back, resting on a heating pad. Reports were spread on the blanket. He had worked every night that week. Laurel saw his fatigue. She hated to see him in pain, but still she said, "Mark, we can't live like this any longer."

"Like what? We'll go out next week."

"I don't care if we ever go out. It's the bed, your work, our life, moving. It's crazy."

"Can't you see I don't feel well?" He pointed to the documents that surrounded him. "I'm working hard."

"For all of our sakes, you have to take it easier."

"New job, new place..." Mark shook his head. "Everything is stressful...but you."

"No," Laurel said, "what I see is you having a nervous breakdown. You have to do something. See someone. Get therapy, acupuncture. Anything."

"There is no such thing as a nervous breakdown," he said with irritation. "I work with millions of dollars at the office. I'm preparing a huge case. I solve people's problems. Successfully. I have a bad back. A reaction in my arm. That happens to people at our age. The warranty runs out."

"A crisis of character, maybe," Laurel replied softly. That's what Mark had once told her about a friend in Boston who went into a drug rehabilitation program for a cocaine habit. "Call it whatever you want."

"That's absurd." He threw the report he was reading on the floor and slowly got out of bed.

Laurel stepped close to him. "Mark. I love you. I'm worried about you." She eyed him as if she were seeing him for the first time. He had the beginnings of a belly and his hair was thinning. "Maybe you don't want to be married anymore. Maybe you're sleeping with someone. I don't know."

Mark shook his head again with impatience. There was a time, Laurel knew, when he would have taken both of her hands and kissed the fingers and palms and told her, "Don't be silly; I love you." Now he arched his brows in annoyance. "After fifteen years, can't you have a little confidence?" he said. "Can't you have some sympathy? Can't you see I'm pressured?"

"And what about me, about us?"

Laurel decided she wasn't worried about Mark in a fundamental way. His health problems might be part of a private madness, a way to wrestle with himself. She thought of Mark's other brother who lived in California, worked sporadically in carpentry, and surfed. Maybe Mark was more like this brother than he imagined. Mark always spoke of him disparagingly. "He's a health-food nut. The problem with him is that he's never found himself."

Laurel was finally offered a job as a landscape designer working for an architect who had an office in her home. Six others worked there, too, and Laurel struck up a friendship with a man ten years younger. Peter wore his dark hair back in a ponytail. He was living with a woman and involved, but he went to lunch with Laurel and they flirted. They talked about plants, flowers, and ways to design gardens, and toured magnificent yards.

"You have a gift with plants," he said. Laurel strolled by Peter's side and felt as if this was what she was meant to be doing, being outdoors, talking about things important to her. They never had an affair. Peter played the bass in honky-tonk joints on weekends. Laurel went to see him once at a music club with Christopher. Peter played the bass as if he were stroking a woman.

Peter studied tai chi at night, too. Laurel went to some of the classes. She bought a pair of tight blue jeans with rhinestone studs on the pockets, and some high-heeled cowboy boots.

She started to work in the garden at home, in the warm spring weather. Emily and Jimmy helped. Laurel marveled at the variety of vegetation, the long growing season here. With the upheaval of moving, she had almost forgotten how she loved to kneel on the grass and scoop dirt in her hands. She knew everything about the outside, instinctively, what to expect in every season, the way wind or weather would affect trees or flowers, how to prune and spread soil. She loved the feel of moist dirt beneath her fingernails. Sometimes when she was pruning, she imagined this was what life was like, always the shaping, reforming, making more out of what might look like less, salvaging what was usable, and discarding the rest. She had tried to teach Mark about this. Even in Boston he'd never had the time. She supposed he could tell her the same about his world, and sometimes he had—the satisfactions of balancing figures and getting them right, the beauty of a good legal argument, the grace of the numbers. Mark had talked about the pleasure of using a sharp pencil with a clean eraser, streamlining a legal brief, choosing the perfect words. The efficiency. The charts and graphs and interpretations.

In Boston, she had thought of his busyness as a disease, of the soul perhaps, though she never told Mark this unless they were arguing—or unless she felt like arguing and provoked him, he had sometimes said.

He was a success at his new job. At a dinner for the company, his colleagues shook Laurel's hand heartily and said, "We're thrilled to have Mark on board. He's doing a phenomenal job." Mark had already gotten a raise, and there was promise of a bonus.

After the two beds had been in their room for ten months, Laurel came home from work one afternoon and found that the mattress on the floor was gone. Only the queen-size bed stood there. A bouquet of yellow roses lay on the pillow. When Laurel saw this, she felt alarmed, as she had felt when Mark first complained he wasn't feeling well. But this time, she realized she felt the panic for herself.

Mark came into the room and draped his arm around her. "I have to apologize to you for all these months. Maybe my back will never feel perfect. I don't know. The bed probably wasn't the problem."

He held Laurel close and kissed her neck. "Maybe I have been too pressured. This big case has settled, and we've got to get back to normal. I apologize for arguing. We'll make a good life here. We'll be happy."

"It's not that simple," Laurel said.

"It is if you make it."

That night they lay in their bed together. "This is how we were meant to be," Mark whispered. But Laurel stayed awake after he fell asleep. She remembered how her mother had once said after Laurel apologized for something, "It's always easier to ask for forgiveness than permission."

It was raining outside now; the rain wasn't lazy as it had been the last few days, but focused and steady. It seemed as if it would never let up. The room felt stuffy, but Laurel didn't want to open a window. She lay in bed, tossed the blanket off, and moved to find a comfortable position. Then she realized she was unbearably warm, sweating, not from the room or from desire or illness, but as if she were shedding some part of herself.

In the early morning, she tiptoed from bed. She took her purse and some money they kept hidden in Mark's *Constitutional Law* book, and threw a few things into an overnight bag. She left a note for Mark on his desk, next to the list of suggestions about his back: *Couldn't sleep. Went for a drive. Will call later.* It was a Saturday, so it wouldn't matter if she was gone. Emily didn't have a skating lesson today.

Laurel thought of her father suddenly. She had never understood why he'd abandoned the family. Her mother wouldn't talk about it, and the few times Laurel saw him, he wouldn't either. What had he felt on the day he left? she wondered.

She drove to the airport and decided to buy a ticket to Portland,

Maine. Laurel had visited there before she'd married and had loved the ocean and the lighthouse. She would fly there next week and stay, walk by the sea. She might meet someone like Peter. She would have the most casual intentions. In the late spring, she would plant a garden. Practical things would spill away like water. In the winter, she would go to a warm island.

She thought it was a mad thing to do, buy the ticket, but she did it. She had always blamed her father for abandoning the family, she knew. She had never tried to imagine his point of view. Then she got in the car and drove to a jobsite to see a friend there, and then out to the country. In the late afternoon, she started back. But when she turned off the expressway, instead of veering right, she turned left. Instinctively, without thought. The rain had stopped. A thin white mist hung in the air. For a moment, Laurel didn't recognize where she was going. Instead of the familiar commercial strip with Arby's and McDonald's, the road became another highway, and after a few miles, it intersected with still another. For a while, her car was the only one on the road. There was just the hazy sky around her and white industrial buildings. Then another car joined her. Soon fields and miles of empty land surrounded the highway.

Maybe her father just hadn't been happy in the marriage, she thought. Maybe that had been enough to propel him to leave. Had he climbed into his car and driven away?

Laurel phoned Mark from a pay telephone at a gas station eighty miles away from Nashville and told him she would be home in the next day or so. She had forgotten her cell phone at home.

"The next day?" he said. "I thought last night we decided to get our lives back in order. Are you losing your mind?"

"I told you. I took a drive in the country and then some wrong turns. The car broke down. Now I'm stuck." She knew he would know this was a lie. She had never lied to him before. "Honey. It's silly for you to come out here. There's food in the refrigerator."

Mark didn't answer.

"I'll water the garden when I come back. With the rain it doesn't need a thing. The children will be okay. Be careful with your back."

He was silent.

"Mark, we're grown-ups. I'll be fine. No one is here with me. Don't worry. It's not an affair."

"Affair," he yelled. "Then what is it? I think you've lost it. I think the move and my not feeling well has been harder on you than I realized. If something is going on, tell me. Laurel—"

The operator interrupted to say Laurel needed to insert more coins.

Laurel fished in her purse for dimes and quarters. "Mark, I'm almost out of coins. I'll be home tomorrow or in a few days. I need time to think. The kids can go to school like always. Honey, if there's a change of plans, I'll let you know."

"A fucking change of plans? Give me the number of the pay phone. I'll call you back."

"Mark." She said this to reassure him as much as herself. "I'm happy. I love you. Don't worry."

Again the operator interrupted, but this time Laurel was out of coins. "I'll call tonight or tomorrow," Laurel said, "and—"

When the line went dead, Laurel stared at the receiver. She placed it in the cradle of the telephone. She didn't call back. She could give the gas station attendant dollar bills and ask for coins in exchange, but she didn't.

She would drive to Chicago or Detroit and stay a few days, then go home. What did you owe another person, she thought, and what did you owe yourself? Was she her father's daughter? She wasn't going to use the ticket yet. She couldn't leave the children. Not until they were ready. As for Mark, she had always loved him, but maybe they had been leaving each other all along.

Second Wife

You've never written a story in second person—no, that's not true. You wrote one in your former life when you were teaching school in the inner city. You've never looked at your life as if you were outside of it, an observer, but that's how you're assessing events now. You're beginning to think your life is just a series of former lives.

You wanted to be a writer then, but now you work in the research department of a college library and also ghostwrite books. You enjoy your work, the variety. You've just finished a project about Chicago. Facts still float through your mind. You can recite how many Lithuanians, Germans, and Poles lived in Chicago in 1930. You know the dates when streets were named there and when the names were changed. You know that "avenue" is a title applied to streets running north and south, though there are exceptions, and that a boulevard in Chicago doesn't allow trucks over five tons. These facts are obscure, but even so, they ground you and give you a feeling of control, a feeling that's missing from the rest of your life.

This morning you receive an email from your ex-husband. You don't read it yet. He has been your ex for five months, and the process of detaching has been tough. After thirty-one years of marriage, you thought: what's the point of splitting up? But the point was, he told you, he didn't think he wanted to be married. You felt devastated at first, but on some level you accepted what he said. He was difficult to live with. He had a big ego. He's a transactional lawyer with a firm in New York. He writes contracts and arranges deals. He tells people what to do all day long, and used to come home and do the same with you. He wasn't like this at the beginning. He used to do a lot of pro bono work. He was softer then. But these last few years, if you washed a plate and didn't set it correctly in the dish rack, he showed you the right way to do this. He complained you bought too much clothing for yourself and the children, and you didn't throw out old catalogues and magazines. He said you wasted time talking on the phone to friends. You took his words to heart. Not that you were a supplicant. Your parents argued with each other every day of their sixty-five years together, and you wanted a different life. You wanted peace in your home. And you wanted to recapture the rapture you and he shared at the beginning, even after the children were born, when a night together at home, reading in the same room, talking, and making love, felt like a womb of safety.

You didn't realize until he announced he wanted a divorce that his accumulated discontent with the marriage had fueled his complaints.

You went through the divorce like a trooper. That's what friends say, and you think this is true. What they don't know is that in the middle of the night when you can't sleep, too often now, a surge of panic rises. You read books to distract yourself, classics like *Great Expectations*. But all kinds of feelings rumble inside you. You try to sort and identify them. Panic, despair, fury, disappointment, anxiety, need, relief, hope, even wonder. Thirty-one years of marriage, two kids who have graduated from college and are working at jobs they like, and now you're on your own. Death and illness are worse, of course. As you look forward in life, you'll slam into that wall sooner or later— death—like everyone does, but still, it would be easier if he died, the ex, though this is a cynical and cruel thought. You've discussed this with divorced friends. It would be easier, a friend said, because then the ex is simply not around. Complete closure. No emails about the kids. No feeble attempts to be friends. No curt calls about something you were supposed to do but didn't. No unexpected encounters at a restaurant or social event. It's over.

But this. The divorce. You're living with the shadow of him for the rest of your life.

And the holidays. You split up the holidays, you split up the kids. Your heart is split in two, although you know you'll get used to it.

Everyone says the adjusting takes a while.

You've given a lot of thought to the marriage. You can't place all the blame for failure on him. You weren't a perfect wife, but you tried to be a good one. The old cliché is true: the road to hell is paved with good intentions. Your intentions, nonetheless, were good. You raised the children, created a home. As he became successful, you entertained for his firm, and you loved his family as if they were your own. You loved him. You never wanted to hurt him, but you weren't direct with anger. That's your flaw. If he asked you to do something and you were angry at him, you completed the task late. You started to prepare slipshod meals, using Hamburger Helper, and sometimes prepared elaborate ones, spending too much on gourmet food. You strived to be truthful, but you lied about money. You're not proud of this. He was parsimonious. The last years of the marriage, you took out more cash from the joint bank account than you needed and saved it to use for a new coat or dress more expensive than he would approve of. You gave gifts and cash to the kids. Of course, the marriage wasn't about approval, but you wanted to keep the peace. You thought about other men. You considered having an affair with a coworker, but didn't go through with it. Did this qualify you as a loose wife or just a fanciful one?

You wonder if what a person wants—if the wanting itself—ends up being his or her undoing. You longed for harmony, and in the end, the marriage disintegrated.

These days, you think maybe your ex had a point. It's okay not to be married. You've gone on dates and had a lover since you and he split up. Nothing serious, but still. You felt awkward at first, but you appreciated that there were no arguments, no criticism or complaints, at least not yet.

Sometimes you think back to the days before you met your ex-husband. The world seemed to unfold seamlessly, and you filled your life with whatever hopes you wanted. It was okay to be single then. It's okay now.

That's what you thought before you opened your ex-husband's email. It's Saturday morning, and you're sitting at the kitchen table in your apartment, facing your laptop. Autumn sunlight streams in through the window. He's called a few times, and you haven't returned his calls yet. This is self-protection and gives you a feeling of control. It's hard to hear his voice. A voice you associated with love and trust. There's coldness in his tone now, a hostile reserve. The voice usually dispenses bad news.

The email is no different.

Dear S,

I called three times and left messages, which you did not
return. The reason I wanted to speak to you is I am planning
to get married. I wanted you to hear directly from me, rather
than from anyone else. Our kids wanted me to tell you, so that
they would not have to. I agreed with them. I wish you every
happiness in the future.

—L

You read the email twice. You wonder what's worse—getting a
message like this or ending a relationship on a Post-it. Or maybe
they're the same. You dated a man last year after you and your ex
separated. The man wanted more of your attention. You went only so
far with him sexually. "It's been a long time since I've had a warm body
next to mine all night, all weekend," he purred. You realized you didn't
like him enough to have sex with him. He called a week later and said
he thought you and he should stop seeing each other. You said, "That's
been on my mind, too." Then he said, "My daughter told me I should
call you. She said not to break up with you on a Post-it." He'd made
a toast at dinner a few weeks before your conversation with him. "To
us," he'd said to you. He told you on the phone, "This changes things
for us."

And you replied, "There is no us."

But the email. Your mind is spinning. You've been divorced five
months, and your ex-husband is getting remarried. You read the
message again. You're a rational woman, and you know this happens.
People remarry. But you're shocked. You immediately telephone him.
As you begin to punch in the numbers, you forget he's your ex. You
can't believe he's not man enough to tell you in person. This astonishes
you; he has been slick and weak and dishonest. When he announced
he wanted to split up, he said he didn't want to be married anymore. "I
want my independence," he said. "I won't marry again."

You were his second wife, and when he asked you to marry him,
you hesitated. If he could split up with the first wife, he could split
up with you. You wondered then if he was a man who left easily. You

know there are men who leave and those who stay. But you were in love with him, his long arms and full laugh, the way he kissed you. And his mind. You loved that he knew obscure facts about history, court decisions, and politics. There was an ease between the two of you, a level of comfort you hadn't expected. You loved something about him then that you could not name.

After the two of you separated, he began to see a woman who lived in France. She was a lawyer and taught at a law school. You know this because your daughter mentioned it. You wonder if he knew the woman before you and he split up, if he slept with her then. You assume he did.

You are sitting at the kitchen table, the telephone receiver pressed against your ear. You advise yourself to hang up. To ignore his message or send a brief reply. But you don't. You can identify the feeling inside of you immediately: fury. You've been civil in the divorce. You have your pride. You didn't want the kids to see you fall apart. For the most part, you haven't called him names. You haven't yelled. Oh, he yelled when the lawyers were negotiating about money. You weren't surprised. Generosity isn't a strength of his, but you realized you made excuses for him during the marriage. You thought of him as conservative rather than cheap. As impatient rather than judgmental. As forgetful rather than evasive. You accepted the good and bad. You allowed him to get away with things. Now there is only bad.

His voice drops when he realizes it's you. He's annoyed you haven't returned his calls. You tell him you've been busy with work and wrapping up the myriad details from the divorce. And then you lay into him. It's not your nature, but you suddenly feel set free in the most humiliating way.

"I can't believe you're getting married," you shout. "We've only been divorced five months. How can you tell me in an email? God will curse you and your marriage. You'll see. The karma is bad. You can't build happiness when you've destroyed it for us. That fucking woman." Your heart is thumping. You don't even know if you believe in God.

"You're crazy," he yells back. "If you were getting married, I'd want the best for you."

What's the right reply: Fuck you? Give me a break? If he wanted the best for you, he wouldn't have divorced you? "Oh, please," you shout. "You've ruined our lives and the kids' lives. I'm telling you, God is going to punish you." You suck in a breath. What you've said is not exactly true. He hasn't ruined your life or theirs. He has derailed yours for a while. Stolen time. He has filled your thoughts with mind-numbing details and sadness. He hounded you to move faster with the divorce after your father died. Your ex has become a toxic personality, and his toxicity has spilled into your life.

What you don't say to him now is absolutely true: You detest him. You detest him and want to blot him out of the last decades of your life.

He is complaining about the things you did and did not do when the two of you were married. You're not listening, just as you often didn't listen when you and he were together. You want to tell him calmly what you learned last week from a project at work: there's a common language to all religions. Most adhere to a variation of the Golden Rule. He's not religious and neither are you. Facts swirl in your brain as he talks: Christianity: *All things whatsoever ye would that men should do to you, do ye even so to them.* Islam: *No one of you is a believer until he desires for his brother what he desires for himself.* Judaism: *Thou shalt love thy neighbor as thyself.* Hinduism: *Men gifted with intelligence should always treat others as they themselves wish to be treated.*

Why couldn't the two of you practice the Golden Rule? You want to reach him in that place of his you once loved.

"Are you there?" he snaps. "Did you fucking hear me? Say something."

You are about to recite these facts and talk about kindness, but instead you yell, and you don't even know what you're saying. This is unlike you. Your hands shake.

Whatever it is you've said, the words elicit a reaction. The two of you are locked in an argument like ones you used to have. Only then, you tried never to go to bed angry.

"I can't believe you're so bitter," he finally says. "You're so sweet to everyone, and I can't believe you're bitter about this."

"You don't understand human nature," you say. "You don't understand people. I loved you. We loved each other. We have children together. You're nice to everyone else, and you treat me like shit."

"Don't turn me against you. Someday you may need me."

When you and he separated, he said, "We can have an amicable divorce. We'll be friends. I'll come over and help you. There's no reason to fight."

"I don't think that will happen," you replied softly. You weren't prescient, just realistic. "I see what divorce does to people. I just don't see how we'll be able to be friends."

"You're so pessimistic," he said then. "That's what I hate about you."

The next day, you're more sanguine. Let him do what he'll do. It's not anger you feel but hurt. You don't want to be married to him, but you're being replaced. Replaced by a French floozy. She's heavyset, with mousy brown hair, and not even pretty. You saw a picture of her once on the internet. The kids will be involved with her. Maybe they'll prefer her over you.

These are not rational thoughts. You wonder if you might be crazy after all when it comes to the divorce. Your friend Carla said to you last month, "So he has a girlfriend. She doesn't know it, but she's walking into hell. Kids are tough on the new love interest. Don't worry. The kids always come back to the better parent."

You want a happy ending to this story, but all you wish him is unhappiness. It is not in your nature to wish him this. These feelings are an illness festering inside you. You plot ways to ruin his life, or at least to make him uncomfortable. Slashing tires, breaking into his apartment and destroying his things. Confronting the woman and warning her to stay out of his life. Slapping her face. Accusing her of breaking up your marriage. You stop yourself. All you want to do is sit and weep. Or walk out of this life. You don't even want to call a friend. Friends will commiserate. They will say, like Carla has, that he is arrogant. They will say "Ouch" when you tell them about the remarriage. They will say you are better off without him. So soon, they might say. It's just like him, plunging into marriage without thinking.

It doesn't matter what they say. They all have ups, downs, and problems. This is your life and your problem.

What is the appropriate response to his email? You've given him the response on the phone. But you write to him anyway. He has a retirement account and owns the apartment the two of you once shared. You write: *I'm going to stick my two cents into the situation. If you're getting married, you should get a prenup. You have to protect the kids.*

He writes back: *I agree.*

Sunday, you wander around your apartment. You're still amazed at how affection is a chameleon. The only thing that saves you is work. You can't wait for the weekend to be over. You have to be sedate at work, precise, gracious, and calm. You long for this calm in your life.

You are amazed that love is so fickle. That loyalties change. You have lost friends because of the divorce. Lost his family. Your situation is not new. Millions of people get divorced. It's the way of the world, Carla says. She's married for the second time. People marry three or four times. Fourth time is the charm, your friend Neil said. It's always the last marriage that works. He's been married four times. At that point, is a person just tired? No spouse is perfect. Maybe by then, you don't have the energy for the changes and machinations.

You don't know the answer. You suppose you'll have to live longer and look back with hindsight.

You finally talk to Carla over coffee at Starbucks on Sunday afternoon. You tell her about the remarriage.

"She'll have to put up with his bullshit," Carla says. "It will be mixed for her, too."

"Maybe." You gulp your coffee. "He's not easy to live with, but I loved him."

"Just wait." Carla nods emphatically. "You'll watch his new marriage unravel."

"Or maybe it won't," you say.

"Whatever happens, in the end he's stuck with himself. I'm stuck with myself, and you're stuck with yourself."

"True."

"We're all on our own, married or not."

Monday, on your way to work, you bump into a friend and neighbor, Arthur Rhodes. He is a lawyer like your ex-husband, dressed in a suit and tie, and teaches at a law school. You wonder if he knows your ex's wife-to-be. You stop yourself from asking. Arthur is a warm man, but he complains about the school administration now. "They are technocrats, dictators," he says. "I'm telling you what I think, but I hope you won't repeat it." He pauses. "I say whatever I want. I learned that when I was young. I was born rich."

You think this is an odd admission, but there has always been a patrician quality about him, so you're not surprised.

"You're probably healthier saying what you think," you tell him.

"Oh, yes. I'm sure of it."

You still need to divide up some possessions with your ex. You thought the divorce was over, but you realize you are still in the middle of things, even though he's moving on. You wonder how the kids feel about the remarriage, but you're not ready to talk to them about it yet.

Tonight he calls; his name glows on your cell phone. You hesitate, then answer. He doesn't mention the last conversation or anything that's happened between the two of you. All he says, in a weary voice, is: "When we divide the rest of the things, let's just do it. I don't want it to be a big deal."

"Okay," you say, and end the conversation. You don't want to argue with him anymore.

That week, you stay at work late every night. You don't listen to your personal messages, and they accumulate on the machine. Your cell phone voice mail is full. At home, you wander around the apartment. You're confused by your emails, as if you're lost in a forest, a thicket that needs to be trimmed. You don't return phone calls. This isn't like you. Your efficiency has gone to hell.

You can't quite remember why you fell in love with your ex.

You can't get any traction.

You read an email from a cousin, but don't reply. She's moving to Chico, California, to be near her daughter. Your college roommates worked at a camp there. You remember only their first names now. You know your ex would remember the last names, but you won't ask him. Instead you do a Google search: Chico, California, camp directors. You follow link after link until you're reading the cost-of-living data and salaries in Chico. Maybe you should move there, too; you indulge in the fantasy. Then you stop yourself from clicking on *View All Job Titles in Chico, California.*

You don't need to do research at home. Every day you do research at work. But the internet maze distracts you. You've become an expert at distraction.

You pay the month's bills late and rack up interest and fees. You intend to clean your desk. You do not. You cancel the appointment for a colonoscopy. You don't call the kids. You cancel a date, and a dinner with Carla.

You still miss your ex next to you at night and the sense that the two of you could weather life together. Were you too dependent? You don't know. What you want is not only fucking. You want stability, a partner, the life you had with him.

But this is where you are now: alone. A fact as indelible as those in your searches at work, as solid as a fact you found for the project about Chicago: in 1925, a street there, now called Marine Drive, had no name. You began to think of this place as: the street with no name. This thing, the divorce, this new way of life, is for you: a life with no name.

You've always been determined to have a good attitude. Attitude and character are all a person has. You believe in self-reliance. In the last two years you've lost your father, your marriage. You pride yourself on coping, functioning. Moving forward. You're surprised by this torrent of grief.

Three weeks later, on a Monday morning, your daze of confusion begins to lift. You wake up early and notice there's been a shift in your state of mind. Like the shift that occurs when you realize you love someone. The stark recognition. You realize you feel differently about your ex. You don't wish him harm. What you feel for him is indifference. He'll do what he'll do, and you'll live how you'll live. Maybe that's called perspective.

You feel suddenly philosophical, as if you've survived a destructive torrential storm. In a marriage, you think, one needs respect, good will, and love. Sometimes the relationship is held together by sheer will until the rhythms change and improve. You knew things were changing between the two of you, and you had no solutions. Did you forget that intimacy is what you wanted in marriage? Did you forget because the world marches in and sometimes takes over? The car breaks down, the freezer doesn't freeze, there is a pay cut at work, one of the kids breaks her arm, you lose your job, your son gets arrested for possession of marijuana.

This morning, you feel calmer than you have in months. You fling open the curtains and look outside. It's a clear, sunny late-autumn day. You sit on the edge of the bed. You're not penniless. The children are doing well so far. You have a job you like and friends. The future will have to take care of itself. You think: really, you're lucky. Marriage is just a word. No. Much more than a word. A contract. A vow. A promise: to protect and love your spouse, not to hurt him or her. When the promise is broken, what's left? Crushed hopes, disappointment, and hurt feelings. Disbelief. Psychic pain. Grief. People cope, and you will, too.

You drink your morning coffee, scan the headlines, and check email. There's a message from your ex. This time, he's contrite: *Let's try to be friends. We can work on it. We'll talk. I don't want us to go forward with hard feelings.*

You consider how to answer, but instead press delete.

You log off and dress for work. Divorce isn't illness or war or terrorism or murder, you think. Really, you're nothing special. This recognition is a relief. You're like a fact you've read about at work. How many Lithuanians lived in Chicago in 1930? How many women with X number of children have divorced in the last year? You're just another statistic. Yours is just another marriage that crumbled.

You take a deep breath, square your shoulders, and hold your head high. That's how you want to greet the world. Who you want to become. You gather your purse, keys, and coat. You march out of the apartment like a woman who knows what she wants and where she's going. Most of this is bravado, but you don't care. At least it's a start. You slam the door.

It's Me, Lydia

Rae and I are out walking. It's February, a hazy day. The palm trees are in bloom and the grass is green, making the winter landscape, even here in Florida, seem unreal. A light drizzle begins to fall and brushes the air with a moist, cloudy mist that makes it hard to see where you've come from or where you're going.

I'm visiting Rae in Tampa for the weekend. In high school, we were best friends. We're sixty years old now and still best friends. We haven't seen each other for over a year. She and I like to walk and talk. We debate sometimes: does talking create intimacy or can silence? "Both," I said once, "you need both."

"Talking can help solve a problem. Relieve a burden. I want to believe it, Laura," Rae said then. "I want to believe there's a solution for everything."

Winters in New York City, where I live, are gray and cold, and in Minneapolis, where we grew up, they were bitter. I'm happy to be in Tampa for a few days.

The thing about Rae and me is it doesn't matter how much time elapses or how infrequently we speak; we dive in right where we left off.

"That's where my friend Janet and her husband live." Rae points to a yellow clapboard house. "He's an alcoholic."

I don't know the couple well, but Rae likes to narrate the neighborhood as we pass each house, as if every story can instruct us how to live. As if we aren't merely gossips or voyeurs, but are striving to learn a lesson.

"That's too bad," I reply. My ex-husband hated gossip. *Lashon hora*, he called it—loose tongue. Though I never admitted it, such stories intrigued me. One of the many things I didn't admit during our marriage.

"Janet's husband is an alcoholic just like Owen was," Rae says. "I don't know how she lives with him."

I nod. Owen was Rae's second husband. She's had three.

Rae wears an olive green fleece jacket that matches the green of her eyes. Her black exercise pants cling to her shapely legs; her sneakers are Nike and new. She jogs every morning at six. I'm tall and a little chunky, dye my hair chestnut—my natural color—to hide the gray. I'm wearing black stretch pants and sneakers. My hair is wound into a ponytail, and my sweatshirt has the words emblazoned on the front: *Still Pure After All These Years*. A hand-me-down from one of my daughters. Rae is an inch or so shorter than I am, not slender, but with lovely curves. She dyes her hair blonde, really several shades of radiant gold. She's the kind of woman who looks beautiful whether she wears makeup or not.

"Stuart Lewis and his wife live here," she goes on. We stroll at the same pace, and she points to a large white bungalow trimmed in blue. "Do you remember them? I think she's having an affair with Max Greenwald."

"I remember her. I've never met her husband," I say. "An affair. Really?"

"Yes. And Max Greenwald lives next door to Lydia."

"Who's she?"

"She worked at the hospital with me. An older woman. Seventy or seventy-five or so." Rae laughs. "I mean, we're older now, so she'd have to be almost elderly. A social worker. The nicest woman you could meet. She lives with her daughter. We can stop and say hello. You'd like her."

"Sure."

"When I first moved here, she was like a mother to me. Lydia was smart, independent. She took me under her wing."

"I remember now, you talking about her. She was the opposite of your mother, you said." Rae's mother was like an army sergeant. A perfectionist. A big woman with brassy blonde hair who didn't believe in explanations and barked orders.

"She was a real looker, Lydia," Rae says wistfully. "Dressed impeccably. Men fell all over her."

"She was lucky. Like you."

"It's just like you to give a compliment," she responds, pleased.

The wooden houses, some Victorian style, are painted bright

pinks, whites, or yellows, and are framed by lush yards, flowers cascading in gardens. The landscape is like one in a fairy tale. The air smells of a fresh, moist sweetness. I inhale the lilac scent, like perfume.

"I feel great at the moment," Rae says. And she looks that way, exploding with energy. In high school, she was a cheerleader. A little wild. The first one in our circle to have a boyfriend and sex. I spent a lot of time in the library then. We all envied her. "All my aches and pains are in remission."

"I guess that's all we can hope for at this stage in our lives. Remission." I sound more sour than I intend. "I have arthritis in my left elbow. No more tennis."

"Oh, Laura, I'm sorry. But everyone has something. I used to think there was a designated Job in a family. You know, like your brother, someone who has lots of burdens. Now I think everyone is part Job. Not to be grandiose, but everyone has struggles, whether people admit it or not."

"Maybe so."

"You'll take up another sport. Don't be discouraged. We can hope for a lot more."

"Such as?"

"White teeth." She grins. Her teeth gleam, the color of clouds.

"Nice." I pop open the umbrella, though just occasional raindrops splatter to the ground. I smile. I've whitened mine, too.

"Good for you. Very becoming," she says. "And great sex. We can look forward to that."

"With Paul?" I say. Her husband. "Things are better with him? That's good news."

"Sometimes. He still has that, you know, erectile problem. Do not say anything to him about it. Ever. Promise me. But I'm not a monk."

I turn to look at her. "So you're sleeping with someone else?"

"In fact, I am."

"Who?" I'm surprised Rae is having an affair. She hasn't had an affair while she's been married, as far as I know.

She's quiet. I can see she isn't certain she wants to tell me, although we tell each other so much.

I respect that. I won't pry or moralize. "That's okay. I don't need to know."

"It's complicated." She pauses. "He's the husband of Max Greenwald's lover."

It takes me a moment to process her roundabout way of telling me. "Max, he's the guy who lives next to—what's her name—Linda?"

"Lydia." She presses her lips together. "Yes."

"Oh." I let the information sink in. Rae's lover lives in this very neighborhood. Wasn't that reckless? I've had one husband. No lovers while married. I don't use sex toys. Rae once extolled the virtues of them. But I've had lovers since my divorce. Still, I sometimes think: I don't know how to live. I'm sixty years old. When will I live? "Isn't that dangerous?" I say.

"God, Laura. I'm careful. We use condoms. I can't get pregnant. It's disease. That's what you worry about at our age. Disease. Don't you worry?"

"All the time. But I mean, isn't it dangerous to have a lover in your neighborhood? You have to be careful."

She seems to consider this. "Really, it's pretty convenient."

"What if Paul found out?"

"That would be a problem. We're very careful." She hesitates. "Paul would be furious. He'd leave me."

We stand closer together beneath the umbrella. The mist is turning to light rain. Rae's first marriage ended in divorce—an annulment, she likes to joke. She was twenty-one and discovered her husband didn't like sex. The second husband was the alcoholic. And now Paul. He rescued her from that. I can tell the idea of Paul leaving her is more than she wants to bear.

"Then why do it?" I ask.

"Why do anything?" She frowns. "Loyalty. I believe in loyalty and commitment. I love Paul. I'm loving to him. I'm not abusive. I'm not really hurting him. But I'm very attracted to—his name is Stuart. We have so much in common. I know you'll like him. But if you meet him, don't mention anything about this. I promised him I wouldn't tell anyone."

"Just one more of our secrets." We are still girls—in women's bodies.

"We must be the queens of secrets," she laughs. "I wonder what it's like to live a normal life."

Since my divorce, I've experimented, slept with perfect strangers, using condoms, of course. Met men online, flirted, talked dirty. Lied about my age and attributes. Described myself in the best possible light. Rather than mentioning I teach students with developmental challenges—children with autism and those who struggle with learning disabilities or social issues, who are mainstreamed in a city school—I explain in my online profile that I supervise programs to help students with special needs and special gifts. I note that I'm tall, attractive, and willowy, though the truth is, I need to lose fifteen pounds and a few wrinkles.

Another old friend of mine, Joe Benson—I had a crush on him in high school—tutors me in dating at our age. He lives in the city, too. He's silver-haired and came out as gay years ago. He showed me websites and told me his dating tales, how he likes to cuddle in bed with men, not even have sex, he says. Just the touching, wrapping his arms around someone all night, is often all he needs. You don't always have to tell the absolute truth to a date or anyone, Joe advises me. Besides, the truth about yourself can change from moment to moment. He's tall and lanky, like he was in high school. He had jet-black hair then, with the same beautiful cerulean eyes. We all had a crush on him. Rae dated him. How many men has he dated since he and his partner split up a few years ago? Hundreds, he told me. "If you don't like one, there's always someone else. Online." Endless choices. This seems overwhelming to me. "But sometimes," he said last month, "I think if I could meet a nice woman, I might even get married and have a normal life."

"A normal life," Rae says again. "Do you think anyone has a normal life?"

I shrug. "In fairy tales that end happily ever after. In the suburbs maybe."

She shakes her head.

"But how would we really know what kind of lives people lead anyway?" I ask her. There is a private zone in every person. What's Rae's?

This is mine: loneliness. My one-night stands, cruising the internet late at night, phone sex with a college friend who lives in New

Mexico, on his third marriage, like Rae. I used to judge such acts harshly. Three marriages. Though I understood Rae's. Phone sex. You have to be desperate and debauched, I used to believe, to talk on the phone and be able to get off. But not much surprises me anymore, except that doing such things can actually bring pleasure, connection. And now I've met Len. He supervises the band and teaches music at a high school in Denver. His instrument is the piano. Jazz. Twice married. Wears a hearing aid. We met through friends. I see him every month or so.

"Lydia lives there." Rae interrupts my thoughts. "That house at the corner."

I squint. She points to the street intersecting with this one, at the end of the block.

"She was always kind. Genuinely. Not gratuitously." Nostalgia creeps into Rae's voice. I notice she uses the past tense and wonder why. "She used to call and say, 'It's me,' or 'It's me, Lydia,' and I'd say, 'It's me, too.' Just like you and I do, Laura. You don't need any introduction, any hellos or formality."

"A kind of intimacy," I say.

"Yes. Exactly. Her husband was a jerk. A player. I don't know how she put up with him. Lecherous old guy. But she did."

"Sounds like you knew him well."

"He'd come to the holiday parties or stop by to see her at work. He even hit on me once. She has Alzheimer's now, Lydia does." Rae's voice drops. "It's sad. Lucky she won't remember all the grief that guy caused her. He's dead now. Heart attack. Years ago."

"That's terrible, Alzheimer's." I take a deep breath. "But the way you describe it—maybe there's something redeeming about losing your memory after all."

"Something redeeming for sure." She picks up her pace. "You can rewrite in your mind what happened in your life."

"I don't know about that. But the distance helps. Helps you try to make sense of it all."

"They say hindsight is twenty-twenty." She shakes her head, amused. "Paul hates when I use clichés."

We step around puddles that have gathered from this morning's rain. They glisten like mirrors, reflecting the white of the sky and the bright colors of the houses around us. The drizzle is letting up. Rather than proceeding to Lydia's house, Rae ushers me in the other direction. "I want to show you a house where they're building an addition. Pink stucco. You only see this kind of thing in Florida or Vegas." She studies me. "What happened to your glasses? I just realized you're not wearing them."

"The eye doctor told me I don't need them."

"That's great," she says.

"But I've worn glasses all my life," I protest. "I told the doctor he made a mistake. He's young, arrogant. Went to Harvard. He said there's no mistake. I asked him to check again."

"Did he?"

"Yes. No glasses. I'm nearsighted in one eye, farsighted in the other. He said my vision has changed with age. The two eyes balance each other now. There's no need for a correction anymore. Just what I thought, he told me."

"You're free."

"But I don't want to be." I shrug. "I like my eyeglasses. The routine of them."

"You're lucky to have good news. I wish I had more routine. It's been one thing after another the last years." Rae's legs glide effortlessly along the sidewalk, and her sneakers squeak. Her arms brush against her sides. It feels as if we are speed walking. "First, my mother's cancer." She gulps a breath.

"Paul's heart attack," I say gently.

"Yes." She pauses. "And Grace."

Grace is Rae's twenty-four-year-old daughter. She stopped speaking to Rae last year. She wants to "find herself," she said.

"I hate to talk about it," Rae says.

"Then we won't."

My ex-husband, Glenn, didn't want to talk either—about finances. When we were married, he handled the bills and money, eventually put me on an allowance. I loved him, but was a little afraid of him, too, and didn't ask about this. Afraid of his criticism. He was an architect and the chairman of the synagogue social action committee. Creative and dreamy, bursting with ideas. When he left, I knew nothing about our financial life. I should have been the one to leave. It turned out he'd gambled, lost most of our savings, and took out a home equity loan. I always believed marriage should be "until death do you part." But maybe the death is of illusions.

Now I begin to recount the changes in my life, as if they demand attention and still feel like sudden, dangerous cracks in a road. "The last years have been tough for me, too," I say, hoping my list will make Rae feel better, not so alone. "My father's stroke. My brother's son joined that cult. The divorce. It was so hard on the girls." Rae knows I'm close to my two daughters; one works for Google, the other is a teacher. "My mother's death." I stop. We are all starting over, one way or the other, it seems.

"I tried to explain this to Len once," I continue. "We were going somewhere, driving in a rundown area of Denver. I was visiting him. I said: Why can't I just feel lucky? Why can't I compare my life to someone who has real troubles, who's homeless or ill or lives here, instead of comparing my life to someone who lives on Park Avenue?"

"What did he say?"

"Why compare at all?"

"Oh, I like him," Rae says. "I haven't met him, but already, I like him."

"You'll meet him. He's very direct. I love to be in bed with him."

"To fuck."

"Why not?" I laugh. I imagine Len and me on his bed in his small apartment, having vigorous, joyful sex, his skin glistening.

"You should move there," she suggests. "Live with him."

"I haven't been invited. And he's separated. Sometimes I wonder where our relationship is going."

"But he makes you happy."

"He could go back to her, his wife."

"I guess he could."

"When Glenn and I split up, I thought I might die. You know that. Twenty-six years together. Two children." I shiver. "But I'm used to it now, being on my own. I don't want to need anyone like that again. Now with Len, I worry about needing him too much. I guess you can get used to anything."

Rae stops walking. We stand in the waning drizzle and stare at the pink stucco mansion, like a Las Vegas reject plopped right here. I close the umbrella. Stray raindrops splatter in the puddle beside us, disappearing like stones cast into a lake.

"Next time you come to visit," she says brightly, "Paul and I, and you and Len—we'll drive to the Keys. It's beautiful there. We'll go on a vacation. Walk by the ocean. You can see Hemingway's house in Key West. It feels like you're far away, in a foreign country."

The idea of a vacation seems to cheer her.

"And what about Max Greenwald's lover's husband?" I ask. "Stuart?" It almost feels like a betrayal to speak his name.

She flutters a hand through her golden hair. "Oh, I wish. I wish we could take two vacations. Paul and me, you and Len. Then Stuart and me, and you and Len." Her face tenses. "No, Stuart. Maybe he's the one I really love." Her expression grows serious, as if this thought has just crystallized in her mind. "Sometimes I'm afraid that's the truth of my life," she says quietly. "It's been going on a long time. He's the one I love."

Maybe this is Rae's private zone. Maybe that's what love is. She really loves Stuart. Am I beginning to love Len? I'm not sure. How much time do we have for these late loves, imagined or real? "You're lucky to have those feelings. It's complicated but lucky."

"I don't know. He's kind of—it sounds silly," Rae says dreamily. "Stuart is radiant. Smart and funny. Oh, it doesn't matter."

I rarely hear that softness in her voice. Len is smart and funny, direct, and accepts no excuses. Beneath his toughness lies a tenderness I might love.

"I'm too old to leave Paul," she whispers. "But I'm too old to stay with him like this, all the lies."

I nod. What does she expect? To live in a wilderness of pleasure, like an oasis in the desert? Is that what she thinks she'll find with her lover? I remember my divorce—the fighting, the money problems, our life together splintered into pieces. The loneliness. I still sleep on the same side of the bed as I did when I was married, as if I'm waiting for my old life to return. Yet I'm no different than Rae. I want to live in that wilderness. I want that passion and pleasure, that happiness, a chance for it now. I bite my lip.

Everyone has to traverse his or her own life. Me, too.

"All those years with Owen, his drinking," she says. "I used to pray to God—and you know I rarely do that—but I prayed someday I'd find a man who liked sex, was kind, who I loved and who loved me. Who didn't have so many problems. It's absurd, the things you think."

"It's not absurd. It's kind of sweet. Actually, it's hopeful."

"And you know what? He gave me that man. But it's Stuart." There's a quiet vibration to Rae's voice, like the sound of a wounded bird. She turns and begins to walk in the direction we came from.

"I see," I say and follow her.

"Paul wants to move," she tells me suddenly. "Retire. To Las Vegas."

"He does? Can you afford that?"

"No, but he's determined to go. I'm not living there, Laura. With houses like that pink one. The fake mansions. It's grotesque. A wasteland. With people I don't know. I won't leave here."

"That's a problem." I wish I knew how to help her. "But Paul can change his mind. He has before. Like when he had that job offer in Memphis."

"That's true. He has changed his mind." She sighs, as if I've solved her dilemma. "Maybe that's the answer. I like to believe for every problem there's a solution."

"I wish, Rae. When you're a kid, it's easy to believe that."

"But I want to believe it. And talking helps. Makes everything better." She entwines her arm in mine. "When you and I talk, we can solve anything."

"Almost anything." Rae called me nearly every day when I was getting divorced. She was my anchor. I wouldn't have made it through the divorce without her. We talked, and she listened.

"Anyway, here's where the infamous Max Greenwald lives."

"I wonder what goes on in there," I say.

We both laugh.

"And Lydia lives next door. The Alzheimer's, it's just in the early stages. A little problem now."

"Little ones can become big ones."

"You sound just like your mother," Rae says.

This is the last person I want to sound like. She wanted order and routine. When something went wrong, she became anxious, talking and talking. She made little problems into big ones.

The window shades in Max Greenwald's house are pulled down, hiding what's inside. Pink peonies and exotic grasses bloom in the garden. We leave his house behind and approach the white clapboard house next door. A yellow picket fence surrounds it. The house is like a gingerbread house, perfectly appointed for a fairy tale, black shingle roof, clusters of flowers in the two window boxes. Red and purple pansies grow here, even in winter.

A stocky woman shuffles toward the gate, opens it, and makes her way to the sidewalk, just a few yards from us. Her white shirtwaist dress has an old-fashioned feel to it, with a wide, twirling skirt. She doesn't wear a sweater or coat even though it's damp outside. Her dress looks a little damp, too. Her gray hair falls in loose waves to her chin. She must have been pretty once. She has large green eyes, creamy skin, with slivers of wrinkles beneath her eyes, on her cheeks. No makeup. A worried expression.

"There she is. Lydia," Rae says with excitement. She hurries to the woman and hugs her.

Lydia takes a step back.

"It's me. Rae."

The woman stares at her.

"Don't you remember?" she prods. "I came to visit you last month. We had lunch in the yard here. You and I used to work at the hospital together, before you retired. I'm Rae Radner."

"That's a pretty name," the woman says, as if she's never seen Rae before.

"And this is Laura." She motions for me to join her. "My best friend. We've known each other since we were thirteen."

"Twenty years at least," Lydia says.

Rae laughs. "A lot longer than that."

I look at the two of them. Rae is trying to engage in normal conversation, but the woman is half there. Her expression is vacant, puzzled, like my mother's was toward the end. Rae peers at her the way I gazed at my mother then, with a desperation for the indignities of age and illness to disappear.

"What are you doing out here?" Rae asks Lydia. "You should be inside."

"I live here. In the back. My daughter's house. Mickey Mouse." She points to a small cottage attached to the house. "I'm waiting for her."

"It's almost four thirty." Rae glances at her watch. "She'll be home any minute from work, your daughter." She gently grasps Lydia's hand. "At least wait for her in the yard." Rae opens the gate and leads the woman in.

I trail behind them.

A large red-and-blue striped umbrella shields a wooden Adirondack chair in the yard. "You can wait here." Rae glances at the sky. "It could start to rain again, though. You'd better wait inside. I'll help you go into the house."

"Rain won't hurt. You live long enough, you'll know." Lydia plops into the chair and looks up at me, as if I'm the one with whom she shares a history. "What if she doesn't come home? My daughter?"

"She'll be back," I reassure her.

"When you see her, tell her, it's me, Lydia." She tilts her head toward Rae. "Tell her I'm waiting."

"We'll tell her," Rae says. "She'll be home soon. But wait inside. Please. You really should. Let me help you."

"No."

"Well." Rae sucks in a breath, exhales. "Take care of yourself."

"Goodbye," I say to Lydia.

"Thank you," she replies.

"Thank you." Rae rests a hand on the woman's shoulder. "For everything. You were always so kind to me. Stay in the yard or go inside until your daughter comes home."

Lydia doesn't answer. She folds her hands in her lap, on top of her flowing white dress, as if she will be waiting here for the duration.

We leave the yard, and Rae latches the gate tightly, then swings around to smile at the woman.

I try to imagine Lydia when she was young and beautiful, in love, to imagine her failure of a husband, the old lecher, whom she's lucky not to remember. She probably can't remember her own secrets or the truth about herself. But I can't make the leap from age to youth. Then

I think absurdly about a wilderness of pleasure. My friend Joe used to say he lived for pleasure. Now he lives to find love. Is there a difference between the two? And Len. I know I'm too old not to recognize love when I feel it.

"Maybe I will move to Denver," I say, apropos of nothing except my fear of growing old alone, turning into someone like Lydia. What can I say to Rae about Lydia that does her justice? "But don't go to Las Vegas. Stay right here. If it makes you happy, Rae."

"Let's go home."

We walk away from the yellow picket fence and white clapboard house.

"It's a fucking shame," she goes on. "Lydia. The Alzheimer's is worse. I wouldn't have taken you there if I'd known."

"Yes," I whisper.

Then we veer onto Rae's street. After a few minutes, we glance back. Lydia's street runs perpendicular to Rae's; we can still see the white clapboard house.

Lydia has unlatched the gate and is wandering on the sidewalk next to the yellow picket fence, pacing, inching toward Max Greenwald's house. Looking around in agitation.

"She could get hurt there," I say. "We should do something."

"Someone ought to do something," Rae bristles. "It's dangerous. But it won't help to talk to Lydia. Or the daughter. I've tried. People create their own hell. Someday they'll have to put Lydia in an institution. And that will be that."

I hesitate, about to go to the woman. It's the right thing to do, to go to her. But what exactly could we do anyway?

Rae barrels ahead without changing direction, and then I do as well. We walk so quickly now, as if we're sprinting in a race. I think about Lydia and her Alzheimer's, about Rae's love affair. I suddenly want to shake Rae.

"You ought to do something about your life, Rae," I say. "Look at how you're living. Take a look at it."

But she doesn't answer.

"Answer me, Rae," I insist. "I'm telling you the truth."

"No." Her fists slice the air. The leaves of the palm trees stretch upward, as if they're reaching for the heavens. I glance up, too. I don't want to live like Rae does. I'm going to shake away my loneliness, take a chance, and go to Len. Before it's too late. That's what I want to do, I think, relieved my sense of drifting has come to an end.

The sky is still obscured with that thick white haze, as if it's dusk already, as if Rae and I are slogging through a tunnel made of clouds and we will never get out. I step closer to her. She takes a step toward me. We don't touch. We don't talk. No rumbling of thunder announces the rain, but moisture suddenly ricochets down in long, strong spurts, clattering around us. We huddle beneath the umbrella, just big enough to protect us both. Then we hurry past Stuart Lewis's house and leave that behind, too. We don't look back. We just keep pressing forward, without saying another word.

2

A Modern Woman

ANGELA BENDER HAD ALWAYS PRIDED HERSELF on being a modern woman. She thought about this as she rolled her suitcase out of the terminal in Nashville and waited for the rental-car van to take her to Budget. She was forty-nine, with large brown eyes and short black hair, medium height and medium build. Years ago, she had eagerly embraced the sexual revolution. She had been involved with a number of men then. Eventually, she fell in love with Rob and married him, and they had three children. But she had recently come to the conclusion that she wasn't modern anymore at all. In an uncharacteristically honest moment last Sunday, she sat alone in the small sunny living room of the house where she lived with Rob and the children in Brooklyn. She wasn't *truly* liberated, she realized. Not like the young women with whom she worked in the admissions office at the college. They were in their twenties and thirties. Smart, beautiful, and single, they had sex with men, with other women's husbands, without shame or guilt. She listened as they discussed details of their personal lives. Angela marveled at their attitude. They viewed the body and its uses cavalierly, as if it were a commodity.

Of course, these young women had confided to her that marriage and motherhood must be the solution to loneliness. One colleague, Ginger, said this with envy. Angela reminded herself of this as she hoisted her suitcase into the Budget van. She had once tried to describe the limitations of the married state to Ginger, but had lost her focus as she studied the tattoos of pink roses imprinted on the young woman's arm and neck. The generation gap, Angela had thought. This is what she wanted to say to Ginger: marriage was a great divide. If you stood on one side, gazing at married life from a distance, you might long to cross over and bask in its imagined delights. But once you'd made that crossing, as Angela had eighteen years ago, you might have regrets and begin to question, just as she did now, whether the pleasures promised were a mirage.

Angela exited the highway and drove the green Honda through a web of streets until she came to the house in Nashville where she and Rob used to live. They had moved to Brooklyn eight months ago. But the house hadn't sold yet, and the renter had just moved out. She had returned to search for a new Realtor. Rob would join her tomorrow. The children were in middle school and high school. Angela's sister was staying with them while Angela and Rob were away; Angela had given her sister strict instructions to limit phone and computer time for the children.

Rob had worked for a health care company in Nashville, which went bankrupt. An opportunity at another company had come up for him in New York. They had moved to Nashville ten years ago from Pittsburgh because of music. He played piano and guitar, wrote songs, had dreams then of giving up his work in finance and strategic planning, becoming a country singer. Angela liked to think of him at the piano, his lanky frame, his green eyes intent on the keys, wide fingers pounding notes, his thin lips sweetly humming a song.

The house sat in the middle of a cul-de-sac. A small white ranch. It was a mild April day, and the dogwoods were in flower. Glistening white blossoms overflowed from branches like clusters of snowflakes. She and Rob had left a bed in the house, a few pieces of furniture, and odds and ends they hoped to sell or bring to New York once the house was sold. The renter was a teacher at their children's former school, so they had felt comfortable leaving some possessions here.

Angela's footsteps made a hard thud on the dark oak floors now. Even after you moved from a house, she thought, the echoes of your life there remained.

Wandering through the mostly empty rooms, she saw this: books, cookbooks, an old red plastic record player, a cracked black globe, the attic still filled with stacks of boxes. The gray concrete driveway where their son had broken his ankle while playing kickball. The soft blue kitchen she had stripped of wallpaper and painted. This was the room where, on a Sunday afternoon, she'd learned her father had metastatic cancer. The master bedroom was a quiet yellow room with long windows; shadows settled across the floor as the day wore on. This was the room where, on a terrible winter night, she had confronted Rob after she discovered his affair.

An hour later, Sonny Farber drove up. He was early. Angela had just finished interviewing one Realtor, who had left. The woman had been late. Now Angela saw the two real estate agents talking in the driveway. *Damn.* She ran her fingers through her dark hair and pulled on her dangling blue earring. She hadn't wanted the two agents to overlap or compare notes.

When she opened the door, she thought she saw displeasure in the man's eyes.

"Sorry you bumped into the other agent," she said, thinking perhaps this had upset him. "I didn't realize you'd be here at the same time."

"No problem." Sonny Farber stretched out the word "problem" as if it were two separate words. She could tell by his tone that he was annoyed. "Our business isn't like that," he said. "We all work together. We're all in the same *league.*" He smiled tightly and walked in. "But I know folks like to compare and contrast us Realtors." He appeared to be in his mid-forties. He had thick strawberry blond hair, blond eyebrows and a freckled, tanned face. An air of prosperity surrounded him. He wore a pressed beige T-shirt with a Polo insignia, neat khaki pants, and a sparkling gold chain around his neck.

Angela watched him eye the walls and ceiling of the entry. He was frowning, staring at the front hall, which to her appeared suddenly vacant and uninviting. No furniture, just the garish gold candelabra chandelier hanging with its glowing lightbulbs shaped like candles, like a medieval fixture. She had always meant to replace it.

"Exactly what can I do for you?" he asked.

She escorted him through the house, explaining that she and Rob wanted to change real estate agents, that they had to sell the house. They couldn't afford the payments anymore. The renter had moved out, and they were absentee owners.

Sonny Farber listened without comment.

Angela disliked him. He reminded her slightly of the man she had slept with twice in Brooklyn. Secretly. She had slept with him to get back at Rob for his affair. It was pure revenge. Passionate but ultimately unsatisfactory trysts. Her lover, married, a financial planner, had an arrogance that had both attracted and disturbed her. She had felt modern with him, liberated, like the women at the college. Or like her younger, unmarried self. She wore sexy lacy underwear and met him at a hotel. But both times, afterward, she felt a shame and guilt she was sure Ginger and her other young coworkers never experienced.

"The reason you haven't sold this house is that it looks uncared for," Sonny Farber said. "Neglected." He seemed to eye Angela, her face, her short black skirt and shapely legs, as if he might, in fact, be interested in *her*, not the house. "I don't mean to be blunt, but I like to be honest. Look at the door." He marched to the front door, brushed his finger across the dust caked on the molding. He pressed his thumb against the white paint of the wall. A chunk flaked off. "Filthy. The yard." He pointed to the property line by the street. "That dead tree, the weeds."

"Oh," said Angela. "No one is living here now."

"But people did live here, and they didn't pay attention to things. The dead tree and weeds have to go. You'll need to do major repair work here. It's not impossible. At one time, this house was in fine shape. Not anymore. And it's not because a renter moved out. The problems have been here for years. Oh, I can take this house on. Believe me, I'm not going to chase away business. But I want you to know up front, I can't promise miracles."

"I don't believe in miracles anyway," she said.

Angela had discovered Rob's affair four years ago. This wasn't a full-fledged crisis with a separation, the marriage pulled apart. She had seen that happen with friends. Some reconciled, others divorced. His was a quiet affair. A note left on his desk at home that Angela had discovered when looking for the car insurance statement. A note from the woman: *I love you!! Can't wait. Your JS.* Angela was stunned. That night, after the children were asleep, she showed Rob the paltry evidence, and he became paler than she had ever seen him. He blinked, once, twice, three times.

"I found this. What does it mean?"

There was silence. They both knew.

"You've been sleeping with someone," she finally screamed. "Doing *it* with her. You asshole. It's true, isn't it? It's fucking true. You're tired and moody with me, and you're sleeping with her." Angela's eyes filled with tears. Rage pressed inside her chest. She didn't know whether to cry or to slap him. She did both.

Rob looked startled, as if shocked by what had suddenly happened in his life. He stuttered and tried to explain. The woman worked at his company, he mumbled; she was divorced. He had met with her a few times. "Just a few. She had a problem she needed to talk to me about and I…I will end it. Stupid, foolish thing. It means nothing to me."

He later swore to Angela that he had broken off the affair. He apologized over and over, was more attentive to her and the kids. But for months, Angela could not bear to have sex with him. They talked to a marriage counselor. At first, Angela faulted herself for his affair. She had been busy with work and the children, hadn't paid attention to Rob; he had been struggling with his music career then. She wasn't a tolerant enough woman. She held grudges, had outdated values. He had asked for forgiveness. Why couldn't she accept that? She thought of Ginger's attitude toward sex, as if it were sport, of how Ginger seemed to emulate the one-dimensional lives she saw on the television dramas she watched. She had told Angela that she often slept with more than one man in a week.

Angela could not wrap her mind around this concept. The only friend she had confided in about Rob's affair, a friend from college, had said, "If you stay together, you'll have to forgive him sometime."

"I could never," Angela said.

"You forgive for yourself. Not for him."

Yet after that, nothing was as it used to be. If you didn't *do* something to keep intimacy alive, Angela thought, time pounded its fists until any closeness lay like pulp at your feet. Rob's body seemed strange to her now, foreign, as if it had traveled to another country, absorbed another persona, another skin. He did not seem like her husband anymore. The physical space between them in a room, their bed, seemed crowded with secrets. She told Rob this.

"I can't wade through the secrets to reach you," she said. "What happened between you and her. She is in this room with us. I hate what you've done to us."

"There's nothing here," he said. "Just you and me. No more secrets. It's over. I promise you." He extended his hands to hers as if to prove this.

She held his hands. But she mourned what had happened. The private loss followed her like a shadow, even now back in Nashville, in the house. She had always loved Rob. But she couldn't make up her mind. She would stay with him. She would leave. She could accept what happened. She couldn't. She had hoped that returning to this house would clarify her thoughts, help her move on with him, or leave. She was determined to decide.

One of the reasons they had moved to New York was to start a new life.

That night, on the phone, she told him about the real estate agent.

"Maybe you're too hard on him; maybe the guy wasn't so bad," Rob said. "He has a good reputation for selling houses."

Angela shrugged, even though Rob couldn't see her. She had learned not to react to Rob's generalizations about her or anyone else, and she imagined Sonny Farber's tight smile, his tense jaw as he looked with disdain at the house, as he brushed his hands along the baseboards and stared with distaste at the dust. "We'll see. You can talk with him yourself."

"Be positive," Rob said.

"I'm telling you what I honestly think about him," she said.

That first night at the house, Angela slept in the yellow bedroom alone. In the morning, she ate an egg salad sandwich she had bought at the airport. The kitchen counters were cleared of signs of family life. Books still sat on the oak shelves Rob had built, varnished, and mounted. She had been so proud years ago of how he designed and constructed the bookshelves. She used to lie on the couch in the living room then, listening to him play the piano, watching as he taught the children scales and chords. Now, they would leave behind the bookshelves for good, sort through the books they had left here, give some away. Her mother had never liked to discard things, as if having a tangible record prevented the obliteration of one's past.

Angela pulled a cookbook from the shelf. It had a yellowed, torn cover. She thumbed through the book her mother had given her. Hors d'oeuvres, breads, eggs, cheeses, main dishes. When she was growing up, her mother had served pot roast, flank steak, and tongue. Tart and pleasantly sweet tastes, pink meat that seemed like silk in her mouth. Her mother had prepared elaborate meals, and the whole house seemed to burst with aromas of onion and garlic, smells of chicken and sweet meat simmering. The cooking had seemed like magic then. But Angela knew now that no magic was involved. She leafed through more pages in the book: vinegar, brown sugar, white raisins, salt, and lemon. Common ingredients, easy to buy and combine.

Once, her father had come home from work early, and Angela's mother had switched on the radio to a big band station. Her father had taken her mother in his arms, and they had danced, a slow, close dance. Cheek to cheek. Then a tango. He'd twirled Angela's mother, and Angela and her brother watched the blue checked apron swish and swing as the couple moved and laughed. That night, the flank steak had tasted like rich filet mignon or some special delicacy. She had basked in the warmth of her parents' smiles and hoped someday that she would live in a house and dance with her husband like that.

Angela tried to imagine those scents now, willed herself to, but the aroma wouldn't come to her.

The second night at the house, Rob arrived late, and they slept in their old yellow bedroom that was bare now, the walls without pictures. The two long rectangular windows framed the full moon and let in its pathways of light. The room seemed cleared of irrelevancies. The glowing moon reminded Angela of a Hiroshige woodblock, an ukiyo-e she had seen once in a museum. A full moon hung like a perfect buttermilk circle in a blue-black sky; the people below it were tiny, like fine, rounded brushstrokes. She felt so small in comparison with the moon, fragile in the lumpy bed next to Rob.

"You have the body of a young woman," he said as they made love. She could tell by the way he touched her that he was happy, and when she allowed herself to have a kind of amnesia about their past, she enjoyed him, too.

In the morning, he said, "What I've always loved about you is you don't fall into self-pity."

"What?" Angela pulled the blankets to her neck.

"The Realtor sucks. We haven't sold the house. We can't afford to keep up the payments. The kids are still adjusting to the move. They're glued to the computer. And you're still okay about it all."

"I am?" she said groggily.

"One of your best qualities is that you have hope. Like about us. Optimism."

She smiled, did not contradict him.

"You know, you used to be too thin." He turned on his side to look at her.

"Me? When?"

"Two, three years ago maybe. But now you're perfect."

"Oh." She wasn't pleased by the compliment. It struck her as disparaging. But there was no point bringing this up now. "Way too much stress before."

"Stress." He paused. "Really, it happened right here in this room." She nodded.

"You always change the subject." He brushed his hand across her cheek. "Why did you take me back? Whenever I ask, you don't answer."

"No, I try to avoid talking about that."

"I suppose I let you change the subject," he said. "Why didn't you kick me out when there was all that…stress?"

She sat up in the bed. "Do you want me to be honest?"

He closed his eyes. "I don't know."

"It's hard to be honest." She hated to talk about this. She preferred silence. Or distractions. There were no distractions here. "I've always thought I stayed with you because I was scared. I was a coward."

"I'm glad we didn't…" He looked at her, bit his lower lip. "Scared of what?"

"Life on my own with three kids. Of the future. Of what would happen."

"Oh." He stopped. "It's tough to hear the reason. To think of what

I did, how you felt then. I'm glad we stayed together." He nodded. "Grateful."

"But maybe below the fear was love. To be truthful, I don't know, Rob."

"Love. That's why I'm here. Because I love you. Don't you know that?"

They worked in the house, clearing out the garage and attic. In the afternoon, Rob sat on the one chair left in the den. His face was pale. He looked exhausted.

"You need a rest," Angela said.

"I'm worn out. Not from here. The new job. The move. The changes in our life. Pressure about money. I suppose I'm ambitious. Always have been. If I don't succeed at something, I feel like shit. Like with the music."

"But you wrote beautiful songs. Your music was a success. You didn't push it far enough. So what if one artist or a music company didn't like a song you pitched? There were other singers, other companies. You had to get out there and network. Wait it out."

"Maybe."

"I would have supported us the best I could," she said gently. "You gave up."

"But it makes me feel empty. As if nothing is in here." He pressed his hand against his chest. "I wouldn't have asked you to support the family like that. I need those successes to fill me up somehow. Goddamn bankrupt company. I couldn't save them. They didn't listen to me. Having to start over now. I'm too old for this."

"You're not old. And you know those things aren't so important." She knelt on the floor next to him.

"They're important to me. What I do and accomplish is important." He glanced from her to the room. "How I treat people is important. It's something. Being here. All that time we lived in this place. Now it's a memory. All those things that happened here. The good times. The lost time. I lost a lot of time for us."

"You did." She could see he was tired. "Tell me how I can help you."

He sprawled on the floor, arms stretched out next to him. "Let me rest for a bit."

In the kitchen, Angela stood on tiptoes, reached toward a high shelf and pulled out *The Joy of Cooking*. Then she stared at the room as if it were someone else's house. Soon it would be. She could imagine her children in this very room, when they were younger, crowded around the round oak table, laughing or bickering. She could hear the sweet notes of the piano as Rob composed a loud chord, a trill. She could see herself reading contentedly with the family around her, imagine herself in tears when she had discovered his affair, the sluggishness of her movements then, the slap, the scream, throwing a chair then later a broom at him. She still could feel the terrible despair. The anger.

Enough.

She hurried outside, climbed into the rented Honda and drove to Kroger with its neat aisles of carefully stacked products, the pleasant, polite checkers who asked, "How are you today, ma'am?" She remembered the old HG Hill store that had stood a few blocks from Kroger years before, and the employees dressed in red aprons who piled the groceries in bags and cheerfully placed her purchases in the car for her. She thought of Ginger again, who might laugh at such a store, who might be sure Angela's ideas were outdated, obsolete.

At home, she checked on Rob. He was sleeping on the old couch in the living room now. She lined up the ingredients on the white kitchen countertop and used what utensils were here, an old roasting pan, a rusty oversized slotted spoon, an aluminum pot she'd meant to discard because she had read that aluminum caused Alzheimer's disease. She seasoned the beef with spices and vegetables—rosemary, salt, pepper, chopped onions, carrots, and garlic—and set it in the oven. Then she began the pie, combining flour and sugar and butter, kneading on the countertop, the dough like warm thick salve. She boiled red apples and added cinnamon to the mixture until the scents began to fill the kitchen, not the scents of her marriage, but those of her childhood, until the house burst with aromas of sweet cinnamon, onions, and garlic.

She heard Rob's movements. She peeked into the living room.

He was standing up, rubbing his eyes. "Are you cooking?" he asked.

"Yes. I thought we would..." She walked into the room. "Let's pretend no one is here."

"No one is." Rob shook his head, as if shaking the sleep from his eyes. "Or did someone come over? I was out cold." He looked to the left and the right. "It smells wonderful in this house. No one else *is* here."

"You know that's not true," she said.

He didn't answer.

Angela didn't know what or whom he might imagine in the dim light of the room. But she saw the divorced woman now, his lover, like an apparition, floating in a white gossamer dress cut so low that the fleshy curves of her breasts bulged grotesquely. The woman was like filament, pulling at Rob's arm. The room seemed heavy with secrets. The gossamer figure. Angela's lover—a Sonny Farber double—beckoning her. Her own wavering affections.

Rob didn't seem to notice that she was lost in these thoughts. How could he know what she was imagining unless she told him? Perhaps that was as it had to be.

Angela blinked once, twice, and the images were gone. For how long would they stay away?

"So," Rob said. He looked at her expectantly.

"We'll make the most of it." She nodded decisively. "Yes, that's exactly the thing to do." She walked into the den. Rob followed her. She went to the old record player, the worn red plastic machine she'd meant to give away years ago, and plugged the cord into the wall socket. In the den closet, the hidden one she pushed against to open, she found the old vinyl records, 33 1/3 rpm, that she and Rob had owned in college and before. Hers mixed in with Rob's. Joni Mitchell, The Grateful Dead, Roy Orbison, Johnny Mathis, Frank Sinatra. The shiny vinyl records were obsolete now, relics of the past. She pulled out *Johnny's Greatest Hits*, which had belonged to her parents, and placed it on the squeaky turntable.

Rob watched. "What are you doing?"

"Atmosphere." She laughed and felt suddenly giddy. "Atmosphere is everything."

"Almost." He smiled with affection.

"Yes. Almost."

The scratching melody of "When I Fall in Love" floated in the room. She held Rob's hand and pulled him close, leaning into him, and he leaned into her, until their bodies kneaded against each other, hers pressing into the firm warmth of him.

"I'm sorry for everything I have ever done to you. It was selfish," he said quietly. "I've done a lot. Too much. All those things that happened in this house. I wish I could erase the past. Please believe me."

"For all the things not done, too?" She didn't wait for an answer. "Will you forgive me, too?"

He did not ask for what, and she was grateful. She didn't think she would have told him if he'd asked.

They began to dance. Rob hummed the melody. Angela hadn't had a warm feeling for him in so long, and now in his arms, she wished they could go round forever. Here, in this room, in this house, with these very scents. He held her close. They danced in the light of the waning full moon that shone through the window and that, for a brief instant, cast a flickering golden halo across their faces.

Double Helix

TODAY I LEAVE WORK EARLY and will finish a project at home. It's a breezy June day. I do graphic design for an arts organization in Brooklyn, and help with fundraising. The sun is shining, and I feel almost as if I am on vacation. In the lobby of the building where I live, the doorman hands me a padded envelope.

"For you," he says.

"Thank you. I wasn't expecting anything."

"Then it's a surprise," he says, smiling. "I hope it's a good one."

"Oh, I hope so, too," I laugh.

I glance at the envelope as I make my way to the elevator. I immediately know who sent the package. My name is written on the front. I'm careful with how I form letters and numbers when I write, but my ex-husband has always been careless about penmanship. I know the way he shapes the letters of my name: Lucy. The large *L*, the hurried vowel, and the flourish after the *y*. For a moment, I wonder if Thomas is sending something I inadvertently left in the apartment we once shared, and if he has enclosed an angry letter like those he sent to me during the divorce.

In my apartment, I sit at the dining room table and open the padded envelope. He has included a note on a beige card: *Lucy, I want you to have this. We were married for 28 years, after all.* —*T*

I pull out the book, his book, and laugh at the title. *The Heart and the Gut.* This is his first book, and I notice it's published by a reputable press. I knew he was writing a book; our daughter, who is in graduate school in Vermont, told me.

Thomas isn't a writer. He's a scientist. An accomplished one, but not famous. His experiments are published in professional journals, but he hasn't catapulted to being a scientific superstar. He studies diseases of the stomach and heart.

Some days it's hard to remember he's my ex and that we're not married to each other anymore. We have two children, and we once loved each other. There were lies, and he had an affair—a few affairs, I later learned. I was involved in one affair and felt guilty about this, but also grateful.

I stop myself from reliving the difficulties of our divorce two years ago, because what good will it do? He did what he did, and I said what I said. Thomas has a temper and freely wielded words when we were divorcing. "You weren't a partner to me," he shouted, as if raising the decibels would add weight to his words.

People are always falling in love with the wrong person. After we separated, I hung up when he called and didn't respond to his emails. I sent them to my lawyer instead. Even the one in which he wrote: *Your lawyer is stupid. She's wasting our money. If I were you, I wouldn't listen to her.*

That caught me off-guard. I read the message and stared at the computer screen. "You're not me," I shouted in answer, "and I'm not you." I typed this, but then remembered the lawyer had said not to reply to his messages. I forwarded Thomas's email to her with an apology. She replied: *No apologies are necessary. This is a legal case. It isn't about ego. He doesn't like the advice I give you because it doesn't favor him.*

A divorce is like a funeral, a prolonged funeral. This book is a message from the dead. A demand to relive the past. It's too early for a glass of wine, so I make coffee, rummage in the kitchen cabinet, and eat a few chocolate chip cookies. I set the bag of cookies on the table and study the book's cover, black with designs in blue and orange, a double helix, a picture of a human heart, and shapes that are probably bacteria, but look like art.

Thomas led a double life, but as I skim the book, I realize a reader would never know this. The book is about science, I remind myself; a reader doesn't need to know about his double life. Still, I am shocked as I turn the pages. The book purports to be about his life as a scientist, but it's really about his life as a man. Thomas has included autobiographical details, but he's rewritten his life without me in it.

He wrote about our children and people who worked in his lab, about Eric J. Smith, a PhD student from England, who lived with us in our apartment for a year. Eric was a lovely young man, but he left his clothing and damp towels on the floor in the bathroom. We had dinners together, and he joined us on a family vacation, driving through New England to see the fall colors. Thomas wrote about his own scientific experiments with bacteria and diseases of the heart, about the illnesses of his parents, his new wife, his brother, and in great detail about our son's childhood asthma, the trips to the pediatrician and ENT doctor, to the emergency room.

I didn't expect acknowledgment in the book, but I expected the truth. I drove our son to the doctors and the hospital. I told Thomas and the doctors that I was wary of too much medicine. He and I discussed this at length. We made decisions about our children together. I am nowhere in the pages of the book.

I can't bear to look at the acknowledgments page. He probably thanked the new wife. They've been married a year and a half.

The telephone rings, and it's our daughter who's in graduate school. We talk for a while, and then I say, "Your father sent me a copy of his book."

"He did? Why would you want one?"

"God knows. I read the chapter about the time you broke your arm. I was the one who took you to the doctor." I stop myself, embarrassed that I've mentioned this.

"Mom, I know. Everyone knows that."

"I'm sorry, honey. I guess looking at the book brings everything back." I'm usually careful not to put the kids in the middle.

"Then don't look at it. Really, it's not that interesting."

I quickly change the subject and ask her about school.

After we finish talking, I study the book's cover, the double helix. Thomas once described this to me. He talked about science like a man in love. DNA, he said, is a molecule that encodes an organism's genetic blueprint. DNA, he went on with excitement, contains all the information required to build and maintain an organism.

Later, I call my friend Beth. We've been friends for years. I tell her about the book. "I'm humiliated," I say. "Angry."

"He's the one who should be ashamed." She pauses. "It *is* a slap in the face. I can understand that. I would be angry. The book is so *him*. It's all about him. I read a review of it, and the critic said, 'You'll like this book only if you believe the author's theories.' She said he doesn't mention anyone else's. I would never buy the book or read it. Besides, who reads books anymore?"

"A slap in the face," I repeat. "He can write whatever he wants, but why should I see it? Why would he give it to me? The book is undoubtedly on Kindle. Maybe there's an audiobook. He's probably making a fortune."

"I don't think so," Beth says. "It's not a bestseller. I shouldn't be so blunt." She sighs. "He had some good qualities, but he was all about ego. That's who he is."

A walk would help me. I hurry out of the apartment, out of the building, and make my way toward the Starbucks on Broadway near West Ninety-Third Street. I decide to walk along the river, where it's quieter.

The trees are cloaked in green near the Hudson, and the air smells of grass and flowers, fresh, not the odors of diesel and urine that float on Broadway. People stroll on the path, and after a while, a woman who looks familiar walks past. She is walking with a man, talking. They aren't looking in my direction, but I realize the woman is Allyce Wasserman, my divorce attorney. I recognize her short black hair and silver wire-rimmed glasses, the red lipstick and gold bangle bracelets. I haven't seen her since my divorce. I debate whether to say hello, then hurry up to her. She is older than I, in her sixties and divorced herself. I imagine she has met a man, and the two of them are taking time away from work. I'm excited that she's in a relationship. I wonder if they've moved in together.

"Allyce," I say.

"That's right." She turns around, stops, and smiles. "Lucy. How lovely to see you."

"Yes." I look from her to the man.

"It's been a long time. How are you? Oh, this is my brother, Gordon. We're coming from a funeral, and we took a detour to walk here."

He is wearing a dark suit, and nods.

"I'm sorry," I say. "About the funeral."

"It was a cousin. She was very sick. What can you do? Everyone passes. That's what waits for all of us." Allyce looks at her brother. "Lucy was a client. She did very well in her divorce. She has two children, and she's a graphic designer and a painter." Her voice is warm. I'm flattered she remembers me so clearly. When she turns back to me, she asks, "So, how are you? How do you like your apartment?"

I tell her about the apartment and my work. I think about Thomas's book, but don't mention it. I'm not going to talk to Allyce about business now.

"See," she says. "I told you there's life after divorce." She turns to her brother. "I told Lucy that you can be perfectly happy. Divorce is not the end of the world."

As she's talking, I look at her with a perspective I've never had before. I suddenly feel odd, as if I'm large and clumsy, and I'm startled to realize Allyce is much shorter than I am, maybe five or six inches. She's a small, compact, wiry woman, but I never noticed this. Her brother is the same height as she is. At her office, I sat opposite her, on the other side of her desk. She seemed tall then, sturdy, so certain and knowledgeable. For a second, I'm confused. We're almost strangers, I realize, but she knows intimate details of my life, my finances, my divorce.

"It's funny," I say awkwardly. "Really, I'm so much taller than you. You always seemed taller than me." I'm appalled by what I've said. "I mean, you knew so much," I stammer, trying to explain.

She laughs. "You and I were usually sitting down." She eyes her brother. "We're small people. I'm five foot two. Our mother is five feet. But height doesn't matter when you're representing a client in a divorce." She glances at her watch. "We've got to go to the shiva."

For an instant, I think we'll hug, like Beth and I do, as if Allyce Wasserman is a dear old friend.

She thrusts out her hand to shake mine. "I'm so glad you're doing well."

I'd never told Allyce the history of the marriage. She wouldn't have been interested, and she would have billed me. She billed in ten-minute increments. She was interested in the residuals, the demise of the marriage, and getting results.

Thomas and I had been set up on a date by friends. We were both living in Denver. He was from New York, a PhD student at the university, and he wore T-shirts and jeans, and rode around the city on his bicycle. I had grown up in Michigan and moved to Denver after college. On our first date, we took a long walk to a store that sold special cakes with layers of mocha and chocolate. Back then, I ate as much chocolate and drank as much wine as I could. I lived with a kind of abandon, as if I had endless time, and, in a way, I did. We talked about our lives, his disdain for bourgeois, materialistic values, and his desire to live a deeper life, the very same feelings I had. We were young, idealistic, and serious. He was smart and funny, tall and good-looking, with a high forehead and long nose, solid hands, and cocoa-colored eyes. I could marry this man, I thought.

The pastry shop was closed. We should have known. This was Denver, after all, and though the summer nights were mild, the stores closed early. We saw a shower of stars in the sky as we walked. When we returned to the house I shared with a roommate, we stood on the porch, and Thomas said, "Do you believe arranged marriages can be happy marriages?"

I smiled and thought for a minute. "Maybe so," I said, and explained about my grandparents. Their marriage had been arranged in Poland and they had grown to love each other, had been married for over sixty years. "Maybe that's a better way than dealing with the disappointment of modern romance."

He held my gaze steadily, as if he wanted to bore into me.

I had to look away. "Do you?" I asked.

"Maybe. Yes." He laughed. "What do you do with your money?" he asked suddenly.

"I save it," I said, though I thought this was an odd question to ask.

When I think about our first conversation, I realize it is emblematic of our communication. I lied from the beginning. I wanted to save as much money as I could, but money slipped through my fingers. I told Thomas who I wanted to be, who I thought he wanted me to be.

And he lied to me. Maybe he didn't believe in monogamy or marriage, arranged or not. But he knew, even then, that this was not the answer I wanted to hear.

At home, the book sits on my dining room table like an evil eye. I tell myself: this is foolish. The book is nothing more than a book. A divorce is nothing more than a divorce. I have to finish a project for work, but I'm unable to concentrate.

I check for online messages from potential matches, then peruse the dating site, looking for photos of men who seem appealing and seem to be telling the truth. I am better off without Thomas, I know, but it's hard to convince my heart sometimes. To convince my ego. I've met a man through the site who seems promising. Live Love Laugh is his screen name. His profile states he is a nonsmoker. Six feet. Has a master's in education. Physically active. We've spoken on the phone and met once. He looks just like his photo, and he doesn't seem to be lying about his age or anything else. I like his deep clear voice and expressive oval face. His positive attitude. He's a widower. I like his way of saying, "We all have baggage."

I'm unable to concentrate on the website either. I tell myself: if the book is bothering you, throw it out. But I'm drawn to the shiny cover, the design of the double helix. Thomas once recounted the history of this. Thumbing through the pages, I find a section with words similar to those he once spoke to me.

DNA was discovered in 1869 by Friedrich Miescher. In 1953, two scientists, Francis Crick and James Watson, described the molecular shape of double-stranded DNA as a "double helix." Double-stranded DNA is composed of two linear strands that run opposite each other. The strands twist together and form a double helix. In cells, the DNA helix is often overwound, causing a phenomenon known as supercoiling. This increases the stress on the molecule.

I discovered Thomas's last affair. He begged me to take him back. I said I'd consider it. I still loved him, though I didn't know how I'd be able to trust him again, or if I could forgive him. Then I discovered he was still seeing Sandra. His promises had been hollow. He and I had a life together. We had children. I didn't want to lose him. But I already had.

I stare at the book again, at the title, at the overwound double helix. DNA is just DNA, I tell myself. Am I too narcissistic? No. The book is about my ex-husband's life, and he portrays the events as if he handled them alone.

Finally, I open the book and read the inscription he wrote to me: *For Lucy, Thank you! You were present at the creation. Best, T*

That's it?

At the computer, I compose an email to Allyce Wasserman: *Dear Allyce, What a nice coincidence to see you. My ex-husband has published a book and*

What can I say? He left me out of the book? He was difficult in the marriage, in the divorce, and in his book? He owes me royalties? Owes me love?

There is no way she can help. I am divorced. I got in the settlement what I got. There was unfairness, but no one is really happy in a divorce. Whatever was unfair remains that way. A settlement is not love. This book falls onto a trail of injustice that may never end. I'd better get tough. I'd better get used to it.

I pick up my cell phone to call Beth, but decide not to call. This is my problem. I need to handle it alone. It is time to move on. But to what? I am able to flirt online and in person, but I still haven't gotten over my ex-husband. That is the dismal truth.

I pace in the living room. My heart hammers in my chest. I would rather not face the truth, but the truth is staring me in the face. The truth is in that book and my reaction. Thomas has divested himself of me. He has a revisionist view of history. The coldness in his tone on the few occasions we've talked spills into the coldness of his words in the book. He's a stranger to me, like Allyce Wasserman is. I have embraced divorce as if this will set me free.

But I'm not free. I have a list of wants: to fall in love again or move away, finish the large paintings I started before the divorce for a group show. The canvases sit propped against a wall in my apartment.

My mind wanders when I paint now; I mull over the past and murky future. I want to take our kids on a trip. I want to visit the desert and the ocean. To put this marriage behind me.

I pace faster and think about the impersonal inscription. I am upset with myself for dodging the truth. For sugarcoating it. For not saying to Allyce Wasserman, her brother, and myself: Yes, there is life after divorce, but that's not the whole picture. The whole picture is: There is life, and there are scars. To deny the scars is to live in a simplistic fantasy. There's the past, and then the attempt to overwrite it, but the past always remains as an underpainting, lying just beneath the surface of the present.

The book with its shiny cover seems to nod in agreement. Life after divorce! Maybe that is how Allyce and other divorce lawyers rationalize their trade.

What I Said about Thomas:
- Thomas was happy as long as I did everything the way he wanted.
- He was sure his opinion was the right one.
- He was impatient.
- He said he wanted a partner, but that was not true. A friend of mine who married late said he finally understood he hadn't been looking for a partner, but was really looking for a clone of himself. Someone with interests and DNA footprints identical to his. "Do I want a clone," he said to me, "or do I want to be married?" Thomas wanted a clone.
- He was frugal.
- He was loving at the beginning, but later became judgmental and sharp.

What Thomas Said about Me:
- I was happy as long as he did everything the way I wanted.
- I was sure my opinion was the right one.
- I was indecisive and dreamy.
- I did not truly understand his scientific work.
- I let money slip through my fingers.

• I was loving at the beginning, but later became judgmental and sharp.

I feel a sliver of comfort as I remind myself of our perceptions of each other. We didn't understand these things when we met. At the beginning, all we wanted was to be with each other and have sex, to grow old together. Nothing else seemed to matter. In a way, as the years passed, both of us were right. We each wanted something from the other. Our genetic blueprints were the opposite.

At the computer, I leave the email to Allyce Wasserman unfinished. There is a new email from Thomas: *Did you get the book?*

I read his words twice and realize that by the very act of giving me the book and following up, he's shown he really hasn't moved on either. He may have tried to erase me from the past, but he still wants a reaction from me. I don't reply.

There's a message from Live Love Laugh, the widower. He invites me to dinner. I compose a reply: *Thank you. Would love to meet for dinner this week! What works for you?*

Would love to see if we can have a friendship, I think, become emotionally entangled, become lovers, but I don't include this.

I save the message instead of sending it, grab the book and march to the hallway, to the trash room. I pull open the can's metal lid and stop. How can I throw out the book? A book is a sacred object, at least in my world. So I go back to the apartment and set the book on my kitchen counter. Then I rip out the page with the inscription. It's painful to hear the sound of paper ripping. I am not happy to deface a book, even one from Thomas. In my filing cabinet, I search for the thick folders that overflow with papers and notes from the divorce.

I slide the page with the inscription into a folder, place all the file folders and papers in my folding shopping cart, set the book on top, and take the elevator to the basement. In the storage area, I unlock my bin and drop in the bulging folders. Then I make my way to the laundry room. In the back is a small library, shelves lined with books, and a sheet of paper tacked to the wall:

LIBRARY RULES

1. Donations are accepted. ONLY FICTION.

2. Please make sure the book is in good to perfect condition.

3. Check out a book for no more than two weeks, and return it to its place.

4. Biographies, poetry, memoirs, self-help, and other nonfiction books will be disposed of.

5. Appropriate books will be donated to a prison reading program.

6. Problems? Contact the doorman or Chuck Henricks, 5B, librarian.

7. NOTE: We follow the HONOR system. Borrow but RETURN the books.

I shake my head. This is a library in a laundry room in an apartment building and there are more rules for how to borrow a book than rules given to a person for how to master marriage. There is a manual for almost everything, except marriage. Is everyone a beginner? Will my son and daughter need a manual? Marriage should follow the honor system, too.

Thomas married Sandra, the young research assistant, a woman with large breasts and a toothy grin. It's a cliché: married middle-aged man fucks younger woman and marries her after divorcing. Beth and I used to shake our heads at this. Is there a manual for middle-aged men? What does the wife do to deserve the betrayal? Or is the betrayal independent of what one deserves? Is anyone to blame? How can a woman have fallen in love with such a man? I know it's sociobiology, too: men have a genetic imperative to spread their genes as widely as possible, and they turn to younger women of childbearing age after their own mates can no longer bear children. Men need to fight against this. But it doesn't matter what I think of this cliché or how I analyze it. I am living it.

I slide Thomas's book onto the shelf in its alphabetical place in the laundry room library. My feelings aren't about pride or money or sex. This is about disappointment. Disappointment and hurt. Anger fueled by hurt. Anger at being wronged. It is my private sorrow. All sorrows, in the end, are private.

What can I do? I walk briskly to the elevator with the shopping cart. When I reach my floor, I throw his envelope into the can in the trash room, relieved my apartment is freed of his book, his presence.

I pour a glass of wine, drink it, and then have second thoughts. An evil eye is an evil eye. A reminder of a sorrow is a reminder, whether it sits in my apartment or on a shelf in the laundry room. I race to the basement. A few other tenants are filling washing machines with dirty clothing, and we nod hello to each other. Then I pull the book off the shelf, go to the storage locker, and retrieve the inscription page, too.

I heard a rabbi speak once about a passage in the Torah in which Moses goes up to Mount Sinai. I don't go to synagogue often, but this time, the rabbi's words caught my attention. There is a sentence in the Torah indicating Moses wanted to see God's face. God says: "Do not see my face and live." The rabbi explained that this phrase is about the unknowability of God. There are limits to what a person can know about God. There are limits to any relationship, the rabbi said. Limits to what you can know about another person. Limits to intimacy.

Maybe there are limits to memory, I think, limits to the past.

In my apartment, I drink another glass of wine and then find the paperweight Thomas gave me once, a beautiful, heavy piece of blue glass shaped like a heart. It sits on top of yesterday's mail. I've kept it on my desk at home because it reminds me of happier days. We were married for twenty-eight years, after all.

I slide the book and inscription page into a plastic Food Emporium bag, and put in the paperweight, too. Clutching the bag, I walk to the path along the Hudson River where I saw Allyce Wasserman and her brother. They are long gone. Other people stroll there. The air has cooled, and the sun glistens behind the clouds.

At the river, I stand by the railing and think of *tashlich*, the religious ritual Jews perform on Rosh Hashanah, when they look ahead to start a fresh year. People come to the river and throw in pieces of bread. I'm not sure if they cast away their sins, or forgive the sins of others, or ask forgiveness for their own. Do they try to get rid of toxicity in their lives? I wonder about the widower and Allyce Wasserman's brother, even Beth. Do they wish they'd read a manual about how to navigate the differences between people?

I pull the book from the plastic bag, take a last look at the graceful design of the double helix, the intertwining strands, then slide the book back into the bag. I pull out the inscription page, rip it into tiny pieces, like confetti, and stuff these into the bag, too.

Then I fling the bag over the guardrail. Thomas's sins are not mine, but I'm casting away my sins, too: fury, envy, disappointment, regret, blame, need, sorrow. The bag lands with a splash, sinks into the muddy gray water, and disappears, like a sack of rubbish. That's what waits for all of us, Allyce Wasserman said. And though I am not religious, I mouth a silent prayer: Help me. Help me be tough. Help me help myself. Something flutters inside me, almost like tenderness, almost like hope.

The Feather Pillow

THE LONG HALLWAY at the Fairview Retirement Home seemed dark today. Greta walked quickly, holding a bouquet of roses. Light from the patients' rooms usually brightened the passageway, but now most doors were closed. It was just as well. Greta didn't like to look behind doors anyway.

At the nurses' station, Mrs. Johnson stopped working at the computer, walked to Greta, and began to talk to her. Greta glanced into the woman's flat brown eyes, but listened only vaguely. She thought about the roses. Her mother loved roses. Her mother loved the name Greta, too, like Greta Garbo. When Greta had been a child, her mother kept flowers in every room of the house. She would open all the curtains, sunlight and roses spilling through the house.

"Your mother has started speaking German," Mrs. Johnson was saying. "Of course, we can't understand her, but it's the way your mother talks. Her manner is so intolerably derogatory."

Greta took a deep breath and focused on the woman's words. "It must have been Yiddish. She always spoke Yiddish with my father."

"I wouldn't know." Mrs. Johnson shrugged with impatience. "She's becoming hostile. This morning she spit at an aide. We have lots of patients here, Mrs. Williams. We can't give preferential attention to any patient."

"But that's not like her. Not anymore." Greta shook her head. "Something must be bothering her."

"One more thing. She always complains about the food, but she eats. The past few days she's hardly eating." The nurse spoke gently now, and rested a hand on Greta's shoulder. "Try to talk to her."

"She's so thin already. You've got to call me as soon as these things happen."

Grasping the roses firmly, Greta turned away and continued toward her mother's room. The corridor felt warm; the air smelled stale. Greta's thick dark hair pressed uncomfortably against her neck. She unbuttoned her coat, glancing at the polished green linoleum floor, the freshly painted yellow walls. She hated this hallway. Hated everything about the Fairview Retirement Home. Even the other patients. It almost hurt to be near them, as if they were contagious.

In calmer moments, away from here, Greta knew this retirement home was better than most in Chicago. She had looked at many a year ago. Her mother was seventy-three then, but still, it had been a terrible decision to make. Greta taught middle school English and taught in the after-school program and couldn't give her mother the attention she needed. There wasn't room in the house for her mother either. Fairview was clean and its staff was competent, though they didn't care for her mother as Greta wanted them to, as a daughter would or a friend.

At the end of the corridor, the door to room 454 stood ajar. The room was like all the others here, painted white with two neatly made beds, two dressers, and an armchair, except that her mother, Charlotte Nussbaum, sat near the window watching the traffic outside.

As Greta looked in, she noticed that her mother's cheeks seemed hollow, as if someone had scooped out part of her mother's face. Charlotte's angular nose seemed more prominent, too, and a blue cotton dress hung shapelessly on her. Perhaps her mother's body was disappearing, Greta thought, like her mind.

"Greta, sweetheart." Charlotte glanced up, beckoning to Greta. "I've been waiting for you. So long this time since you were here."

"Hello, Mama." Greta bent to kiss her mother's cheek and touched her wiry gray hair. "You remember. I saw you the day before yesterday. That was Tuesday. Today is Thursday. It's not so long." She placed the bouquet in her mother's lap and closed Charlotte's hands around it. "I brought this for you."

"How nice, very nice, Gretie. They probably don't have a vase here; they have no taste. There's a jar in the bathroom. Go take a look."

Greta found a yellow plastic pitcher and filled it with water. She brought it to the night table. "I thought we could go to lunch today, Mother. We'll have a nice visit." She began arranging the roses. "There are things I need to talk with you about, too. It's important." Greta paused. This morning, she had found old letters of Charlotte's, love letters from Mr. Spearman, a family friend. Greta wanted to ask about the letters, about Charlotte's past, things they had never spoken of, unpleasant and difficult things—to talk honestly before it was too late. Greta wasn't eager to begin. "But first, Mrs. Johnson stopped me, and she—"

"Mrs. Johnson." Charlotte waved a hand in the air as if trying to swat an insect. "What does she know? Not an ounce of good in her heart. An idiot."

"I don't like her much either, but she told me you haven't been eating. You've got to eat. You're too thin. You know that. She was annoyed, too. She says you weren't nice, that you cursed; you were speaking German. Were you speaking German? Yiddish? When you talk in another language, she can't understand you. She doesn't know if you understand her. She can't do anything for you then. It upsets her."

"Those nurses always lie." Charlotte pursed her lips. "They don't care about me. They're always trying to touch me and undress me. I've told them to stop. To put up with this now, it's worse than the war."

"Please, Mother, I don't know why they'd lie to you. It's their job to help. You don't have to like them, but don't be so belligerent."

Charlotte turned her head toward the window.

"Just be nice," Greta said. She went to the closet and removed her mother's red wool coat. "If you don't want help, tell them, but don't be difficult and…they won't let you stay."

"Do I want to stay? Come, Greta, you should know better. I'd rather be with you or in my own house." She stood and reached for Greta's arm to steady herself. "Let's not argue, sweetheart. You always like to argue."

Greta sighed. "How about lunch? We'll go to Myer's, the restaurant you've always liked. We haven't gone on an outing in so long. It's been so cold."

"In the winter in Chicago, it's always cold."

Greta nodded, and helped her mother into the coat, fastening the brass buttons and turning up the collar, then wrapping a black silk scarf with a design of roses around Charlotte's head.

It was a sunny March day. The sky was a fine, clear blue. Charlotte breathed deeply, one hand in her pocket, the other holding Greta's arm. "It's good to feel this air," Charlotte said. "You forget, being locked up all the time."

Greta moved closer to her mother. "You're not locked up. That was before, before I was born. Now you can come and go with me whenever we want. You know that."

But during the first days at the Fairview Home, Charlotte hadn't understood. She had spoken German then, too, crying incoherently. There was nothing Greta could do to help and it had made her shudder to see the underside of her mother's past.

Myer's delicatessen wasn't far, but the drive seemed uncomfortably long. Charlotte didn't speak, and Greta didn't have the energy to begin. Greta had taken the day off from work, which she felt bad about because she wasn't sick. She'd spent the morning packing her mother's papers. Renters had moved from Charlotte's house, and there was an interested buyer. Greta would have preferred to use this time to relax in a deep, hot bath.

She had promised to visit her mother, though. It was easier to see Charlotte when Greta's husband, James, and the children came with her. But their twin daughters were in high school, busy with friends, sports, and theater, and James worked long hours at the advertising agency and rarely had the time. So Greta usually visited her mother alone.

As Greta drove now, she thought about outings she had taken with her mother years ago. Greta was an only child, and just the two of them would go. They visited relatives or family friends, and once had driven west just to see the mountains and desert. Her mother used to tell stories or they would sing together. Charlotte had recorded a song once, "South of the Border," a small 45 rpm disk she kept in her bedroom. During car trips she sang that melody, sometimes making up new words as they went along:

> South of the border
> Down Mexico way
> We'll find a new love
> We'll all slip away

Greta's father never joined them; he didn't like to travel. Greta always imagined her mother preferred to go without him. She was certain after their trip to Florida.

The truck in front of Greta's car rounded a corner, and she accelerated, thinking about the spring they had driven from Chicago to Miami to see relatives. She couldn't remember much about the stay, except for the stop in Atlanta. They had visited Mr. Spearman, a widowed family friend. His children were grown and he lived alone.

There was something formal about him, though he was cordial and handsome, with wavy silver hair and the brown tweed jacket he wore even at home. Greta's mother had known him in Europe before the war. He also spoke with traces of a German accent.

Greta and Charlotte had been given a second-floor bedroom to share. That night Greta went to sleep early. She was tired from the drive. She must have been thirteen or fourteen.

When she awakened, the room was dark. The clock on the dresser read four thirty. As she shifted to a more comfortable position, she glanced at her mother's bed. Charlotte wasn't there. The bed was empty, the flowered quilt lying neatly on top.

For a moment Greta wasn't able to breathe. Then she forced herself to, hurrying through the hallway and downstairs, looking for her mother. She stopped at a closed door near the staircase, listening. She waited there for a long time. Everywhere, the house was still.

Greta followed an entrance onto the Outer Drive now. The road was wide and curved along Lake Michigan. Charlotte was smiling and staring out the window at white sailboats bobbing in the water.

Greta remembered her mother and Mr. Spearman smiling at breakfast long ago, how he had placed his hand on Charlotte's arm. She remembered other visits Charlotte made to Atlanta alone. Greta sighed deeply now. Despite the time that had passed since then, she had never forgiven her mother.

Yet she knew what Charlotte had done wasn't as shocking as it once seemed. Her parents had never been happy together.

They both had grown up in Germany and survived concentration camps. Greta's father owned a small hardware store in Chicago. He was quiet and brooding, liked to read books in his armchair. Charlotte always said he had forgotten how to smile.

She refused to help in the store, instead finding jobs as a secretary or travel agent. She dyed her hair blonde, then red, then blonde again, and went to the symphony and traveled alone. When Greta was old enough, Charlotte took her along.

Her mother had always seemed so massive then. Greta remembered standing in the tiny bathroom of her parents' apartment, washing her face as Charlotte undressed or used the toilet. She remembered her mother's large pale breasts and big belly resting near wide hips, the skin like balls of smooth round dough, as if her mother had been shaped by a baker. There wasn't enough space for Greta then; Charlotte's body seemed to expand to fill the air.

Inside the delicatessen, a group of businessmen mingled near the long glass takeout counter, waiting to be seated. The restaurant was bright and noisy. Most of the square wooden tables and blue vinyl booths were filled. Greta would have preferred a quieter place. But her mother had always liked to meet friends here.

A few couples were leaving, and a waitress escorted Greta and Charlotte to a booth at the back. Greta could see the kitchen doors swing open as waitresses rushed by, balancing plates of thick sandwiches and soups.

She helped her mother take off her coat. Charlotte loosely draped her scarf around her shoulders, then slid into the booth. "So much noise, sweetheart." Charlotte pointed around the room. "Like a carnival. It never used to be like this."

"Just relax, Mama." Greta sat across from her. "You used to love it here. You'll see. We'll talk. You can look around. It's a nice change of pace."

Charlotte rubbed her palms across the white paper placemat, as if clearing away crumbs, then pushed her menu toward Greta. "You choose for me, Gretie. You know what I like."

Greta ordered soup and omelets for them both.

"I was so happy to see the lake today," Charlotte said after the waitress had gone. She smiled, resting her hands on top of Greta's.

"I haven't seen it for so long. All my life if someone asked me what I loved, I've always said my Greta and the lake."

Greta glanced at her mother's hands. The fingers were knobby and bent, skin chapped, nails shapeless and uncared for.

Her own hands were so much like her mother's used to be. Greta tried to imagine how it would feel to have hands like her mother had now. Would she grieve or would she even know the difference?

But the hands didn't really matter. What the nurse said didn't matter. Her mother was doing fine, Greta told herself. Today they would talk like they used to, perhaps more honestly than they ever had before.

Charlotte stared at a boy who sat at a nearby table. Greta sipped her water and sighed. She and her mother had always been close, like two fingers, Charlotte used to say. Even after Greta married, they spoke often, about almost everything, except Mr. Spearman and life during the war.

Charlotte had always loved to give Greta advice. "You've got to do for yourself," she would say. "In the end, no one else will help you." Greta ought to choose a sensible career, think twice about marrying James.

There had been times Greta had longed to be free from her mother. After college, she had taught school for a year, though she'd planned to give up teaching, move from Chicago to Boston, and study art. But when her father died suddenly, she didn't leave. There were no other relatives. Charlotte needed her more than ever.

The waitress brought two bowls of soup and a basket of breads. Charlotte twirled her spoon in her bowl, pushing barley from side to side.

What if she doesn't eat? Greta thought. We'll have to see the doctor again. He might put her in the hospital. She's so stubborn, always. "Just try the soup, Mother," Greta said. "Here, let me help." She held Charlotte's hand around the spoon's handle. Then Charlotte began to use the spoon. Soup spilled on her dress, but she managed another taste and another.

If only we could talk, Greta thought, really talk. It was odd what she and her mother never discussed. Greta didn't know the names of the concentration camps her parents had been in. Her mother never mentioned Mr. Spearman. In their house, it was as if nothing had happened, as if Greta's parents didn't have a past.

When Greta was a child, she had asked her parents about the war. Once she brought a notebook to write things down. Her father hit his fist on the table and yelled that she would do better to pay attention in school. He stormed from the room. Charlotte said to leave him be. Then she had kissed the top of Greta's head. "When you're young," Charlotte whispered, "you can bear anything."

Still, there were numbers on her parents' arms, always the numbers, small uneven blue numerals. Greta used to pretend they were odd patterns of veins or a new fashion that could be washed off if one used soap and really scrubbed. Sometimes she wished her mother would wear long white gloves. After a while, when she was a teenager, she stopped noticing.

It hadn't been hard to stop wondering about the numbers; Greta had been frightened of what she would hear. Those were things you never talked about, she decided. Those things, you kept to yourself.

But since Charlotte's illness, Greta had become curious, about Mr. Spearman, too. She discovered a great longing to know. Her mother was the only one left to ask. Greta wanted to understand how her life and her mother's intersected, how they were bound. She wanted a legacy, a kind of communion.

She had even discussed this with James, though he had advised her to leave well enough alone, and for years she had. Then this morning, while sorting through Charlotte's papers, Greta had found a thick manila envelope filled with letters from Mr. Spearman.

When she saw them, her heart froze. Mr. Spearman wrote of his children and garden. He spoke of Charlotte's eyes. Once, he asked her to come away with him.

The waitress cleared the soup bowls and brought omelets on steaming plates. Greta leaned across the table, wiping barley from her mother's lip. "You're doing nicely, Mother. You've got to eat like this every day."

Charlotte bit into a crust of bread. "The food is better than I remembered. But what a beauty you are, Gretie, even at your age. But you're tired, sweetheart, always tired. James should take better care of you."

Greta closed her eyes. She could almost see her mother forty years ago. She imagined her in the bright green dress Charlotte had worn in Atlanta. "Mother, I'm fine. Everything is fine." She looked at her mother and took a deep breath. "But we need to talk about something. I need to know."

Charlotte gazed at her expectantly.

"Do you remember the trips we used to take?"

"Oh, how we would drive and drive, Gretie."

"Yes." Greta forced herself to go on. "Do you remember Mr. Spearman, your friend?"

Charlotte stared at the table, moving her head from side to side as if smoothing a crook in her neck. "He was a nice man, Greta. Wasn't he a nice man?"

"Did you know him during the war, Mama? Tell me about him."

"Does he have a nice house?" Charlotte stroked her scarf against her cheek, as if soothing herself with a child's blanket. "Is it a rich house?"

"You know I don't know that."

"Does he still have his children?"

"Mother, how could I know?" Greta stopped. She could help her mother. She could tell Charlotte about the house they had stayed in, the big white house surrounded by bougainvillea. She could tell her about the letters.

Charlotte was pulling at the coarse white hairs on her chin and staring vacantly at Greta.

"Let's forget him then." Greta spoke softly. She didn't want her mother to become agitated. "We'll just forget. Let's talk about before you came here, to Chicago. I need to understand."

"Does he sing like he used to?"

"Mama, listen to me. It's important."

Charlotte squeezed Greta's hand. "Does he still sit in the garden?"

"Mama, please. I don't know. I don't know anything about him now."

"My arm hurts, Gretie, my leg. They don't do anything for me at that home; they let me rot. I tell them, and they let me rot."

The star-shaped light fixtures in the restaurant suddenly seemed garish to Greta, seemed to glare in her eyes. She wanted to shake her mother, until the pieces of Charlotte's brain spun madly around and resettled into their rightful places.

Instead, Greta tightly held her mother's hand. "Look at me. You're fine. You've got to know that."

Then Greta remembered the one piece of her mother's past that she knew, the only story her mother had ever told her. It floated through Greta's mind.

Charlotte had been in a German jail. She'd never explained why she was there or what happened afterward. All Greta knew is that her mother had demanded a pillow from a guard. "I want a pillow, a feather pillow," Charlotte supposedly said. "Look me in the eyes; I'm a human being, like you." The guard had said nothing, but surprisingly complied.

Greta had never believed the story. No one would have had the nerve to ask. Yet she wanted to believe it. She had even imagined the pillow, with layers of lace and satin, intricate pink embroidery.

Charlotte was looking around the room now. Then she pressed her fingers against her cheeks. "Good God, over there, Greta; it's Mrs. Schnable. She can't see me like this. I can't be seen."

Greta recognized a heavyset blonde woman walking toward the door.

"She can't…I can't stay," Charlotte said loudly.

The boy at the nearby table peered at them, his gaze fixed on Charlotte.

"Calm down," Greta whispered. "She's an old friend." Greta stroked her mother's arm. "Look, she's leaving. It's not important."

"Please." Charlotte covered her face with her hands and began to cry.

"Mama, it's okay. She's left. We should leave, too." Greta quickly signaled the waitress for the check, helped her mother into her coat, and left money on the table.

In the car, Charlotte continued to sob.

"She's gone, Mother. There's nothing to worry about."

Charlotte stared out the window like an angry child.

"What is it? This is supposed to be a nice time for us together."

"We shouldn't have come. You should have known."

"Stop whimpering," Greta shouted. "Just tell me what you want. I'll find a new doctor, look for a new home. I'll visit more. Just talk to me. I know you're there. You don't have to starve or sulk or act crazy to let me know something is the matter."

"Don't yell, Greta. Stop yelling. Just take me home." Charlotte wiped her nose on her scarf and sleeve. "I want to be like I was, to get my own mail, to go to the symphony. Please. Take me home. At home, I'll be fine."

A tray filled with green and yellow circular glass beads and a wire bent into the shape of a flower was sitting on Charlotte's night table. Mrs. Johnson must have put the craft project here, Greta thought. The bouquet of roses Greta had brought for her mother stood in a pitcher on the dresser now. Charlotte was talking about the lake again.

Greta felt bad about yelling. "It was a nice visit," she said. She forced herself to smile, then helped settle her mother into the chair and set the tray of beads on Charlotte's lap. "I'll be back in two days. Saturday."

Charlotte scooped up a handful of beads and dropped them on the floor. "I'll die here, Greta."

"Don't." Greta collected the beads and strung some onto the wire flower. "You'll do fine." She looked at her watch. "I have to meet James. Just eat. Everything will seem better if you eat."

She kissed the top of Charlotte's head and inhaled the sweet scent of her hair. "Saturday," Greta said, placing Charlotte's hands on the tray. Then without looking back, Greta hurried from the room.

In the car, she checked her watch again. She was late. But instead of driving off, she let her head fall into her arms on the steering wheel.

She would visit her mother in two days and another two days, and another. Maybe James would come with her, and the girls, too, when they had time. Maybe not. It didn't matter. Greta would visit until the end.

She wrapped her arms around her chest now, hugging herself, and glanced into the car mirror. Her eyes were dark and wide like her mother's.

Greta shut her eyes. She longed to disappear or drive for days like she used to with her mother, like they'd done the time they went to see the mountains and desert. They talked for hours then. When Greta felt tired, she rolled her jacket into a ball and pretended it was a soft feather pillow. Charlotte sang to her and whispered that Greta should sleep. "Like an angel, Gretie. Sleep. Troubles go away. They always do." Greta slept then, imagining she and her mother would go on like that forever.

Sleuth

SHE HAD GIVEN HERSELF TO HIM in a way she had never done with anyone before. Completely. A kind of surrender. He didn't know it. He would never know, and it didn't matter. This was a gift Helen gave to him and herself. A gift that went nowhere, she sometimes thought. What use were such gifts?

He was married, and Helen used to be married. There had been a kind of parity in their relationship then. Neither of them had wanted to leave their marriages, but even so, they wanted to be with each other. Helen had thought that perhaps her relationship with Edward had even sustained her marriage. But the marriage had ended three years ago. It had been a difficult divorce. Now she was on her own.

She lived in New York, and Edward lived in Ohio. She taught American history at a college, and he taught at a law school and ran the immigration legal clinic there. They were in their sixties, and saw each other when they could. It still felt startling to her that she was divorced at this juncture in life. She'd imagined that with their children grown, she and Philip would feel liberated and would travel and enjoy one another. But instead she felt adrift, constructing a new life, facing the visceral realization that there was more time behind her than ahead.

Helen was tall and slender with wavy brown hair. She walked and jogged to keep in shape. She missed the steady companionship of marriage. She had told her childhood friend Erin this. Erin lived in Boston, and they kept in touch by phone. She encouraged Helen to go on a dating site. Erin didn't know about Edward. Helen hadn't told anyone about him. Some of her friends weren't happy in their marriages, as if marriage sometimes became a truce between two hostile countries, a truce you lived with because of the honor involved in fulfilling a commitment or the fears and complications of unraveling a shared life.

164

Helen had considered looking at the dating sites herself, not to replace Edward; that wouldn't be possible—they had such a long history together, and, in truth, she was in love with him—but to find a companion here, in New York, a connection. She had finally signed up on Match.com six months ago, really dabbling in it, and gone on dates, with a veterinarian, a medical researcher, a teacher, a business professor. She thought of them in this way—an aggregate of attributes, because she hadn't met anyone she was really drawn to. She felt like a sleuth as she perused online photos and profiles, went from man to man, looking for someone who seemed appealing, trying to extrapolate the hidden meaning in the words each man had posted about himself online. Who was this man? What could he give her? What could she give him? Was there a chance they might like each other, even fall in love?

There was something dispiriting about looking at the photographs, and also something hopeful, seductive, as she studied the faces of these men. Some were smiling, some serious, total strangers to her, as if choosing a date was like choosing a shiny product on Amazon. Some men looked ragged and worn. Sometimes photos were snapped from odd angles—you knew these were selfies—while others had been taken years ago and posted on the site with the misleading caption: *I look about the same way now.*

Helen had always been able to set her mind to a task and complete it. She decided to approach dating in this way. She was systematic, methodical. She posted a short profile of her own, saying she taught history and was a mother. *I love adventure, the outdoors, music, art, travel, movies, books.* She was upbeat in the profile, and sounded breezier and more daring than she actually was. She found two recent photos of herself that softened her wrinkles, and posted the photos, too.

Suddenly, there were possibilities. Men contacted her from New York and even from Minnesota, New Mexico, and Boston. They had screen names like Infinity, The Real Deal. The Cool One. Ageless. Some were in their sixties or seventies. One man was forty-two; another was eighty-three.

She discovered considerations she hadn't anticipated. Was she willing to travel for a relationship? No. Did she want to meet a man who'd never been married? Someone who didn't seem to read? Who'd had some college? Most weren't worth meeting. Their profiles or photos didn't appeal to her. Some sparked her interest.

Each time she went on a date, she tried to gather clues, data about the man's essence, just as he was gathering information about her. But Edward was still always in the back of Helen's mind. Was he getting in the way? She didn't know.

Her date, Keith, was sitting at the dining room table in her apartment. It was a Saturday in early June. This was their second meeting, and she had invited him over for a glass of wine before they went to dinner at a nearby restaurant, but she realized now that inviting him here had been a mistake and would give him the impression that she was ready to sleep with him. She was still learning how to navigate the dating world.

He had thinning gray hair, a gray beard, was a little bulky, and wore a neat navy blazer, white shirt, and khaki pants. He owned an art gallery. He was in his late sixties. He was telling her about the art business when her cell phone rang. She went to the kitchen counter and glanced at her phone. Edward's number flashed on the screen.

"I have to take this call," she said. "I'm sorry. I'll be right back."

"No problem," Keith mumbled, and pulled his cell phone from his pocket.

She hurried to the bathroom, shut the door. A few weeks ago, she and Edward had had an argument. They'd resolved it, but she wanted to avoid any misunderstandings. She'd tell him she'd call him back.

"Edward," she said. She pressed the cell phone against her ear.

"Anna found your name on my calendar, that I'd planned to see you last month. I'd written the conference dates, the extra days I was staying, your name, the hotel. She said: 'Why were you there so long after the conference ended? Did you meet Helen? Are you involved with her? Sleeping with her?'"

"Oh, God, no. What did you say?"

"I told her no."

"That's terrible," Helen whispered. She and Anna had been friendly years ago.

"Yes. Then we could never see each other. Or talk to each other."

"Oh." Her heart sank.

"I told her your brother lived there. You were visiting him. I stayed to meet with colleagues. Write to her and tell her you're sorry about her son, that he broke his leg. Say I'd mentioned it. Will you do that? Do it now."

"I will." Helen opened the bathroom door. "I'll be right there, Keith." She hurried to the computer and wrote the message.

This was bound to happen, sooner or later, she thought. People were ambivalent. Sometimes they wanted to be discovered. No, maybe Edward had just been careless. She took a deep breath, shaken, and went back to the dining room, relieved she would be distracted for a moment from what Edward had told her.

"So," Keith said. "Anything important?"

"One of my kids." She took a gulp of wine. "I had to do something on the computer for her."

"It gave me a chance to answer an email from work. You know, we didn't talk about this the last time." He eyed her intently. "I'd like to be with someone four or five nights a week. How was your sex life with your husband?"

She stared at him, taken aback. "Fine," she said curtly. "How was your sex life in your marriages?"

"Not so good with the first. Very good with the second. I'm blunt; I know."

"You are."

"I like to be direct. I've had a prostatectomy. But I can do other things." He spoke as if negotiating a business deal.

She took a sip of wine, considering his words.

"I don't know that I'd ever marry again," he said.

"You'd have to be divorced to get married," she said. His profile had read: *Currently separated.*

"I've never put your name on my calendar," Edward said the next night. He and Helen were talking on the phone. "I did this time. It was a mistake, a stupid accident. I wasn't thinking. She was looking at my calendar for a phone number from the bank I'd written there."

"Are you worried?" Helen asked.

"No."

"I am."

"Don't be. If…I think a marriage can survive an affair," he said, his voice trailing off as if he were talking to himself.

But can an affair survive a marriage? she thought.

"I know you're worried," he went on. "Put it out of your mind." He paused and then said quietly, his voice unsteady. "You can stop this anytime you want. Though it would be painful for me. I don't want to lose you."

That night, Helen lay awake. She thought about Edward with longing. She felt lonesome for him. She didn't allow herself to think about his wife often. She had met Anna almost thirty years ago, and they had begun a kind of friendship when their children were young. Or maybe she had met the woman through Edward. Helen didn't recall.

They lived in Evanston at the time. Anna's children were in the same gymnastics class as Helen's children. Helen saw her in passing. Anna was married to her first husband. Edward had a first wife then and their children were in another gymnastics class. Helen and her husband had socialized with Edward and his first wife once or twice when parents gathered at the gymnastics school to retrieve their kids. Edward was finishing his PhD in American history at Northwestern, and Helen was working on her PhD in history, too. They'd been in a class together. He was tall with dark hair, intense brown eyes, and an angular face. He was quick to smile, quick to become angry. He was older than she was, by four years, but it felt as if they were contemporaries.

They hadn't become involved with each other then. She had been happily married, or thought she was, and assumed he was, too. They discussed history, the Civil War, the ancient world, Epictetus, and the university bureaucracy. They went jogging together along the lake some afternoons when classes ended for the day. Edward was from Michigan and Helen from Chicago. His family had vacationed in a small town near Lake Michigan, Union Pier, where Helen's family had spent time when she was young. Sometimes when they talked, it felt as if they would never stop.

She remembered when he and his first wife had separated. He didn't mention it other than to say, "It's a difficult time for me now. Personally, that is." Then he'd asked to meet Helen for coffee, which wasn't unusual. But this time, he had said, his voice steady, "I wanted you to know I've been seeing Anna Kramer. I wanted to tell you myself. I didn't want you to hear it from anyone else."

Helen had been surprised he'd told her, but when she thought about it, she understood. Anna Kramer had left her husband. Helen had told Philip, "I wonder if Edward and Anna have been seeing each other for a while."

Philip shrugged and frowned as he often did in what seemed like perpetual disapproval. "Don't know," he said. "We'll probably never know. And it's not our business."

Once, Helen went to dinner with Anna. Helen had arranged this, she supposed, out of kindness to Edward, a friend. She and Anna met at an Italian restaurant on Michigan Avenue. Anna was petite and slim, with blue eyes and bouncy blonde hair. She was smart and talkative, a lawyer and the mother of two sons. Anna talked about Edward, tilting her head to one side. "I can't believe it," she'd said. "I almost fainted one day in the hallway outside of the courtroom. I'm so lightheaded since I began seeing him. I'm like a woman who loves too much."

Helen had nodded, thinking this was an odd comment—she didn't know Anna well enough to be her confidante. Or maybe the comment reflected a dependency, a neediness, or really, Helen decided, it was a feeling to be envied. What did it mean to love too much? She had realized she didn't know.

Since then, Anna had been absent from Helen's life. Or on the periphery. Helen had finished her PhD, and she, Philip, and their two children moved to New York. Philip was in finance and had been hired by a large insurance company. Edward had gone on to law school after the PhD. He'd combined the two fields, but, in the end, law was more practical, he said.

It wasn't simple to navigate a long-distance love affair. Helen was surprised to find herself in one, as if she had wandered into it, taken a detour that led in the wrong direction. She was usually adept at controlling her emotions. There was no duress involved or pressure. Edward had married Anna; they didn't have children together but shared a blended family. Helen had lost touch with Anna, and in truth, the woman had become an uncomfortable, troubling fact for Helen.

She had become involved with Edward during her first separation from Philip fifteen years ago. She loved Philip, but he'd become cranky and critical. She never knew if, when he came home from work, he would smile or yell. He finally told her he was in love with someone else. She was shocked. They had separated, gone to counseling, and eventually reconciled.

Edward came to New York for a conference during the time Helen was separated. She was shattered by the split from Philip, a little desperate and ashamed even, of the depth of her disappointment, anger, and sorrow. She went to lunch with Edward and told him, "I'm a mess."

"You don't look it," he'd said. "Messy inside?"

"Yes."

They had gone for a walk in Central Park, and it was a comfort to be with him, a good friend. She had been faithful to Philip, but she said impulsively, "We could meet a few times a year. Wouldn't it be nice if you and I were…involved?" She knew Edward was attracted to her; she thought you could tell those things. At least, she imagined he was—the way he listened with interest, it seemed, and peered into her eyes. She was attracted to him.

"It would be romantic to think that could be so," he said. They walked in silence, and then he'd kissed her.

What had begun with Edward as a need, a distraction, had grown into something more.

It would be easy to piece things together, Helen knew. You didn't have to be a sleuth. If you looked at what happened around you, you would see the clues. She had once called him back in a fit of anxiety— she always reacted to Edward's anger—and he'd answered and was curt. Later, he'd telephoned and said, "I was in the car. With Anna."

Helen was embarrassed she had called, to be in this situation. Maybe if she were tougher she might not feel the guilt she did, the moral confusion, or maybe if she were more practical. Yet she knew the heartbreak of betrayal. Of deceit. She did not want to do anything to jeopardize the relationship with Edward, though she understood, in the end, if he had to choose, she was dispensable.

And she'd sent gifts and cards; once after he'd broken his wrist, she'd sent a card with hearts, flowers, and a sentimental Hallmark message. She was trying to make up for the times she had disappointed him, or couldn't call, just to talk or say, "I love you." To be connected. That was not possible. He said to her once, "There's a saying my grandfather told me: the glass can be half empty or half full. Can't you look at this, us, as half full? Can't you be happy with what is, instead of thinking about what isn't?"

It was very full when they were together. "I am happy," Helen said, and she was. She loved being with him. She didn't admit it to herself often, but at one time she'd hoped they might travel or live together.

The clues were everywhere for Anna to find. Once, years ago, they had all been at the wedding of a mutual friend in Chicago. Philip wasn't able to go; the marriage was rocky then. Helen was uneasy about seeing Edward's wife. Anna had walked into the hotel lobby. Her blonde hair was cut in short waves and pressed against her head. She wore a light blue dress and dark sheer hose. There was something off-kilter about her, Helen thought, unfinished. Helen stood straighter and tried to banish the tension she felt, though she wished she were anywhere else and not in the hotel lobby, facing Anna.

At the dinner, Edward had sat between his wife and Helen. He said something to Helen. She replied, and Anna said to her, "You and Edward have a strange, but wonderful relationship." The woman had noticed something about Helen and Edward, as if Anna had stumbled on data, evidence, was collecting clues, perhaps unconsciously, Helen thought. If Anna considered carefully the interactions she'd witnessed, the relationship between Helen and Edward would become clear.

Anna had later said disparagingly, during dessert, "Edward is always working, on a case, a legal brief, a paper, or a committee."

"But he's productive," Helen said. "He's helping people."

"Yes, no question, but my father spent time with the family. That's the model I'm used to. I put limits on my work." She had sighed, and she'd probably had too much to drink. She looked at Edward. "If I'd known the problems you and I would have with our kids, I don't know if I would have gotten divorced from my ex."

Helen had wanted to be a musician when she was young, but scholarship and history had taken precedence. She still played the piano. Since the conversation with Edward about his wife, Helen played the Beethoven sonata she was working on with vehement concentration, as if this could ease her misgivings about what he had told her.

It was the middle of June, and she was on vacation from school. Mornings she walked or jogged in the park. She liked to go when the sun was shining but before the heat of the day, walk away from the congestion of the streets, into the cool green shade of Central Park or Riverside Park, away from the jumble of humanity that hurried along the sidewalks.

She planned to teach a segment on reparations in the fall and was preparing that. Reparations given to Japanese Americans who had been interned during World War II, and the possibility of reparations for people whose ancestors had been slaves before the Civil War. She liked to discuss ethical and moral values in class. The subject had always interested her: What does a nation owe to people it has wronged? What does a person owe to someone he or she has wronged? Can reparations ever really correct an injustice? What does it mean to live an ethical life?

She had heard from Keith, her date. He was going out of town but wanted to get together with her again when he was back.

She had done what Edward asked, writing to Anna, and this, for the moment, allayed Helen's fears. The next week, she sat at the computer to check the dating site, but first looked at her emails. There were messages from the bank, Bloomingdale's, from her kids and friends, one from Erin, and three from Match.com: *Smile! James just liked you! Send him a message!* and *Romantic Singer likes you! Send him a note!* and *You have 24 new matches!* Her emails were like a traffic jam.

A new message popped up. Anna's name was in the address. Helen's heart sank. She opened the message.

Dear Helen,

Thank you for your kind note about my son. He's had so many issues, and now a broken leg. Sometimes I am beside myself about how he is living his life, not married, not attached as I would like him to be. Your words meant a lot.

Love, Anna

Helen took a deep breath. The last thing she wanted was an email exchange. She felt weak. Maybe this was a test. If she passed the test, she didn't have to worry anymore.

She replied, writing that she hoped the injury would heal quickly.

She didn't receive more emails from Anna, and she was relieved. One night, though, a few weeks later, Helen was listening to the voicemail messages on her landline. She immediately recognized Anna's voice. "Hi, Helen. It's Anna. I thought I'd try to catch you via phone. I know how busy everyone is. My other son, Zachary, is going to New York in the fall for an internship. Would you know of a room or apartment-sharing arrangement? And do you have thoughts about a surgeon, in Chicago? I know your brother is a doctor there. If you have suggestions, please call or just shoot me a quick email or text. I'd appreciate it so much."

Now, in the last weeks, she'd had a few exchanges with Anna. Helen didn't think she was central to Anna's thoughts, but she didn't want to have more interactions with the woman. She would quickly collect information and send it in an email. She didn't know how Anna had gotten the phone number, and it didn't matter. She didn't tell Edward. What could she say?

Today, she was meeting him, against her better judgment. It was July. Her better judgment told her to go online and meet one man after another until she found someone with whom she felt compatible. It didn't have to be love.

She never listened to her better judgment. She said to herself, "One more time. I'll see Edward one more time." But it never was the last time, no matter how many months elapsed between meetings.

She often went to meet him in Chicago if he was there for work. This time, he was in New York for four days, at a conference again.

Edward's thick dark hair was gray now. He was still handsome, solid and fit. He swam, worked out, and used to do triathlons. These were just an aggregate of attributes. What she loved about him was the way they talked. How they listened to each other. The way they made love. Without artifice. Without introduction or inhibition, as if they were resuming the last conversation they'd had, the last encounter.

"You must have a lot going on," he said. He looked at her with tenderness. They were in bed in his hotel room.

"I do."

"I can usually tell what you're thinking," he said.

She nodded.

They were careful with the data they shared. Helen didn't have to be a sleuth to know something might be missing from his marriage. Was it sex? A need for variety? Was he a man who couldn't be monogamous? Maybe he and his wife had a contentious relationship. Or perhaps they weren't emotionally connected anymore. Maybe he was drawn to qualities Anna didn't have now. Or maybe nothing was missing from the marriage. If he had been married to Helen, would he have been faithful? She didn't allow herself to think about these questions often. It was part of the bargain she'd made with herself.

"My cousin died," he said when they were lying side by side. His arm was around her, her hand resting on his shoulder. They had made love and now they talked, as they always did.

"I'm sorry," she said.

"I hadn't seen him for a while. I told you about him before. He had been sick for a long time. It's sad for him."

"And it reminds you of your own mortality," she said.

"We're all getting closer to that."

In the hotel room, mortality seemed a distant concept, inconvenient, irrelevant, even obsolete. The hotel room was like their home. There were no children, no marriages, no obligations, no illness, no drama, no loneliness. Just the two of them in a functional space. The surroundings were plain, as if all else receded to make room for what mattered. For passion. For desire. For comfort.

The next day, at home, after Edward had left the city, she made two lists.

Pros: What I love about Edward
1. Almost everything
2. Who he is in the relationship—intimate, direct, perceptive, loving, sexual. A comfort.
3. Who I am in the relationship—the part of me he taps into. I'm most myself when alone or with Edward. I can be myself with him, discover things about myself. Uninhibited, alive, loving, valued, sexual. Complete.

Cons: What I dislike about the relationship
1. Who I am in the relationship—dishonest to friends and family, capable of deception. Living a public life and a secret one. Taking what doesn't belong to me. Does anyone really belong to another person?
2. I have become both betrayer and betrayed.
3. Who he is in the relationship—capable of deception, compartmentalizing two lives, the truncated secret one with me and his real life.
4. Anna

She made a list of the times she'd seen his wife. She didn't remember the conversations, except the words at the wedding dinner for the mutual friend that she, Anna, and Edward had attended in Chicago years ago. Helen compiled these lists to pull the thoughts out of her mind.

In August, she received a package. Inside the box was a beautiful blue silk scarf and a note from Anna thanking Helen for the help with her sons.

Helen dropped her head in her hands. Then she wrote a thank-you note on plain beige stationery. She labored over the wording: *It was wonderfully kind of you to send it.* No. *It was thoughtful of you.* No. Maybe: *It wasn't necessary, but I appreciate it. It's a beautiful scarf. I'm thrilled to have it.* "Thrilled" was overly enthusiastic. This felt beyond what she could do. She used another sheet of stationery and went back to the original wording: thoughtful, kind. And it was.

She put the scarf back in the box and set it on a shelf. She addressed the envelope, attached a stamp, and mailed the note.

She felt restless and decided to walk in Riverside Park to try to regain perspective. It was a warm day, but the air by the path along the Hudson River was breezy and cooler. Helen remembered reading a book by William Maxwell last year. He wrote about the strength of erotic attachment. He based the novel on an actual experience, an early friendship and its demise.

When Maxwell and a friend of his were in their twenties, they'd slept in the same bed. Sometimes men did this then, Helen knew, even if they were heterosexual. She'd read a history of the era. Sometimes men used each other sexually, for a release. They still did, she knew. Maxwell and the man had a woman friend; eventually, his friend married her. Maxwell was so upset about the marriage that he slit his wrists. A character in the novel did this, too. It was an extreme reaction, Helen had thought. Later, Maxwell married and had a family. Helen had been struck by how the experience with his friendship affected Maxwell and that he wrote about it decades later. The characters in the novel followed the same trajectory as real life.

Some experiences shape you, Helen thought now, never leave you, live inside you, in your emotions, your imagination. She had never really understood that until she met Edward. The strength of erotic attachment. Emotional attachment. This was what she fought against in herself.

That night, Helen's friend Erin called. Erin asked how the online dating was progressing.

"Slowly," Helen said. "It's an education."

"I think it's a numbers game. You have to meet a lot of men before you find someone you like." Erin told Helen about her sister, also divorced, who had finally met a man online.

"They have so much in common," Erin said. "I feel like I'm in college when I see them."

She listed the different attributes and coincidences: he had gone to the same college as her sister, lived near their brother, and was from a large Catholic family like hers. "I know you'll find someone, too. Someone just for you."

"I hope," Helen said. "Thanks."

Once, after her divorce, Helen had confided to Erin that a married friend wanted to become involved with her. She didn't mention names. She didn't mention she was already involved.

"That's a dead end," Erin had said, practical as always. "Not weird. People do it all the time. I guess you just can't judge these things. You never know what really goes on in someone else's marriage."

Helen sat at the piano and played the Beethoven sonata over and over. It calmed her, even when she made mistakes. She shut her eyes and thought about when she and Edward had parted this last time. She hated for him to leave, but felt almost relieved, too. For the first time, she thought now: maybe he should go back to his life, and I will go back to mine.

They had left his hotel room, had lunch, and then walked together along Central Park.

"I don't want to have a problem," Helen had said. They were talking about Anna. "For us to have a problem."

"What about me?" he said.

"I know. I don't want you to have a problem."

"I don't. And it's not your problem."

"But—"

"Nothing is going to change. I don't want anything to change between us." They walked in silence for a while, then he took her hand and said, "Helen, don't worry. I'm sorry, I have to go. I'll call. I need some time to think."

He kissed her, and she hugged him and said, "Goodbye, Edward." Then he turned away and began to run. He must be late, she thought, or worried. She didn't know which. He had to give a presentation at the conference that afternoon. She watched him bounding away from her, wishing she could go with him, and then, for a moment, she was cheered just by the sight of him. Why on earth had she said goodbye in such a dramatic, final way?

She didn't know. Was she trying to see what it might feel like to say a final goodbye to him? Or confirming aloud what she already knew, what was painful to imagine: the relationship could suddenly end?

Whenever they parted, she worried this might be the last time they would meet.

He looked like a young man as he ran, determined, agile, and love for him swelled in her. She watched until he was almost out of sight. Then she turned and hurried along the park in the opposite direction, away from him. A warm breeze blew. The sun shone, a beacon of light. She retraced her steps home.

By the end of August, there had been no more messages from Anna. But Anna could call or send a message again, Helen thought. She did not go to see Edward when he next had the time. He planned to be in Ann Arbor to consult on a legal case. She had a work commitment she could not change.

This felt like a punishment to her and to him. And perhaps it was a way to do penance, to make temporary reparations to Anna, paltry ones. But there was no way to really make sufficient reparations. It was too late.

Helen played piano and prepared for teaching in the fall. She perused Match.com. She went on a few dates, and to dinner with Keith again, the man who had asked about her sex life, just to be sure she hadn't judged him incorrectly. After the dinner, though, she knew he wasn't for her. She'd googled prostatectomy. This was part of her education, she thought, about dating at this stage of life. She didn't know if he'd had a radical one or standard.

She told Keith she had enjoyed meeting him, but they weren't a match.

"Think about it," he said. "There's plenty of time to reconsider. We'll be in touch."

The next morning, he sent her a text: *We need to have a talk.*

There's nothing to talk about, she texted back.

If you choose not to speak to me, that is a BIG MISTAKE! Make time to see me.

She didn't reply.

U will REGRET this!!! he texted again.

She deleted his number and the messages.

One man had kissed Helen and whispered in her ear, "I have erectile dysfunction. It doesn't have to be anything fancy. If we plan, there's Viagra." Another man had been married three times and told her he used to be monogamous but he probably wasn't anymore. "I take precautions," he said. "There are diseases out there. Every man has a woman on the side."

A third said he'd been divorced for twenty-five years and on the dating site for twelve. He'd fallen in love three times since then. The relationships had been long ones. Two or three years each. That didn't seem long to Helen. "And you?" he asked. "How many times have you been in love?"

She thought for a moment. "Four times," she said. "In high school, college, with my ex-husband, and…" She paused and forced herself not to show any hint of emotion. "Someone else, in between." That was the only way she could describe Edward. But he wasn't "in between."

"Now that sounds interesting." The man took her hand. "I want to be with a sensual lady."

These were the currencies of the dating world, in the online profiles, in what men said: I like to snuggle. I like to hold hands. I like a good long kiss. I can do things. I'm a nice guy. No one said it directly: I like to fuck. I want a sexual partner. I want sex. I want adventure. To live before time runs out. No one said: I want comfort.

Kaleidoscope

WHEN DOREEN AND WILLOW invited Lenore to a surprise birthday party, they wouldn't take no for an answer. "You'll meet new people," Willow said, "expand your horizons." This was exactly the kind of thing Lenny didn't like to do—attend a gathering where she wouldn't know many people. But a man Doreen wanted her to meet would be at the party.

"If I wasn't in a relationship already," Doreen said, "I'd have my eye on him. He's gorgeous."

Lenny worked as a nurse at the Veterans Hospital then, and they were all living in Denver. Doreen was a lab technician at the hospital. She and Willow had steady boyfriends and liked to set Lenny up on dates or give her advice about her wardrobe. Willow had wavy black hair that fell to the middle of her back. She liked to wear tight black low-cut leotard tops and gauzy, full, colorful skirts. Doreen favored flowing dresses with floral prints, and she wound her shiny blonde hair into a single braid. Although Lenny often dressed like Willow or Doreen, she felt happiest in her hose and simple dresses.

She went to the party, and as she would later recall, she fell in love with Adam Thompson immediately. That became her clear, irrefutable memory. The house had been brightly decorated with red and white balloons, and a good-sized crowd filled the rooms, but even so, Adam stood out with his dark curly hair, fine aquiline nose, and radiant smile. When someone asked him to give a birthday speech—the party was in his honor—he had smiled gratefully. "Thirty is a beginning," he'd said. "My fellowship in the laboratory at the university is almost over, and what's next?" Then he added quietly, "I must tell you that I love life. It's that simple. I love you all, and life itself." As she watched from the edge of the group, Lenny had no doubt he was right for her.

Lenny often returned to this moment when she was considering her life, wondering if there had been a grand scheme after all or if the events had been mostly chance—moving to Denver, meeting her two best friends, then Adam.

As planned, Doreen had introduced Adam to Lenny. Later he walked her home. He said he'd noticed her right away. They strolled with a group of his friends first, then took a long, meandering walk by themselves on the dimly lit city streets, their arms at their sides, until gradually they moved closer and Adam rested his hand on hers. He talked about finishing his graduate degree in cell biology and finding a job. Then he asked, "What do you like about your life now?"

Lenny thought about her desire to work with children, to have her own children—she believed this would fulfill her—and her fear that this might never happen. She had always felt a bit plain and awkward with her dull brown hair and thin body, dressed in her nurse's uniform, a little too quiet and tossed about by other people's wishes. But she said, "My life now? I like almost everything about it, I suppose."

"Does that include me?" Adam smiled.

Lenny looked at him, then eyed the sidewalk self-consciously. "I don't really know you."

"You can start now." He pulled her into his arms and kissed her boldly.

In the late 1960s and early 1970s, young people in their twenties like Lenny—people looking for a new beginning, a second chance, a turn of the page—drove west, toward California, in large numbers. They were driving away from social conventions, they believed, to a place where there were no expectations of how to live. They zoomed west on Interstate 80, past flat fields of corn, and some veered south at the exit for Interstate 76, which led to Denver. After a while, the landscape became hilly. In the summer, when Lenny had entered Colorado, the grassy verge along the highway was brimming with sunflowers. The sky seemed wider and bluer than the one she'd left behind in Wisconsin. Then Denver appeared, Oz-like, with the stark grandeur of the mountains that rose beyond the city.

Lenny had come with friends on a lark. She'd finished college a few years before, had quit her temporary job at a rehabilitation hospital, and was living at home with her parents in Milwaukee. One of her friends had known someone in Denver who lived in a big house and was looking for roommates. When the others moved on, continuing their journey to California, Lenny decided to stay. She liked the city and being close to the mountains.

She found a job and her own apartment near Cheesman Park, a grand expanse of green in central Denver. She joined an organization for medical professionals and went on hikes in the mountains with a Sierra Club group. Sometimes she felt desperately lonely. She had left everyone she was close to in Milwaukee. But she became involved in activities she'd never experienced. She enrolled in classes at the Western University for Enhancement of Self-Awareness and took courses like "Law for the Lay Person," "How to Unleash Your Creative Powers," and "The Joy of Kundalini Yoga." The creativity class involved meditation, fasting, and learning to trust yourself. Doreen had been in the group. Lenny had met her in passing at work. Later, Doreen introduced her to Willow.

The three women began to meet at Doreen's small apartment nights after work and weekend afternoons. They sat by the large picture window in the living room, and they painted with watercolors and talked. During the day, sunlight burst into the room. Willow had studied with Elisabeth Kübler-Ross in England and was passionate about the subject of death. Doreen loved to talk about garage sales, bacteria, and men. The snakelike figures she painted on the thick, textured watercolor paper were sure and unwavering; she layered pigment thickly. Willow drew wildly uneven shapes. Lenny experimented with small, precise strokes; she diluted her paints with water.

Doreen explained that at work she peered at tiny particles under a microscope. "Sometimes I spend days searching for what I'm looking for."

Willow laughed and twisted her long black hair into a ponytail. "The answers to the universe aren't floating in the air, waiting for you to find them."

Willow lived with her boyfriend, Teddy, then, a passionate snare drummer from Alaska. One afternoon, she confided that even though he was wonderful, she wasn't interested in a future with him. "I've had affairs. Lots of them," she said. "I'll always have them. I love sex. I want to experience the moment, now. When I marry, I don't want sex to become another wifely duty."

"I'm attracted to noncommittal Romeos, unfortunately," Doreen said. "They're everywhere. But it's hard to be close enough to a man for me to feel I'd want to be with one forever. In the end, you have to rely on yourself." She was considering quitting her job, going to law school. "I don't know if I'll ever settle down."

Lenny had been involved in a few brief relationships before she met Adam. Willow talked brightly about Lenny's flings, but they often seemed to Lenny like sad dead ends.

"There are women who need men," Willow said one evening, "and women who need women, too." They were drinking green tea and wine in Doreen's kitchen. Willow gazed at her two friends, then shook her head. "Not sexually, I mean. Emotionally. I can talk to you both about my period, psychic phenomena, and death. Orgasms. Fucking. I know you'll understand."

"I need both women and men as friends," Lenny said.

"I do, too," Willow replied. "Sometimes when I look at Teddy, I feel weak. Metaphorically speaking. When we met, I said to him, 'It's hard for me to look at you without feeling faint.' I expected him to say something important and memorable. That he was attracted to me like that, wildly in love with me. But he looked at me, kindly really, and said he felt fine. Was I sick?"

An ex-lover of Willow's had created business cards for her, which Willow liked to distribute. One said *Willow: Writer*, with her address and phone number. She handed these out when she was trying to find business in freelance PR. Another had the imprint *Willow Raymond: Book Connoisseur*, which she gave out in connection with her job at a bookstore. A third was printed in deep purple ink with a silhouette of a naked woman: *Willow: Alternative Woman*. She passed these out at parties. Conversation openers, she said.

Sometimes she shared pot with her friends. Not really a drug, she said. "A way to control your destiny. To see life clearly. That's the key. One day it will become legalized. You'll see." She took LSD and mescaline, although neither Lenny nor Doreen did.

One Saturday, Lenny and her two friends sat cross-legged on the floor in her apartment, holding hands. Doreen had dimmed the lights. They vowed they would stay friends forever, no matter what happened or what man they were with or where they each ended up. "We will help each other lead extraordinary lives," they whispered in unison.

Lenny told them her real name that afternoon, saying the nickname "Lenny" had stuck when she was a child, and she was glad; "Lenore" sounded stuffy, old-fashioned. Doreen had stopped using "Dory," her childhood nickname. She wanted something stronger. Willow told them her real name was Susan.

"A name is like anything else. Utterly disposable," she announced the day the three of them went to the courthouse so she could have her name legally changed. "Life is about taking risks. Are you going to dive in or not? If you don't like something, take action and change it. You can't sit on the edge forever."

"I suppose there are people who plunge ahead in life," Lenny said, "and those who watch or float…plod maybe."

"Too pejorative." Willow flung her hands in the air. Her four silver bangle bracelets jangled. "Cautious. I could tell from the moment I met you."

Adam and Lenny began seeing each other after the night of the birthday party. Adam sought her out. They went to movies, on walks, cooked dinners together at his apartment or hers. Even if he hadn't called her, Lenny was certain she would have contacted him.

He said he'd noticed her not just because she was pretty—and she was, he told her, with her soft brown hair and trim body—but because there was something different about her, something solid, grounded. He had seen that right away.

When Lenny was with him, she felt like someone other than herself—not plain or quiet or awkward, but somehow freed. There was the pure pleasure of being together, making love. She and Adam had discovered a new world, she thought, and she had discovered a secret self.

Adam liked to ask her questions. He liked to talk about what was important, which was home and family, values. These were important to Lenny, too, although she had almost forgotten about them since she'd arrived in Denver. How important could these values be to her, she wondered, if she had forgotten them so easily? But they were essential to her, she knew, though she rarely discussed this with Willow and Doreen.

"I want to know everything about you," Adam said, "as if I were you or you me. Do you ever feel that? Wanting to understand exactly how someone else thinks? That close."

"I want to know how you think," she said. She didn't discuss her longing to be more like Doreen and Willow.

Adam told Lenny he'd had relationships in the past but they didn't work out. He had been concentrating on finishing his degree.

He said the timing was perfect for him to fall in love now. He hoped it was for her, too. "We're lucky, you and I. We've found each other. So many other people are still looking, wandering around."

At first, Lenny imagined everyone would get to know one another: Willow, Doreen, their boyfriends, and Adam. They would be close friends, their lives intertwined. But when she made plans with the others, Adam would say, "I don't want to be with other people right now, just with you alone."

Once, she arranged a backpacking trip with Willow and the others to the Never Summer mountain range in the north, near the Wyoming border, a rugged, gorgeous place. Adam cancelled at the last minute.

"But if you want, go on the trip without me," he said. "Whatever suits you."

He had to finish a project for work and wanted to start rebuilding a bicycle. He hoped Lenny would look into a class in ballroom dancing with him.

"I'm not going to force you to do what you don't want," she said. But she wasn't happy to leave him. "I wish you *wanted* to go on the trip."

He said he didn't want to disappoint her, but he had no interest in the trip; it was a matter of temperament. "I should have told you sooner. I wanted to be honest. People are who they are." Lenny decided to stay behind with him, and they went to the dance class.

The studio had a dark oak floor and floor-to-ceiling picture windows. One other couple was dancing. The woman, her hair pulled back in a bun, wore a turquoise shirtwaist dress and black high-heeled shoes; the man wore a white suit. He draped his arms around the woman gracefully. They danced in unison to the music in slow, even steps. Their bodies dipped and swayed; the man spun her around. The teacher, dressed in a black suit and bow tie, watched Adam and Lenny dance. They were more awkward but had great promise, the teacher assured them.

At work, Lenny ate lunch with Doreen. She spoke with Willow on the telephone. The three of them didn't get together as much as they used to.

Doreen was applying to law schools. She was tired of keeping track of particles, she said. She had gone on a macrobiotic diet. Willow had begun consulting with a psychic and drinking diluted hydrogen peroxide flavored with herbs to improve her ozones. Willow and Doreen often visited the psychic together. They gave Lenny a gift of a consultation.

"It's a waste of time," Adam said. "What can a psychic tell you? Everything is luck or chance. They're charlatans. She can't see farther than you or I do."

"You sound as if you're jealous," Lenny said. "Or afraid. This has nothing to do with you."

Lenny went with her friends to the psychic's house the next week. Inside the small wooden bungalow were shelves crammed with books on the occult. Three black cats paced the floor. One curled on Lenny's lap.

She and her friends took turns going into the dim meditation room. The psychic was a heavy elderly woman with short, straight white hair, like straw, and wide, swollen legs. When Lenny was with the woman, she felt afraid of being there, of the future.

The woman propped her thick legs on a blue tapestry ottoman. "I will go into a trance," she murmured. Then she shut her eyes and began to chant, swaying as if praying. "I am with you now. I have come here and I am Laughing Waters." Her voice rose and fell, and became deeper. She grasped Lenny's hand and began to mention details about

Lenny's life. "You moved here from a place far away, Michigan or Minnesota or perhaps Milwaukee." Then she said, "You are a healer. Your womb is empty now, waiting. But there is a man in your life." The woman waved toward the ceiling as if she were a magician, ready to perform a trick. "Or maybe he will come into it soon, an Arthur or Abraham or perhaps Thomas, someone who is steady and understands life. He will lead you into the future."

"It's not the gospel," Willow said later when they were driving from the psychic's house, "but there's a thread, something in everyone's life that's…inevitable." The woman had predicted that Willow would have many husbands and travel, that Doreen would live across an ocean one day.

Lenny wasn't sure what she believed about psychic phenomena. Adam didn't approve of any of it. But he liked to have a good time, like anyone else. That's what Lenny told Willow and Doreen after the psychic consultation.

"Handsome, yes," Willow said. "Smart, too. But he's so conservative and careful. How long have you known him? Six months? I thought he'd be good for you to have a fling with. I didn't realize he was so… conventional. But I suppose you have to follow your heart. He'll want lots of children someday."

"That will change your world," Doreen said.

"You're taking this personally, both of you," Lenny said. "As if I've abandoned you for him. I haven't."

"We want to save you from an ordinary life," Willow said.

"This has nothing to do with ordinary or not. It's the way I feel about him. That weakness. You talked about that when you've been in love." Lenny could imagine living with Adam, having a family together, growing old with him, although she hadn't told him this. "Maybe you'll never understand how I feel about him," she said to Willow.

Willow shrugged. "Maybe that life is something I'll never want."

The night of Willow's summer solstice party, the last night Adam and Lenny spent with Lenny's friends, Adam got drunk.

Willow stripped off her blouse and bra and danced alone. Adam pinched her thighs, stroked her arms, and embraced her. He kissed

Doreen's neck. He said he would miss her when she became a great barrister and that the macrobiotic diet made her more attractive. He tried to play the snare drums.

Later Lenny drove him home, and they sat in the kitchen of his apartment. She made coffee and watched him, his drunken transformation.

Adam stared at her, the smell of vodka strong on his breath. "I'm going to ask you all the questions I want now," he said loudly. "All the things you never volunteer, you with your sweet, quiet ways and crazy friends." He leaned back into the chair, crossed his arms on his chest. "Just what are you going to do with your life? Spend your time with psychics? Live alone forever? What do you want out of life? Tell me."

"Is this an interview?" Lenny snapped. "Or a performance?"

He kept staring at her with his big, dark, beautiful eyes, and she felt something give in her heart. A wave of love for him. A wave of disgust. Handsome, precise Adam who loved life but who now was a sloppy drunk and unleashed. She talked about nursing and then she put her finger to her lips. "Shh. It's late. Let's not talk anymore."

"No, I fucking want to talk. That's why you need other people, to make sense of your life. You go to psychics and God knows what else. Are you going to hang around with Willow and those friends like a refugee from the sixties for the rest of your life? Is that what you'll remember when you're old? I want to know."

"You're drunk," Lenny said. "Really drunk."

"Just tell me." He watched her intently, and she thought for a moment he might cry. "You never tell me," he said. "I want to understand. Just what are you going to do with your heart?"

"My heart," Lenny repeated uncomfortably. "If you weren't so drunk," she whispered, "maybe I'd give it to you."

Lenny became Lenny Thompson after she and Adam married. They moved to Wichita, where he had gotten a job at a university, teaching cell biology and doing research.

Willow was in England by then, just a year after the summer solstice party. She had left Denver a month after the party, left her boyfriend, too. She said she wanted to explore the world and expand her romantic horizons. Doreen had been accepted to law school for that fall and quit work to travel in Mexico until school began.

Adam, remorseful and embarrassed by his drunken behavior at the solstice party, had gone to Lenny's apartment a week after the party, brought her a bouquet of white roses, and apologized profusely. He had called Willow and Doreen and apologized to them, too. He hoped they would forgive him and that Lenny would. He had been offered a job in Wichita, he told Lenny, and hoped she would move there with him. He asked her to marry him. Lenny didn't hesitate. She said yes.

Lenny told Willow and Doreen the next day about her engagement and plans.

"We're all dispersing, aren't we?" Willow said a little wistfully.

"But we'll write to each other and always keep in touch," Doreen said.

Willow had stopped at Lenny's apartment to say goodbye a few days before she left for England. She brought a present to help Lenny remember the years when she was free, Willow said, when the three friends lived in the same city. To help with the future. To shape an extraordinary life. She gave Lenny a large white envelope. Inside were two sheets of gray parchment paper. Each sheet was decorated with silhouettes of purple watercolor flowers. The bottom of one sheet, painted in Willow's flowing handwriting, read: *Upon Lenny's departure from Denver, for a new life.*

Willow dug out three pennies and a gray book from her brightly colored woven handbag. She began to toss the coins on the floor, each time recording heads or tails on the parchment paper, using precise lines. "Hexagrams," she explained. Then she opened the I Ching. "I use the book now as my guide. Much better than a psychic. More comprehensive." She described the meanings of the configurations— the Judgment, Images, and Lines.

"A quiet wind is your image," Willow read aloud. "There is gentle success through what is small. It furthers you to have someplace to go. Always. The wind's power depends on its ceaselessness."

"I don't know," Lenny said. "I feel like I'm at a crossroads. Of someplace to go. But where? Getting married. Moving away."

"And I'm off to England." Willow laughed lightly. "I suppose we all zigzag from one life to another. At least we both have someplace to go. Adam's quite a catch after all, I think. We talked about that at the beginning, didn't we? Doreen and I. Oh, he has flaws. He was horribly inappropriate at the solstice party. But at least he apologized to Doreen and me. To you." She dropped the pennies in her bag and pressed the I Ching into Lenny's hands. "Here. You keep the book. Read it. Think of me."

Lenny set it on the table, and she and Willow hugged.

"I could never be happy in Kansas," Willow said. She walked to the front door. "But maybe that life will work for you."

The I Ching accompanied Lenny wherever she and Adam lived. At first, she kept the book on a special spot on a shelf. With the jumble of different moves and the births of the children—three sweet daughters—the book lost its place and lay wedged with old photo albums, folded maps, and scratched, discarded 33 1/3 rpm records. Even if Lenny had wanted to find the book, she might not have remembered where it was.

Her life took on a different shape. She worked as a nurse in a children's hospital and cared for her own children, too. Adam had taken a job with a large pharmaceutical firm in Minnesota, and he, Lenny, and the children moved there from Kansas. His work involved traveling. Sometimes it seemed to Lenny that these changes in her life had happened overnight. It was as if she had switched the style of clothing she wore or colored her hair; she had felt this way, too, when she first arrived in Denver, when she met Willow and Doreen. Astonished by change. Ambushed. As if something was fundamentally different about her now, as if she had grown taller or happier. Or, perhaps, less plain.

From time to time, she heard from Doreen. Doreen had gone to live in Japan after finishing law school. Lenny wrote to Willow in England once after the wedding. Willow sent a letter in response and wrote that she would be moving, but she never sent the new address.

Sometimes Lenny imagined that earlier period in her life and allowed herself to indulge in memory. The way sunlight glistened on a car reminded her of a burst of golden afternoon light rushing through Doreen's picture window. Or a small, rundown house and a nervous, pacing cat might jog her thoughts about the psychic's words. Lenny often recalled these moments when she felt exasperated with the children or work, or when she was sitting with her new married women friends and talking of practical things—houses, children, and husbands. She thought about Willow and Doreen when she and Adam argued. She and Adam had never argued until they had children. He was, it turned out, a moody perfectionist, and he sometimes drank too much and spent too much money. He said she drove him crazy with her slow, free way of making decisions. "I can't tell what you're thinking," he said. "And you don't tell me."

"Everything doesn't have to be settled and perfect," she replied. Sometimes she thought about divorce.

He had started balding and liked to wear a baseball cap to hide that. Lenny knew she had fallen in and out of love with him and back again. That's what she would have told Willow. He still had that wide smile and liked to say they were lucky. Sometimes she would catch a glimpse of the Adam she had met at the birthday party. She remembered that night, their beginning, the bold kiss. She wanted that time, when anything could have happened, to happen again. Lenny could have fallen in love with him, just as she had. They could have parted or never met. She might be traveling with Willow or Doreen now. She could have stayed in Denver or perhaps never stopped there at all. She imagined people and events, the possibilities, like particles connecting and dispersing, a kaleidoscope.

Twelve years after she'd last seen Willow, Lenny received a letter from her. She immediately recognized the flowing handwriting on the thin blue aerogramme. She carried it to the small backyard to read, where the children were playing.

Willow wrote that she was living in India. She had never married but was a mother of two children now. After she'd split up with their father, she became involved with an anthropologist. *But then we had a falling-out,* she wrote. *Isn't that always the way?* Now she was learning self-healing—pulling the negative energy from her body, and fasting in complete silence three days a month. She was doing secretarial work and saving money so she could return with her children to London.

Where does the time go, dear friend? I thought you'd vanished from my universe. But Doreen passed through here last month and told me about you. We marveled, she and I—you're the only one we know who married and has stayed that way. Extraordinary. How do you do it? You must write and tell me. I'm ready for that stability, too. As for me, I have two boys now. I've had more lovers than I want to count. Thankfully, that's behind me. We all have our weaknesses, hopes, illusions. You and I will have to talk about the experience of giving birth one day, all that follows from that. Quite remarkable.

I must go—and I apologize for not keeping in touch. Or is it you who should apologize to me? Who can remember? But you have children to take care of. You must know how they dominate one's life. I suppose there is no need for apologies. That's what our lives are like now. Aren't they?

Always yours,
Willow

Willow was right, Lenny thought. She stared at the wildly uneven handwriting on the page. Yes, that's what their lives were like now. She glanced at the children running in the sunshine and thought of Adam's balding head and smile. She shut her eyes and lay on the soft grass. Perhaps you travel from one moment to the next, she thought, without understanding why or being quite ready to part with what came before. To part with the possibilities. But you have to know what makes you happy, what you were looking for in the first place. That's what she would write to Willow.

She and Adam had been spared tragedy so far, but that would come, she was sure. It would come to them all. She would tell Willow that, too. You couldn't wrap yourself in illusion forever.

Then Lenny breathed in the warm summer air and slowly reread the letter. As she did, she couldn't recall if that earlier time in her life had been just as she liked to remember it, or if the memory itself was what always brought her such pleasure.

Woman Wanted for Travel—No Romance

1

ELI GROSSMAN HAD LIVED A GOOD LIFE. He knew this. He'd been a grocer and had worked hard before he'd sold the business and retired. At eighty-two, he was in relatively good health, despite the aches in his left knee and right shoulder, a few minor operations he had endured over the years, and the incremental loss of energy that came with age. He prided himself on his strength, independence, and stubbornness. He'd gone to college after World War II and won his wife's hand. He had turned his grocery into a thriving specialty store and pushed to buy a house in a good Chicago suburb so their kids could go to the best public schools. He'd even fought for and kept his sanity when Edith had died six years ago.

His son, Jonathan, who lived in Telluride, had called every day back then, encouraging Eli to build another life when Eli had given up hope. There had been tension between them for years, but Jonathan put that aside for a time in the wake of his mother's death. And miraculously, Eli had found a new life. He was traveling to Florida next week with a woman he thought he loved, a woman he was going to ask to marry him. Irma Leonard.

Eli didn't use the word love carelessly. He had loved his wife, Edith, a love that shrank or stretched depending on the year. When she died, he'd fallen into a depression and thought he would never recover. He had experienced blue moments before, but nothing like that. But his determined will to survive had burst to the surface and pushed him to take the steps that led to Irma.

Friends had told him about online sites where someone even eighty or older could post a personal ad. You might find someone you like, they said. Eli was stubborn and, he supposed, old-fashioned. You didn't just go shopping for love as if it were a pair of socks. And he thought these suggestions were dismissive of his grief. But he started reading the ads in the local suburban newspaper, and finally, three years ago, he'd placed his own.

It had taken him weeks to compose.

Wanted.

What did he want? He wanted Edith back and life as it had been before. He sat at the kitchen table and tried different combinations of words. Finally, he settled on this: *Woman Wanted for Travel—No Romance. Widower aged 79 seeks female, age 70 to 77, for travel and conversation.* He didn't want complications; it was too late for romance. And every word presented problems. What ages should he include? What could he offer a seventy-year-old woman? She would be from a different generation, at a different stage of life. But he decided he could offer a woman companionship, not a small thing.

Besides, it was true: he had opinions about the world, and he wasn't bad-looking. He had a respectable head of gray hair, though his hairline was receding; his eyes were blue, his nose long, his height medium. He'd never finished college, but he'd taken classes at the community college after he retired, courses about the Depression and World War II. One about the computer. He read biographies and walked every day outside or at the mall in winter. His freckled skin was wrinkled, his broad body flabby from age, despite the exercise. How long would he live? His father used to say: I don't have a contract with God for how long I'll live. Eli didn't either.

To his surprise, he received ten responses. He interviewed five women. He took one to dinner at Mario's Restaurant downtown. She ordered too much food. This reflected, he felt, a fundamental flaw in her character. Rather than following his lead, she did what she pleased. She seemed greedy and would require too much of everything, he decided. He didn't remember her name. But he remembered every dish she chose: the melon and dumpling appetizer, a salad with exotic lettuces, and veal—the most expensive entrée on the menu—plus two glasses of wine and dessert to boot. She was pleasant, in her mid-seventies, but not for him. She had heart problems, too. Another woman lived in Florida half the year, divorced three times. He wondered about her fidelity. A third no longer drove; she would become too dependent, he thought. A fourth owned three cats.

Everyone came with baggage.

Irma was the only one who had invited him to her apartment for dinner. He suggested they go out, but she insisted he come over for a "home-cooked meal." It would be a date, just like in a restaurant, but she enjoyed cooking. Did he mind?

He drove downtown to the sleek high-rise on Diversey, parked, and rode up in the elevator to the twelfth floor. The apartment was elegant—Edith would have said so. White brocade French chairs, flowers in a crystal vase, wallpaper covering the dining room walls, the nubby beige grass cloth Edith had admired. Large windows. The lights of the city sparkled against the ink-black sky outside. Irma was attractive, a few inches shorter than he was, with wavy blonde hair, blue eyes, and a warm smile, a confidence, as if she had known him all his life. She wore a blue silk dress that draped her slim figure.

They sat across from each other at the small dining room table. She had prepared a simple meal: barley soup, salad, roasted chicken and asparagus with fancy mushrooms—the mushrooms were the only foray into luxury. An array of breads. The meal was delicious.

These interviews were often awkward. At dinner, he asked her, as he had asked the others, "So, do you have, you know, any health problems?" He didn't want to bring someone into his life he'd have to take care of. What could he say? Are you sick? Any incurable diseases? He had called Jonathan for advice. Jonathan said, "Just be direct and kind. These women may be wondering the same thing about you. Look, Dad, don't rush into anything."

"I was going to ask you, as well," Irma replied. "My birthday was last month, and I'm seventy, but, thank God, healthy. They say seventy is the new fifty. Oh, I have back problems sometimes. Years ago, I had my appendix out." She laughed gaily. "It was an emergency, but I found I could live without an appendix."

"You can live without a lot of things you thought you needed." He laughed, too. Then he became serious. He didn't want to offend her. "I only ask," he said, "because of our ages. You might be a little young for me. I'm sure you can find someone your own age." He paused, embarrassed by his frankness. "My wife, my late wife, had small problems at first. The foot, the knee, the gallbladder, and then the cancer."

"I'm sorry," Irma said.

He didn't like to talk about the cancer, how it had ravaged Edith and turned her into a frail old woman overnight. It was too painful to think about. "As for me," he went on, "I'm seventy-nine, in pretty good health. My cholesterol is good, and my blood pressure. Even my heart isn't so bad." He didn't mention the small melanoma the doctor had removed from his right cheek last year. He didn't tell her about the arthritis in his neck, his shoulder, his knee.

"The heart is the most important. You look like you have a good heart." She smiled. Her teeth were evenly spaced and a soft white. "My husband died because of his heart. He had polio as a boy and limped. It was the heart that killed him at sixty-three."

"He was young."

"Yes."

Whole lives were reduced to this, he thought—a sweeping description, and a lifetime was summarized and dismissed.

Later, over coffee, Eli explained his reasoning. "You understand, we're both adults. We have our own children. At this point, I'm interested in someone I can travel with. There are so many places I've never seen. We could go out on weekends and see if we like each other. Really, that's enough, to travel and spend a couple of weekends together."

She nodded.

"Sometimes, of course, I could take you where we decide to go."

"Oh, no. I can pay my own way." She fluttered her hands, as if pushing away this gift. "Arnold provided for me. To tell the truth, I'd enjoy the company."

Eli liked Irma right away. She'd been born in Iowa and her family moved to New York City when she was fourteen. Later she moved to Chicago with her husband and raised her two children here. She had a flair that some New York women have, one Edith had envied. Mixed in with everything, Irma exuded a Midwestern softness. She had a deep, warm voice, and she played piano. She was interested in acting, had acted in local productions, even done voice-overs, she told him. Whatever it was, Irma—with her wavy golden hair, blue eyes, her pale skin streaked with delicate wrinkles that befit her age—drew him.

He drove home to the suburbs, pleased. He lived in Lincolnwood, in the Towers area, in the house he and Edith had shared. A solid brick Tudor, it remained just as it had been when she was alive. A photograph from when she was younger sat on the piano, a small light shining on it. Jonathan had once called it a shrine. Eli liked the photograph. It brought him closer to her memory somehow, even though there were times now when he could barely remember her scent or the high, clear sound of her voice.

Three months after he had placed the ad, Eli planned their first trip. He and Irma had been out to dinner six times on weekends and twice to a movie. He came into the city each time and picked her up, and at the end of each evening, he walked her to her door and formally shook her hand. Their conversations were pleasant. They talked about their lives, politics, their children, friends, places they wanted to travel. He told Irma that Jonathan was willful and stubborn. "He's hard to get along with," Eli said. "We don't see each other so often, but we talk sometimes on the phone."

"Perhaps you can do something to change the situation," she said gently.

"I doubt anything can be done."

He told his daughter, Cynthia, about Irma. He and Cynthia had a warm relationship. She was a journalist, and she, her husband, and two of Eli's grandchildren lived in California. He also told Jonathan about Irma in one of his infrequent calls. Jonathan was a lawyer, with a wife and two children as well.

Eli was eager to travel. He had never traveled much with Edith. They'd gone to Europe once, but at the time he couldn't be away from work or bear the expense. He'd promised her they would see the world when he retired, but that was not to be. When the children were young, he used to drive the family past the replica of the Leaning Tower of Pisa that stood in a park on Touhy Avenue in Niles, a suburb near Lincolnwood. Eli had never been to Italy, but the Leaning Tower captured his imagination, the six stories with terraces, the bell tower, the flags on top waving in the wind. "Someday, you'll see the real one," he used to tell the children. "It leans just like this one does." He had no idea what the tower in Italy looked like.

"How does Dad know?" Jonathan asked once.

"Your father," Edith answered, "knows everything."

Eli decided he and Irma should go someplace domestic, rather than Europe or even Mexico. What if, in the end, they didn't like each other when they spent more concentrated time together? What if he found himself stranded in a foreign country wishing he had chosen a different companion, the woman who ordered too much in the restaurant, for example? Maybe he'd misjudged her; maybe she knew how to enjoy life.

He suggested New York.

Irma liked the idea. "I went to high school there and used to visit with Arnie. My late husband. It's a perfect choice."

Eli felt an unexpected twinge of jealousy. They hadn't talked about Arnie much. Now she spoke his name with clear affection. But good enough, he thought. She would be comfortable there, and so would he.

At first, he imagined they would stay at the Plaza or someplace grand, but then he realized this was a romantic notion, and he didn't want romance. Edith had always wanted to stay at the Plaza, but they never had. He settled on a hotel in Greenwich Village that Jonathan recommended, the Washington Square Hotel. Eli liked the idea of being in the Village, as if this would infuse him and Irma with youth.

The airplane trip was uneventful. He'd booked a room for each of them in the hotel. The rooms were smaller than he expected, but this was New York, after all. The hotel was full of young people and middle-aged European tourists. As he and Irma drank coffee in the small restaurant, with its colorful murals on the walls, its tables crowded close and young waiters who spoke with accents Eli couldn't identify, he felt as if they were in Europe.

It was January and chilly, but the sun was shining. Irma knew the city well. Every day they walked. His arthritis flared in the cold, but he gulped Advil and pushed himself to keep up with her. When they were tired, she led him underground to the subway. Good, he said. Why waste money on cabs?

A blizzard swept over the city at the end of the week. Snow

fell at a miraculous pace, nonstop, as if they were traveling inside a paperweight filled with white particles that someone shook again and again. The flakes flew horizontally. Wind whipped across the streets. They spent the day of the storm in the Metropolitan Museum of Art, in the Egyptian wing, venturing out unsteadily onto the slushy, icy streets to ride the subway back to the hotel. It was an adventure and made him feel young and strong. He had brought his galoshes, luckily, and Irma wore boots and a black down coat. He held onto her arm as they walked. He'd done this on other occasions to be courteous, but now he grasped hold of her firmly to steady her in the snow. She was bonier than he'd imagined her to be, and he felt the frailty of her form.

That night, they ate dinner in the hotel restaurant. They sat in a booth, facing each other. Jazz floated from the restaurant speakers. As they ate their salads, Irma said, "I think we should really try to get to know each other, Eli. I don't mean any entanglements or, as you said, romance. But as people. Don't you think so?"

He shrugged. "I thought that's what we were doing. I thought we knew each other well enough."

"Oh, we do." She laughed. "But I meant to try to really understand the other person. That's a big task. But here we are in New York, with all the time in the world. So." She paused, her soft blue eyes intent. She reached across the table and put her hand on his. "Tell me about Edith, your wife. Your late wife. We never talk much about her or about my late husband."

"Edith," he repeated. "No, we don't talk about them so much. Maybe it's better." He put his hands in his lap. How could he describe her? Edith was Edith. What came to him as he looked from Irma to his plate littered with lettuce was this: how Edith had been when she was young, her shiny black hair, her firm body moving through the rooms of their apartment and then their house, the sway of her hips, her brown eyes and high-pitched laugh.

"Edith was Edith," he said. "She's…she's hard to describe." Even when she was older, she went to modern dance classes, until her foot and knee acted up. She had an almost youthful appearance until the cancer.

Irma nodded.

"She was a good wife, a good mother. She helped in the store. She was..." Tears gathered in his eyes. He stopped. She had been like another limb to him. She wasn't the best housekeeper. She didn't always like sex, and they argued about this. She could be cranky and critical and imperious. She was...a bulwark against loneliness. "We had a good marriage," he said, pushing away his feelings, the sentiment of his thoughts. "It was up and down, and up and down. I used to kid her: 'We're in love this month.' In those days, we didn't think so much about that. I didn't. You put up with what you didn't like, until you couldn't anymore. Sometimes, you didn't even notice what was wrong." He thought of Harriet, the woman with whom he'd had an affair. It grated on him, this transgression.

He had misled Edith, deceived her, lied, and she never knew. She died an innocent. It was better that way, he thought. Maybe she would have left him. He had lied to protect Edith, to prevent her from feeling pain, from being hurt. "Excuse me," he said to Irma, eager to change the subject. "I'm not usually so clumsy with the words. And your husband, what was he like?"

"Arnold?" Irma smiled a wistful smile. "He was smart. The valedictorian of his high school class. I told you, he was a lawyer. In the beginning, we had fun. We laughed. We had the children. He had, I think, a brilliant mind. Wasted it. He wrote wills and defended criminals. But he knew facts about all sorts of things. Like the heights of mountains. The origins of words. Or the Red River in North Dakota. The river is 550 miles long and runs north, just like the Nile River does. Who else would know such a thing?" She paused. "He was a philanderer."

"I see," Eli said, trying to take this all in. "I'm sorry about the last."

"That's who he was. After a while I accepted his imperfections, as much as a person can. I looked the other way. I considered divorce. If he had been really wealthy, I don't know what would have happened. Maybe I would have left, or he would have left me." She laid her hand on the table. Freckles of age spotted her skin. Her nails were polished a pale pink. "Then he got sick and I thought: what's the point now, to divorce?"

"How could you leave a sick man?" Eli said.

The waiter arrived with their entrées, interrupting their exchange. Later, Eli sipped his coffee and waited for Irma to return from the bathroom. Edith used to complain that he never talked about what was inside him. Was that what Irma meant? She wanted to know what was inside him? Sometimes he didn't know himself. It was how he was made. Those were the days, when he grew up, when people didn't talk about feelings—his family didn't—when psychiatrists were secret shames. He loved to talk to customers at the grocery, to Edith, but not about what was most important to him.

Would he ever understand what lay inside him? He had done what he needed to: wife, children, making a living, and only once had he strayed for long: the affair with beautiful, sandy-haired Harriet Wiser.

Who knew where she was anymore? He used to keep track of her, but that had fallen away. He had heard years ago she'd divorced and moved to Palm Springs to be close to her daughters. His relationship with her—it was one of those things that just happen. Her husband owned a furniture store and played cards with Eli.

Eli had told Harriet right away, at the beginning, that he loved Edith, though this was not the most politic way to begin an affair. She said, "And I love Henry." But this didn't stop her from kissing Eli, meeting him in a hotel, or, a few times, coming to his house when he could get away from work and Edith was gone for the day, taking care of her ill mother. They used the bed in the spare bedroom, out of some misguided respect for Edith. This helped Eli organize his life. He was good at that, Edith always said. "Eli, you put us all into little compartments in your head. The children, me, work. Work is the biggest." He had used work as an excuse, he knew. "You have no hobbies," she'd said. "What will you do when you retire? The children will be grown and gone. You hardly pay attention to them now."

Harriet had made him feel young. She taught English at a community college. Then she and her husband moved to Arizona. That ended the affair—the logistics were difficult, and Jonathan was a teenager and rebellious, had started skipping school. Eli needed to pay attention to life at home. And Jonathan had once seen him having coffee at a restaurant with Harriet. Yet Eli sometimes longed for Harriet, for how she had made him feel, and regretted he'd let her slip out of his life.

After dinner, Eli walked with Irma to the hotel's elevator. They rode to the fourth floor in companionable silence. At the door to her room, he didn't know what to do. Their conversation at dinner had been so personal. Still, he thrust out his hand. Irma responded as she always did, shaking his hand. Then she rested her fingers on his arm.

"Oh, Eli," she said. "There doesn't need to be a romance, but you don't have to be so…formal."

"No, I suppose not." He debated. "Would you like to come over to my room?" he asked. "For a drink? I could call room service."

Irma sat in the white stuffed armchair in Eli's room after placing her black leather pocketbook on the floor beside her. Eli did something he'd never done: he telephoned room service and ordered two glasses of white wine. He had always considered this too extravagant.

The room felt even smaller with two people in it. There was no place for him to sit except on the queen-size bed. He faced Irma, his legs dangling down the side of the mattress.

"I'm glad you invited me in," she said. "I was about to ask you to my room. I thought it would be nice to talk more. I don't want any regrets. My earliest memory is of regret. This may seem silly, but I think about it. When my sister was born, I stood with my aunt outside the hospital. I was five. I still remember. January, like now." Irma leaned into the cushions of the chair, sipping her wine. "My aunt looked up at the sky and said to me, 'Look, look, Irma, the stork just went by. You missed it. The stork brought you a sister!' I always regretted that I missed the stork. When I grew up, of course, I knew there was no such thing. Still, after my sister became ill five years ago, I made sure I was with her when she took her last breath. I had missed the stork; I didn't want to miss the Angel of Death." Irma stopped. "I don't want to miss anything."

"Everyone has regrets," Eli said.

"Yes," she said suddenly. "Let's be honest. Absolutely honest."

"About?"

"About our lives, Eli."

"What do you have in mind?"

"Let's play a game. Arnold and I used to do this. True confessions. First I confess something to you that I might otherwise want to hide.

And then you confess to me."

Eli looked at Irma skeptically, but she was already at it.

"I confess to you that I wasn't always truthful with him."

"No?" Eli said, curious. He had not been entirely truthful with Edith either.

"I used to sneak a look at Arnold's mail," Irma said. "It was in the days when a letter would arrive, and you could hold it up to the light and read it, without opening the envelope. The days when mail meant something." She sighed at the memory. "If I held the envelope just the right way toward the lamp, I could read what was inside. Oh, I'm not proud of this. But I did it from time to time with Arnie's mail. I don't know why. It was a feeling I had."

Eli nodded.

"Once, I saw the letter was from a woman, Florence Magliocha. I remember the name. She worked in his office. She wasn't even pretty. I could see in the thin envelope a piece of paper. A love letter. It was disgusting. *I love you with my life, Your Flo*, she signed it."

Eli just listened.

Irma's face grew blotchy with anger. "So I pieced it together and realized Arnie was having an affair. I didn't know how many others there had been. I didn't say anything to him. Maybe I should have. Instead, I did something I'm not proud of. I had my own affair."

"You?"

"I'm ashamed to admit it."

"An eye for an eye," he said. Would Edith have done the same?

"Something like that. I'll make this short. It was with an old friend who lived in Iowa. We met sometimes. We talked on the phone. The long-distance calls were expensive then. I suppose it pleased me that Arnie had to pay for them. My friend and I met whenever he came to Chicago on business." She paused, blushed, and then whispered, "We had phone sex. They didn't call it that then. But that's what it was."

Eli laughed—not to make fun of Irma, but with pleasure. She was as human as they come.

"You're laughing," she said.

"Not at you. It's nothing to worry about, this affair. The phone.

I've had my share of…" He took a deep breath. "Now it's my turn." He debated what to say. "I strayed with a secretary from a coffee company on a business trip, once in a hotel with a woman I hardly knew. It happens. We're not meant to be monks and nuns." He didn't mention Harriet.

"Have you ever…the phone sex?"

He hesitated. "Yes. The phone…it's titillating." Harriet had suggested this. He decided to be truthful with Irma, but only as truthful as he could bear to be.

"It happens, yes, people stray," Irma said. "Even though I myself had an affair, and you tell me you did, I think it's wrong. When you marry," she said with force, "and you value someone who's faithful…"

"Enough with the confession and philosophy," he said. "With getting to know each other. With regret. Let's enjoy the night and the wine."

"Oh, Eli. Come lie on the bed with me. Will you? Or is it absolutely against your policy?" She rose from the armchair, walked to the other side of the bed, and reclined on it, shoes and all, her dyed blonde hair shining like a crown against the white pillowcase.

He joined her, against his better judgment. They lay side by side.

Then she inched closer to him, and he leaned toward her and kissed her. The past fell away. It didn't matter to him, this confession of hers; it fueled his sudden desire.

They held hands and kissed again. They began to explore each other's bodies, tentatively, then with a passion he had almost forgotten. He greedily touched her, pressing her blouse against her breasts and inhaling a whiff of her lilac perfume. He wanted his body to be like an engine, to work just as he wished. But his mind was racing ahead of it. After a while, Irma slipped off her blouse and her bra. She slid off her shoes, wool slacks, her hose, and panties. She pulled in her tummy. "It's a little flabby," she murmured, embarrassed. "Age. Not enough time in the gym."

"You're fine," he said more gruffly than he had intended. "And me, I could lose a few pounds and a lot of years. I'm not as…not as fast as when I was younger."

"We have all the time in the world."

He slid off his trousers and unbuttoned the white Oxford cloth shirt, slipped out of the green plaid boxers, a gift from Ruby, his youngest grandchild. Irma scooped up their clothing and, naked, laid it on the chair.

Beneath the sheet, all that mattered were the sensations that rippled through Eli, the soft mounds and curves of Irma's body, her sighs that grew louder, his own ragged breath. Slowly his body began to work, and finally they both came. He felt such relief and exhaustion. She lay curled next to him, like a young woman, her head resting on his shoulder. Without a word, she drifted to sleep.

His eyes were heavy with the sudden need for sleep, too. His body felt spent and satisfied. For a moment, he worried he might collapse from the exertion and die in bed right beside her. But his heart, miraculously, thumped on. He thought: how foolish he'd been. He remembered the ad he'd crafted. He had found her, the woman he wanted. She was taking him traveling, but to a place he hadn't realized he wanted to go.

It felt strange to be in this hotel—not her home, not his—this room with its huge bed, the piles of pillows. The flat-screen TV hidden in a mahogany cabinet. Everything sterile and neat, as if real people didn't exist here. He looked out the window; snow still whirled. Making love to Irma here felt out of time, out of place, not quite part of Eli's life, but more real than anything else. This would be an aberration, he thought, the sex. They had made an agreement. And he didn't want to need another person again, like he'd needed Edith and Harriet. He didn't want Irma to need him either. After all, how long would he live? He didn't want to disappoint her, for her to know he was more like her husband than she imagined.

But as he fell asleep in her arms, he knew they would do this again.

2

Though they were intimate now, they adhered to the weekend-only schedule. They had followed this routine for the last three years.

"What do you do during the week?" Eli once asked Irma.

"I play the piano and bridge, sometimes even do a voice-over," she said. "See the grandchildren. Visit the doctor."

"Doctor?"

"The checkups. An ache here, a pain there. You know about the creeping of age and what it brings."

"I admit I go to doctors myself," Eli said.

He didn't tell her about the pain that ripped through his neck and shoulder, his knee and elbow, the arthritis getting worse. He didn't tell her about the melanoma or that his mother and two uncles had died of colon cancer. Eli avoided doctors. He hadn't had a colonoscopy in twelve years.

Sometimes Irma asked: "Are you alright, Eli?"

"Fine, fine," he would say. "A stiff neck. I bent in the wrong way. I knocked my elbow into the dresser."

He pretended he was fine. He didn't want to lose her. He couldn't bear to lose someone again.

Of course, she wasn't just a traveling companion anymore; she was his lover. He smiled at the thought—he, now an eighty-two-year-old man, with a younger lover. If he'd been sixty, she would have been fifty-one; when he was forty, she would have been thirty-one. He usually went to her place in the city. He liked her apartment, the warmth of it. He liked how she played the piano for him, Mozart or Chopin. Sometimes her hands trembled, but she played on. She rarely stayed at his house.

Irma cooked his favorite foods, Italian dishes, and served green grapes and chocolate cake for dessert. She bought shirts for him from the L.L.Bean Catalog, the right size and fit. She rearranged the photographs on his piano when she visited his house. Only once did she comment on the photograph of Edith.

"That must be your Edith," Irma said.

"Yes," he replied. He thought perhaps he should put the photograph away now, but he couldn't bear to. During the week, he liked to see Edith. "I'd like to have a photograph of you," he said.

"I don't have a good one. On our next trip, we'll take one together. Let's go to Florida, Eli. Or someplace warm. It's winter. That's what people do."

"Then Florida it is."

That night, they returned to her apartment. Waiting for Irma to join him in bed, he lay in his blue cotton pajamas beneath the blankets and thought of his honeymoon with Edith. They had gone to Rocky Mountain National Park all those years ago, dwarfed by the towering mountains. They made love fiercely every morning and night, in the middle of the night, too; he could come three times a day or more then. When Jonathan moved to Colorado, they visited him in Telluride before touring the park to find not much had changed, though their ardor had cooled.

Edith had wanted to travel to visit Jonathan again, but Eli wasn't interested. He was working hard and struggling to save for retirement. As the years spilled away, a rift began between him and Jonathan— gradual, insistent—over Eli's refusal to visit, to see the grandchildren. He noticed he spoke to Jonathan less and less.

Jonathan had been attentive to him after Edith died, but then the old tensions resurfaced. He wondered if Jonathan remembered seeing him with Harriet in the restaurant, and suspected the affair. He and Jonathan talked on occasion, but they rarely saw one another now. Eli had wanted Jonathan to bring his wife and children to Chicago. Why should Eli schlep to a small town in the mountains where he could barely catch his breath? "Rigid" is what Jonathan and Cynthia called Eli in anger. Edith had told him this, too. Though Eli denied it, they were right. He hated change. He hated this falling-out with his son, but he couldn't seem to do anything about it.

His children viewed him as just a grocer, he knew. But he'd had aspirations when he was young; he'd wanted to write poetry, secretly scribbling clumsy, heartfelt verses, trying to understand what was inside him, to capture what he saw in the world. When his father went bankrupt and had to close the clothing store, his parents quickly moved to a smaller apartment, and in the process they tossed out lots of stuff, including the boxes crammed with Eli's school papers and books, with his poetry. He was shattered; he believed his parents were cruel and ruthless.

Though he tried to write again, he found his parents' actions had shaped him. But after he grew up, he understood they had simply been too immersed in their own worries to pay attention to him and his dreams. It was just a thoughtless act, dumping those boxes in the trash. Maybe in his own way, he'd been just as thoughtless with Jonathan. Eli had forgiven his parents. Why couldn't Jonathan be more forgiving of him?

Irma appeared, wearing a lime-green silk nightgown that dipped to reveal the curve of her breasts. Her blond hair fell in waves against her forehead. She slid into bed next to him.

If he'd met her when he was young, would he have married her instead of Edith? He wished he could write a poem about Irma.

"Where are you, Eli?" Irma said. "You're drowning."

"Drowning?"

"Drowning in thought. Rumination."

"I'm right here," he said, grateful she had pulled him into the present. "I want to *shtup* you. C'mere, my pumpkin. If my body obeys me."

"I'll help it obey you. Oh, I love everything about you," she cried with abandon. "Your cock."

Edith never said the word "cock," but Harriet had. The word excited him, how Irma trilled with pleasure when he touched her.

This was the first time she used the word *love*.

3

Although Irma planned the details of their trip to Florida, Eli made plans of his own. He thought he might ask her to marry him there. He wasn't completely sure, but he bought a ring. A pearl with two small diamonds set in gold. He purchased it from a friend in the jewelry business, whose store stood next to the furniture store that had once belonged to Harriet's husband. The jeweler said he would give a full refund if Eli decided he didn't need the ring.

In the last years, he and Irma had traveled to Rome and Pisa, to Tel Aviv and Jerusalem, to Michiana Shores. They had seen the actual Leaning Tower—taller, grander, and more beautiful than the replica in Niles, Illinois. They went back to New York, though not in the winter, and once visited Canada. Eli didn't have endless money. But he'd read a book called *Live Rich, Die Broke*, and his children advised him to live while he could. They seemed relieved, too, Eli thought, that he'd found a companion, someone who would take care of him.

His children encouraged him to get married again. Cynthia had mentioned this a few months ago on the phone. "If you're away from home and something happens to one person, they won't let the other make decisions unless you're a spouse," she had said intently, just as Edith would have. "Dad, it happens. Jonathan agrees. We think you should consider getting married."

Eli almost said, "And why doesn't Jonathan tell me himself?" but he didn't. He was silent. He had a loving relationship with Cynthia and didn't want to inject tension into the conversation.

"Did you hear what I said, Dad? Jonathan says if you're worried about the financial aspects, don't be. That can be taken care of."

"Taken care of," Eli repeated. "Marriage. I'll give it serious thought."

"Don't think too much," Cynthia said with affection. "Irma wouldn't replace Mom. She can never be replaced. But…" Then Cynthia changed the subject and talked about the children, asked how he was feeling and if he was eating properly.

"Irma feeds me. So I suppose I'm really okay."

Eli had considered asking Irma to marry him even before Cynthia brought this up. He decided he would talk to Irma about the matter if he could find the right moment.

He and Irma were staying at the Ambassador Hotel in Palm Beach for two weeks, right on the ocean, in an apartment they could rent by the week. It was December. At one time, years ago, some people derogatorily had called this area the Gaza Strip or a *shtetl* with its terraced apartment buildings populated mostly by Jews. The buildings had elegant *goyishe* names, like Sutton Place, The Carlyle House, Sloan's Curve, and Beach Point.

Though Eli was Jewish, he stayed away from large gatherings of Jews. When Eli was a child, his father had been president of the shul and put his own name on the shul mortgage. During the Depression, the synagogue had no funds for the mortgage payments. Eli's father had no money for the mortgage payments either. He'd been pushed into bankruptcy then; the family had been forced to close the clothing store. Not one person in that synagogue helped them, Eli's mother had said bitterly. Eli blamed the whole religion for his parents' fate.

Blamed it for his father's first heart attack that year, for the move to the smaller apartment, the loss of the books and poetry.

The Ambassador was a yellow stucco building with ten floors, large shiny brown tiles in the lobby, and an electric menorah and small Christmas tree gracing the space during the season. Forest-green carpet with a pattern of white swirls covered the hallway floors where the apartments were, as if the guests had stepped into the 1950s. A second, smaller lobby was furnished with rectangular forest-green armchairs trimmed in white plastic and rectangular sofas of the same green. A Yamaha spinet piano that no one seemed to play sat there, too.

Eli supposed the hotel had once been elegant. Now it was merely comfortable. A musty smell floated in the hallways and the apartment as they walked in.

He opened the windows to let in the ocean air. The waves washed up and back outside.

"We'll go to dinner tomorrow. At Ta-boo or the restaurant right here, in the Ambassador," he said.

"No, Eli," Irma said. "Why should we? I'll cook. We'll sit and look at the ocean. What could be better?"

It was true. From the dining room and bedroom there were fine views of the water. The white foam of the waves rose like whipped cream and melted into the sand. The pale sky, the blue ocean, people strolling, the sun cascading through the clouds. Some people wouldn't think much of this and would want to visit someplace exotic. To Eli, this was heaven.

"We'll watch the sunset," she said.

"You're right," he said. "Chicken cacciatore. I can almost taste it."

"Would you like that?" She slipped her arm through his and rested her head on his shoulder. "Grilled vegetables. Even a kugel I can make for you. We'll be multicultural." She laughed. "Isn't that what people do these days?"

He kissed her forehead. He thought of his great need for her, to talk to her, touch her, of how she came in a way Edith never had. And his body still worked, slower, with effort, but like a miracle, he came, too. Each time he did, he worried he might collapse. He was too old for Irma, really. He knew that. She knew it, too, he was sure, although she never said so. He was grateful she never said it. Even so, they were like two souls breathing in tandem. He would ask her to marry him tonight.

Eli had visited Florida with two of his grandchildren, Ruby and Sam, when they were young, before the tension began with Jonathan. Edith had wanted to come here then. They'd stopped at TooJay's, the delicatessen, for giant black and white cookies and delicious rugelach, the chocolate, the raspberry, and apricot.

He and Irma stopped there to buy dessert now. The rugelach reminded him of his youth. His mother had always baked. Eli had written poetry inhaling those scents. He used to believe she loved to bake, but when he was an adult he realized she did this out of necessity. Still, her baking had created memories, smells like these, infused with hope.

He pushed away his thoughts. All his life, he had been plagued with thoughts.

"I want you to meet the grandchildren," he said to Irma as they left the delicatessen. He drove the rental car toward the Ambassador. "Sam and Ruby, the grandchildren from Colorado. I told you she's in medical school in Seattle. You'll meet Cynthia and her children— Oliver and Liza. And especially Jonathan. I'm working on him to meet you."

"Darling," Irma said. "How many years has it been since you visited him?"

"You mean visited Jonathan, where he lives?"

"Yes."

"Oh, that."

"Yes, *that.*"

He calculated. "Maybe seven years or so?"

"Thirteen years, Eli. You told me once exactly when you last went to Colorado to see him. Why have you waited so long?"

He kept his eyes on the road. He didn't have an answer.

"I'm sure I'll meet him, but this is his punishment for you. Anyone can see he's angry you don't visit him. Maybe he's angry at you for something else, too. And what about your grandchildren?"

"He paid attention to me when Edith died."

"She was his mother."

"If you want the truth," he said, "I'm angry he doesn't visit *me.*"

"But you're the parent, Eli. That's childish. He's your son, your blood. Don't push him away. You'll see; blood is always there. When you need him, he'll be there. Remember my words."

"You'll be right next to me. You'll remind me of them yourself."

Pulling into the parking lot at the Ambassador, he knew it was true: he'd pushed Jonathan away. Eli didn't have much of a relationship with his grandchildren. He had always imagined it would develop. But maybe it never would. He had been rigid and unyielding. Childish. Irma was right. True, true, true. All this would be listed on the scorecard of his life in the World to Come.

"Do you remember when we played our true confessions?" Eli asked at dinner.

"Of course," Irma replied. "Our first trip to New York."

They were eating in the dining room of the Florida apartment, the curtains open. They watched dusk creep across the ocean.

"I lied to you," he said simply.

She set down her fork.

"I've had a health problem, a small melanoma," he admitted. He wanted to be honest with her before he talked of marriage.

"Is it…is it serious?"

"No. The doctor removed it before I met you. 'That's that,' he said. The doctor said if I was lucky, it shouldn't come back. So far, it hasn't."

"I see. Is there anything else you didn't tell me?"

"A little arthritis. My neck, my elbow, the knee. Sometimes the shoulder. It's not a death sentence, so I didn't want to mention it."

"I thought as much. I could see it, Eli. The way you limp sometimes. I hate for you to be in pain." She frowned. "Anything more?"

"No," he lied. Harriet. But what good would it do for Irma to know?

"I suppose after all this time I can trust you." Irma took a sip of her wine. "That's one of the things I liked about you right away, that I thought I might be able to trust you."

"I wanted to clear the air," Eli said with regret. "Be completely honest." He should have mentioned this before. Or maybe he shouldn't have said anything.

"I didn't know the air had to be cleared," Irma said. "But I'm glad you told me. I might as well admit: I wasn't absolutely truthful either."

"No?"

"I have health issues, too."

He looked at her with uneasy expectation.

"My heart," she said simply.

"What about it?"

"I didn't want to tell you at the beginning, and then I liked you so much, I didn't want to go into it. It's nothing, really. A murmur here, a palpitation there. It's true; at some point I may need surgery."

"What kind?"

"For the valve. They can do so many things these days. When there's something to worry about, I'll tell you."

"You feel okay?" he said. "You're not tired, no tingling, no pain?"

"Oh, Eli, since when did you become a doctor? I feel perfect." Irma laughed. "Someday, we'll live in a senior community together. When we're very, very old. You'll see. We'll reminisce about our ailments. We'll have real problems then. What would you do if you lived in one of those places?"

"One of those?" he said with disgust, aware she had changed the subject. "They're holding pens. Those places warehouse people until they die."

"No. There are all sorts of situations, reasonable ways to live: independent or assisted living. I've looked into it."

"I may not make it to one."

"You're solid as a rock."

"And what would you do there?" he asked.

"I'll write poetry," she said happily.

"Poetry?"

"Oh, I used to write when I was a girl, silly rhyming verses. And when I met Arnie, too—no, I scribbled until we had the children. I've always wanted to again."

"Then you will."

"I hope. I'll write about you. What would you do?"

"I'd read," Eli said cautiously. "Biographies. Play poker. I'd think about writing poetry, too."

"You, poetry?"

"Yes." He was sorry he had mentioned this. No, he was happy he'd said it. He wanted Irma to know. He had never told Edith this or Harriet. "When I was a boy, a teenager, I wrote poems, pages of them, notebooks. I saved them in two big boxes and put my favorite books there, too. But during the Depression we had to move to another apartment. My father went bankrupt. We had no money. My parents threw the boxes in the trash. All the poetry gone."

"Oh, Eli," she said. "How cruel."

"No. They didn't know what was in the boxes. And what did they understand anyway? My father lost a business, got sick, and then worked in an apron factory. What did they understand about words? What did I?" All those poems: where were they? Those thoughts? He had forgotten them. "It's a silly, stupid thing, but then it was a heartbreak."

"It's not stupid. We'll write together when we're in one of those holding pens."

He nodded. He thought of his sister-in-law, when she went into a home. She had cried and clutched his arm. "Do you see what my children want to do to me?" she said. "I won't survive a year. It's the terrible end of something." Eli had felt goose bumps. He imagined the sterile buildings, the ersatz cheer, people crammed together in awful states of decay. She had been right, had died before a year was up. A goddamned holding cell.

That would never be him. Irma would save him from that. He would save her.

"What are you thinking?" she asked.

"Those homes. My sister-in-law was in one. I was thinking about endings, beginnings."

"I think," Irma said, rising to clear the dinner dishes, "life becomes more about endings than anything else."

"And us?"

"Thank God, so far, we're the exception." She lifted his plate and stacked it on top of hers. "When I look at you, I think: I'm blessed. It's unbearably sentimental, and you know I don't have much faith in religion, but that's what I think."

"I want to tell you something," he said. "All my life, I've felt ten, twenty years younger than I am. Even with the arthritis. On my good days, I feel sixty or sixty-two. Like a young man with you. It's something. Of course, I don't have the energy I used to."

"You have plenty," she said.

"And you do, too." A wave of fatalism washed over him. "But sooner or later, life will dwindle away."

"Don't be so dark, Eli. Enjoy the ocean, the moon, the night. Maybe life won't be like this in the future."

"Why not?"

"You know what happens. You're healthy until you're not." She walked toward the kitchen. "You're happy until that goes, too."

That night, he carried the small black box that hid the pearl-and-diamond ring and placed it on the night table next to his side of the bed.

In his pajamas, he waited beneath the blankets, eager to give Irma the ring, a little nervous, too. She slipped into bed next to him.

He kissed her, surprised he still had it in him, this desire. He wrapped his arms around her, almost afraid to release her, as if she might disappear.

"Now I understand why Arnie had so much fun in his life," she said, easing away.

"Your late husband?" Eli replied, startled she'd mentioned him.

"Yes." She lay on her back, in her lime-green nightgown, and pulled the blankets up to her shoulders. "I told you he was a philanderer."

"So what are you saying? And you are, too?"

"Oh, no. Not anymore. I'm a philanderer only to his memory. But with you," she said softly, "I feel like I'm having an affair."

"But you said an affair is wrong."

"It's true. I think it's wrong if you're married. But you and I are free. And this, ours is an affair of the heart. I want us to be honest, no more hiding things. But let's talk in the morning. Tonight I'm tired."

"Wait. Irma, would you ever consider..." He slid onto his side, to face her. "Consider getting married?"

"Oh, Eli." She laughed, with pleasure, he thought. "That's nice." Then she was quiet.

"So what do you think?"

"It's wonderful you asked. Why do we need it? We're happy as we are."

"Well." He felt shockingly sentimental, disappointed she didn't throw her arms around him with joy. He wanted to say: We need it because I love you. Irma, I think I love you. I didn't think I could love someone again. But he couldn't squeeze out the words. "So tell me what you think," he said.

"Do you really want to know?"

"Yes, yes." Though he wasn't sure he did.

"On the one hand, I think: why have you waited so long to ask?" She turned to face him and stroked his cheek. "On the other, I think: at our age, why do we need it?"

"At any age, if it's right, it's right. We could have a regular, normal life."

"We could have a regular one now." She slid closer to him, looked into his eyes. "What do you feel about me, Eli? You never really say."

He didn't answer at first. He had told her he was very fond of her. "I feel...I feel so much for you, Irma."

"And I feel love for you."

"Irma, I have a gift for you." He eyed the box, about to reach for it.

"This, this marriage, this gift, can we talk about it in the morning?" Her voice was soft and dreamy. "Then we'll see what we'll do. Is that okay with you?"

He wasn't going to beg. He could see she was sleepy. "In the morning then, we'll talk," he said.

"We'll greet the day that way. Oh, Eli. Sometimes, I've wondered... is this, the sex," she began. "Passion is what they called it when I was young and we studied literature. We didn't say sex then." She sounded half asleep. "Is it just biology? You, me, a man, a woman. I suppose it doesn't matter. It works."

"It works all right. I'm lucky my body works. You're lucky. I'm no scientist. But they talk about chemistry. It's the body and the mind."

"The body and the heart."

"The heart. Exactly. That's a poem, Irma. We'll get married, and I'll take you on a cruise around the world."

She laughed.

"Tell me where you want to go." He couldn't stop himself. He talked as if he were rich.

"The most important is how we feel about each other," she whispered. "Don't look that way, Eli. This isn't a yes, but it isn't a no." She laid her head on his shoulder and sighed with the clear need for sleep. "I am so happy you asked. One of the things I like about you is: you're next to me at night. Arnie traveled so much and then died. If I stopped to calculate, I've spent so many nights alone." She laced her fingers in his. "Too many."

"I like that about you," he said. "That you're next to me."

"I love that about you. It makes me feel..." She paused. "Safe."

"I like that about you, too."

"Oh, I love you, Eli. I love so many things about you. I miss you during the week. But when we travel, we're together all the time." She brushed her lips against his. Then she eased her head onto the pillow and closed her eyes.

He heard her breathing slowly, heard her drifting into sleep. The room was dark, except for waves of moonlight that spilled in at the edges of the curtains.

In the morning, the sun was shining. Eli could tell it was late. They'd overslept. Sunlight shimmied in through the thin white curtains. He eyed the box with the ring. It sat just where he'd left it on the night table, bathed in a spiral of light.

When Irma awoke, she said she hadn't yet made a decision about Eli's important question. She needed time to consider it, digest it. Was that alright?

He said yes, of course, and he thought maybe it was just as well. What did they need marriage for? Maybe she was right. Maybe marriage would ruin what they had. Maybe marriage had ruined his love for Edith. Even so, he showed Irma the ring.

"It's beautiful," she said.

Then he closed the box and put it in his suitcase.

For the next two weeks, Irma seemed to forget about their conversation, although she seemed happier, more carefree. Eli couldn't quite describe it, but there was a mood about her, as if their discussion about marriage had released her somehow, maybe given her confidence in the staying power of their relationship, he thought. Sometimes, though, she seemed to fold into herself, quiet, preoccupied.

Eli, however, felt emotion expanding inside him and, though he didn't tell Irma, he would sometimes catch a glimpse of her face, the gathering of wrinkles as she smiled, and he would feel his heart catch in a way he hadn't thought any longer possible.

He said to her, "I don't know if what we have together is affection or gratitude."

"But I know," she said, taking his hand as they strolled along the ocean one late afternoon, the rays of sunlight warming them. "Love and gratitude. They're the same."

They went to the forest-green lobby after the walk, and Irma played the Yamaha piano, a Mozart sonata she knew by heart. Eli sat listening. He never wanted to leave Florida, the Ambassador, this lobby, he thought.

On their way back to the apartment, Irma addressed the matter of marriage directly. "I'm grateful you haven't pushed for the marriage," she said.

"Are you ready?" Eli said more eagerly than he would have liked.

"I still don't know if it's necessary."

"Things that are good don't always have to be necessary. At least take a look at the ring again." They walked into the apartment. He found the box at the bottom of his suitcase and opened it proudly. The pea-shaped diamonds sparkled in the late afternoon light.

"It's just beautiful, Eli. But maybe we're too old. If we were actuaries, we could calculate how long we each have left."

"Don't say that. The question is on the table. You'll tell me in the morning or when we're back in Chicago. If it's yes, then yes, and if no, then not. This is no ultimatum." He set the box on the night table in case she decided tonight.

Later as they prepared for bed, Irma said, "I told you, Eli, I love you. That's what I want to hear you say. That's more important than a ring."

He had told Harriet Wiser, too, that he was "very fond" of her. He'd said to her, "Love is too important a thing to lie about." Now he said to Irma, as he'd said to her before, "I feel so much for you." He stopped. "No. The truth is, I feel love for you."

Irma smiled. "Of course you do. I see it in your expression. It's just your natural reticence, Eli. Your natural caution. What does it matter? I suppose words don't matter in the end." She wore her lime-green nightgown and slid into bed. "But the point isn't a ring. The point of life is emotion. You're never too old for emotion. And please, call Jonathan in the morning. I've been thinking about him, about you and me. You don't want to be estranged from your son. No matter whose fault you think it is. You don't want to leave things unfinished. Unfinished is not a way to live."

He nodded and stood next to his side of the bed.

She sighed and studied him. "If you don't say what you feel, how will anyone know? Not just how you feel about us, but about so many other things. How will anyone understand what it's like to be you, walking on this earth? You'll leave the world, and no one will know." She shook her head. "What I said is an observation, Eli. Not a criticism. I saw how you were frowning. So we'll talk more, and decide," she murmured. "I don't want anything to come between us. I feel this question has come between us. I need you beside me."

He lay next to her beneath the blankets.

She stroked his hand. "I know you want to honor me, Eli. You're old-fashioned, and I guess I am, too. But I don't need protection. You've honored me so much, already. Maybe your children want us to marry. I…I can't explain it. I love what we have. So much has changed in my life already. I don't want anything more to change."

"I didn't think I wanted romance, Irma, but I do."

"Oh, I didn't mind your ad." She laughed. "I answered it in the first place because I could see you were practical. At our age, we have to be practical. Romance isn't practical, and marriage is rarely romantic, at least after the beginning. But Eli? What we have, I think, is a great romance." She kissed him. "A surprising and great romance. If you don't agree, tell me in the morning. I'll listen. I promise I will." She closed her eyes, and soon she fell asleep.

Eli lay there in the dark. He thought of his many happy years with Edith and his bright intense fling with Harriet. Had either of them really *listened?*

He didn't know what he would say to Irma in the morning, but at least he wasn't alone, and she would listen. He would listen to her, too. No silence, no echoing void. He watched her sleeping silhouette and rested his hand on hers. What more could anyone want?

Artifacts

NINA IS SIXTY-SEVEN and has joined a dating website. There is something odd but exciting about being on her own at this juncture in life—not widowed, but recently divorced—scouring a site to find a match. A companion. As she studies the photos of men online, she feels young and energetic, but when she glances at herself in the mirror, she sees a pleasant face, a once-pretty face, wrinkles fanning the sides of her green eyes, a few wrinkles on her cheeks, snaking down her neck. A respectable face for a woman her age. But no longer young.

She applies makeup before leaving for her date tonight, and uses a magnifying mirror—her vision is not as precise as it once was: white powder on her eyelids as the salesman at Bloomingdale's suggested; she draws a dark shadow on the crease of her lid to create the illusion that her eyes are wide. Then she applies mascara, foundation, blush, lipstick. She slips on her round tortoiseshell eyeglasses, making a mental note to buy a more fashionable pair. She'll go to Warby Parker and find something dramatic, chic.

The strangest thing about aging, she thinks, is that inside she feels more and more like herself, but to the outside world she appears less and less like the younger self still alive inside her.

It is six thirty, a cold night in early January, and she sits on the crosstown bus, going to the Upper West Side. Remnants of the holidays—wreaths and strings of lights—still grace some of the buildings the bus drives past.

Rick Friedman lives in an apartment on Riverside Drive, in one of the grand old elegant buildings, he said. She has always loved that part of the city, though in the winter the wind is merciless, and it can be almost impossible to walk there then because of the force of the weather. She lived in a tiny apartment on Riverside Drive decades ago, when her ex-husband was in graduate school, before they moved to

Milwaukee and then back to New York.

She's written Rick's address on a piece of paper, to be sure she won't forget it.

He wanted her to see his apartment and invited her over for Italian food. "My favorite," he said.

"Will you cook?" she said.

"Of course not. This is New York. We'll order out, and get it delivered."

This is the first time she has gone to a date's apartment, and she's a little wary. However, she is a grown woman, a grandmother, she tells herself, and has had dinner with Rick three times. Twice on the East Side, once on the West Side, as if he is keeping score, or maybe she is, making sure everything is geographically balanced. He seems smart, decent, appealing even, more so than most of the other men she has met online.

He doesn't seem to have more than the usual accumulation of baggage in his past: two marriages, two divorces, last divorce four years ago. Kids from each marriage who seem to be doing reasonably well as he's related it. He left the first wife for the woman who became his second wife. She eventually left him. Forty years of marriage total. Both wives were in the medical field, like he is, one a doctor, the other a nurse. Rick is a nephrologist.

"I've never dated a teacher," he said.

Nina laughed. "Then maybe you'll learn something." And tonight, she hopes she will, too.

Nina is an art teacher and now does substitute teaching. She also volunteers, working one-on-one with middle school students in Harlem, helping with reading skills. Her ex-husband taught economics at a college, and, in a sense, she was more ambitious than he was. She went back to school for a master's in counseling. She has worked as a school counselor, administering tests and counseling parents and children. She's fluent in Spanish, an asset in her work. She suggested her ex-husband consult with businesses and go to conferences. He did this grudgingly. She knew he enjoyed it, though, the recognition, the extra money. He was the kind of man who liked to be in control and didn't like change until he decided to change his life and leave. He moved to New Mexico, remarried, and now lives in the wilderness. He doesn't resurface in Nina's life except on occasion, when he comes to New York to see their grandchild. Sometimes they all meet for brunch at their daughter and son-in-law's apartment—Nina, her ex-husband, their children, their grandchild, her ex-husband's new wife. These gatherings are awkward for Nina but have become a new tradition, the sequela of a late divorce, she thinks. She wants to please their daughter, who likes the family to be together.

There was an unexpected poignancy the last time Nina saw her ex-husband, two months ago. He looked older to her, his brown hair completely gray, his shoulders slumped, a tension in his jaw. He walked over to her at the brunch, standing too close, she thought, telling her that his tennis elbow and right hip had become so painful he was considering surgery. Then he handed her a photograph he'd taken of Zoe, their granddaughter. "Here, sweetie," he said to Nina. "I thought you'd like to have this." He used the same endearing and loving tone he'd used when things were good between them. She took a step back from him. Still, his words made her heart catch.

Rick is a nephrologist at a university. In truth, she's not sure about him, just as she's not sure about so many things. She has become less certain as she's grown older. Rick is in his middle or late seventies. She doesn't know his exact age; everyone subtracts years from ages online. She wonders whether something unexpected will happen to him, his health—maybe he's too old for her. Really, she worries about becoming attached to a man again, facing another rupture, a split. To be widowed confers a nobility, she thinks, but divorce is a failure, in her mind. Though an end to a new relationship begun online can't compare to the end of a thirty-year marriage. But perhaps the ending of illusions is what hurts the most.

The last time she and Rick were together, he joked about taking her to a great Greek restaurant in Queens. They could drive in his car there. "Of course," he said, "you don't know if I'm a serial killer." He laughed, and she did, too.

She doubted it, but she'd googled him and found his profile on the university site.

The building is an elegant old red brick structure facing Riverside Park. White stone cornices line the top of the building, and white molding surrounds the windows. Nina checks the address twice. She walks into the lobby, which is under construction. There is an abandoned air. Three tall ladders and sheets of new drywall lean against the wall; part of the ceiling is open. The sharp smell of fresh sheet rock fills the space, and for a minute she's a little disoriented and wonders if this is the right place. She spots the doorman behind a desk at the far end.

She walks over to him. "Rick Friedman," she says.

The man nods, picks up the phone, and announces she's here. "Elevator is that way," he says, pointing.

She walks past cans of paint lined up in the hallway, wondering how many other women the doorman has directed to Rick's apartment.

On the tenth floor, she finds his door. She takes a deep breath, slips her eyeglasses into a case in her purse, and pauses, then knocks.

Rick opens the door immediately. "Come in," he says. "You found the place."

"Yes," Nina says. "Nice to see you."

She is tall and fairly slender for her age, with brown shoulder-length hair, her waist thicker than it used to be. Rick is a few inches taller than she is. He's not heavy, but solid, broad, with a bit of a belly from what she can see, well-preserved, with a handsome face, an upturned nose, gray eyes, and almost a full head of thinning gray hair. He looks appealing tonight, she thinks.

He smiles, brushes his lips against hers in a way too familiar for their relationship. "I'll take your coat."

She slips out of her blue down coat, putting her hat in the pocket. He hangs up her coat in the closet. There is something formal about the gesture, awkward, and she wonders if the whole evening will be like this.

She is wearing gray wool pants, a black sweater, boots, a gold necklace with a charm of a heart, and gold earrings. He wears brown corduroy pants, a white shirt, and a black wool vest. Somehow even in the casual clothing, he seems formal.

The apartment has a cavernous feel, and sprawls. There are several hallways, and they walk down one now.

Nina is reserved, but determined to fight against this. She wasn't reserved with her ex, until the end when they had problems and she folded into herself then. One of her resolutions—she believes in making New Year's resolutions—is to be less reserved, to climb out of herself.

Her dinners with Rick haven't been formal, but there is something about being in his home, his space, that brings this out. She looks around, and her thoughts are clicking. The ceilings are high, with molding, and the apartment has been renovated, has a modern spacious feel, an elegance. Japanese prints of landscapes hang on the walls, and prints of flowers, carefully placed and aligned. She is surprised. This is more of a home than she expected.

"You have lovely things," she says.

"Thanks." He smiles with pride. "I'll give you a tour, if you'd like."

They walk into the living room. The windows look out onto the Hudson River. The lights of New Jersey twinkle in the distance.

"This couch," he says with disdain, "was from my marriage. My ex-wife wouldn't let me take the couch that would fit here. I'm going to get rid of this."

She nods. It's a gray corduroy couch with huge pillows, a little worn, too big for the space, and sits in front of the windows. "You'll find something else."

"I'm still organizing. I still have stuff in boxes."

The white cabinets and counters in the kitchen are gleaming. Nothing looks out of place. The counters are mostly bare. She wonders if he even eats here.

"This way." He escorts her down another hallway. At the end is a room he describes as a den, with a couch, television, and bookshelves. "My kids sleep here when they're in town. The two who live in Denver. I wanted a lot of space. A nice place. My wife was the one who left. I told you. She wanted to keep every last thing we owned, didn't want to give an inch. She told me, 'I'd like an open marriage.' I said, 'Fuck you.'"

"Sounds like she was angry. You were angry. I know about anger in a marriage, from my own."

"God knows what the problem was. She's not happy now. My therapist says possessions mean nothing. Let everything go. Move on. That's what I'm doing."

Nina nods again.

Rick's jaw tenses for a minute, then relaxes.

He has told her about his therapist. She's told him she is seeing one, too. What you don't say, she thinks, is that a whole industry has developed around divorce, professionals whose purpose is to guide people through divorce and the aftermath—the lawyers, analysts, accountants, psychologists who treat one or both partners and sometimes the children. An endless list, and Nina is relieved this is mostly behind her.

Rick pulls a book off a shelf. "This prayer book belonged to my grandmother. There's writing in the back. Hebrew. You're a nice Jewish girl. Can you read it?"

She laughs. She isn't sure if his calling her a girl is flattering or condescending or a joke, a figure of speech. "No one has called me a girl for a long time. Or nice, in the same sentence." She flips through the pages. "I can't read much. A few words. Here. *Shalom. Mayim.* Water."

"Someday I'll have it translated. No one is all that nice anyway, I've come to believe."

They walk back into the hallway, and he stops at a closed door. "This is why I'm here, in this apartment." He pulls open the door. Behind it is a large walk-in closet, almost the size of a small room. Shelves line the walls, floor to ceiling, filled with sculptures, vases, wooden and ceramic bowls, jugs, pitchers, clay pots, figures of people. "I'm interested in South American and Mexican art, Egyptian, old artifacts. It's my retirement."

"This is like a museum." Nina eyes the collection. That's what it is, a hidden collection. The objects gleam beneath the fluorescent lights that hang on the closet ceiling. Some objects are painted bright colors, reds, browns, and green pigments, some pink and white, others the color of pale clay, all lined neatly on shelf after shelf. This seems like a portal into another world, another part of Rick.

"Those," he says, "are anthropomorphic. People. And that one..."

"Cycladic art."

"Exactly. Marble. You can only afford small pieces like this. A kandila, a vessel, 3000 to 2800 BC."

She admires the graceful shape, the yellow-white color of the marble. "This one is especially beautiful."

The piece next to the kandila is a foot high or so, a clay sculpture of a house, painted in browns, pinks, and white, the two front doors flung open.

"I thought you'd like to see this. You appreciate art. That one, the house, is from Brazil. Look inside. There are two people. A man and a woman. They're..." He pauses. "Copulating."

She doesn't turn to face him. She looks closely at the figures inside the house. They are fucking, she thinks.

"On the top shelf is something tamer. The jug. Egyptian."

"Where did you get all of this?" she asks.

"Oh, over the years, I've collected it. I found bargains. My ex-wife and I bought some together. I've traveled there—South America, Mexico, Greece, once to Egypt. I gave her the couch. I gave her the apartment. I gave her what she wanted. But I wanted this."

"I can see why."

"I've bought some myself. When I travel, it's for work, to go to a conference or give a talk, but still I've bought things if I could afford it."

On the bottom shelf sits a pile of what looks like Japanese wood block prints, similar to some that hang on the living room walls. "Those?" she asks, turning to look at him. "Will you frame them?"

"Ukiyo-e. From Japan. I don't need to display them. I know they're here. I can appreciate them whenever I want." He steps into the hall. She does, too. He shuts the door.

They sit side by side on a couch in the room next to the kitchen, studying the takeout menu from Gargatto's. She thinks about the closet of artifacts. Copulating. An odd word for him to use. Perhaps she and Rick don't know each other well enough for him to state the obvious. But why not? It is a polite word, reserved; perhaps he's picked up on her reserve, restraint. Or maybe that is just who he is.

Her parents never used the word "fucking." When they talked about sex, the few times they did, they said "relations." Did Rick's parents refer to it as "copulating?" Maybe the way she and Rick each speak is part of a generation gap.

She glances up from the menu and realizes there are no photographs here, and the order, the neatness, appeals to Nina. Though his apartment seems like a home, there is a pristine feeling to the rooms, as if they aren't quite lived in, as if Rick hasn't found his place here yet; he has plunged into a new life, ready or not.

Maybe she's projecting. Her apartment, the one she and her ex-husband once shared, still has objects everywhere: from the children's childhoods, drawings they did, books, photographs—even of her ex—books he didn't take with him, her own paints and brushes that sit on the kitchen table. She's thought this makes her apartment seem warm, lived-in. Why has she been keeping all of it? She doesn't need those things to remind her she has a past.

"I've been divorced four years, like you. I lived in a small rental, a studio, for a few years," Rick says. "Stored my stuff and then found this. I wanted a place I could call home. How about penne al vodka?" He points to the menu. "Let's get a few dishes and we can share."

He orders dinner, and they talk more about his collection of artifacts. When the food arrives, Nina finds the forks, knives, plates, and napkins in the kitchen. She sets the table in the living room, and she and Rick sit facing one another.

"I'll retire in a few years," he says as they eat. "The university doesn't have a mandatory retirement age. But I'd like to do something else, work with kids, in a school."

"When you're ready," she says, "I can help you get started."

"That's great. I appreciate it. To be honest, I'm a little worried about retiring, though. I'm not in private practice. The 401(k)."

"Your collection, your artifacts. That's your retirement, you said."

"Part of it. I'd hate to sell anything. But I'm not there yet. Who knows what it's really worth? I had to split retirement with my ex-wife. You must have done that with your ex-husband."

"Yes. I'm still working. I figure I'll have what I have when I retire.

I try to be careful."

"Of course," he says kindly.

They talk about their children and he asks about her work.

After dinner, she collects their plates and closes the plastic containers that house the ravioli, penne, and salmon they haven't finished. "I can put these in the refrigerator," she says.

"No, I'll get rid of them." He jams the containers into a plastic garbage bag. "Be right back."

Nina watches him warily. He will throw out perfectly good food, waste it, and not recycle the plastic either. "You're going to throw that out?"

"Yes."

"Why don't you save it? It's food. It could be lunch tomorrow. Dinner."

"Well." He considers this. "I'll try that. If you'll come for lunch."

She laughs.

"Okay. I'll save it. Do you want some tea? Coffee?"

"How about wine?"

"Good idea. I don't have much." He swings open the refrigerator door.

She peeks inside. A bottle of Manischewitz Concord Grape sits on the second shelf.

"That's all I have." He sets the containers of Italian food on the shelf, too.

"That's fine," she says. The apartment is put together, she thinks, but the refrigerator is almost empty, except for the wine, an orange, half a gallon of milk, and now the leftovers from dinner, as if the veneer of order, mastery, is here, but something is missing inside Rick.

"What did you present at the conference?" she asks. "You said you've been out of town."

"It's not that interesting."

"To me it is."

He shrugs. "People want answers. I have no answers."

"None?"

"Oh, I can help with certain things. When I was young, younger, I thought I could solve everyone's issues. I was good at diagnosis. I would keep lives going. I'd make great discoveries. I don't have those illusions now. Sometimes I can; sometimes I can't."

"What about your research?"

"Fifteen people used to work in my lab. Now there are two." He shakes his head. "There isn't much money for research grants anymore. Hypertension treatments for cardiovascular disease in patients with chronic kidney disease. I talk about it all day."

He sounds disappointed, Nina thinks. The shrinkage of his lab must be hard for him.

"And your art?" he says.

"I love it. Watercolors and some sculpture. But I'm still teaching, and I work with kids on reading. I have my granddaughter. It's a full life."

"Better not to have too much time on your hands. I'd like to see the watercolors."

They are standing close to each other, so close, and he sets the bottle of wine on the counter, kisses her, and she responds. It is a tentative kiss, his lips fuller than her ex's or the few other dates she's kissed.

Then he steps back, pours wine into two glasses, and he and Nina sit on the couch in the living room. She had forgotten the sweetness of Manischewitz, almost like dessert.

He presses his head back on the pillow of the couch, gulping his wine. "It's *basheret* that we've met," he says suddenly.

"Excuse me?"

"You know. *Basheret*. Meant to be. That we met."

"I didn't know you were religious."

"I'm not. Spiritual. Maybe this wine brings it out." He pours more into their glasses. "I really like you."

She smiles. "I like you."

"Well." He scoots closer. He leans and kisses her again. She likes the feel of his lips on hers and his arm around her. It may not be love—and how could it be, when they hardly know one another—but it feels like enough now, enough of something without a name.

"Manischewitz," he laughs. "An aphrodisiac. Who knew? Part of the seduction."

"A multi-use wine."

"I thought I'd make my move. I'd like... I'd like us to become lovers," he says softly. "Do you want to?"

She sees his neck from an angle she hasn't before. The skin is sagging beneath his chin. And his face. There is something a little wounded about him, his expression. We're all wounded, she thinks, but that vulnerability makes him appealing.

His bedroom is next to the living room. He turns on a lamp. Stacks of books and magazines sit on the night tables, an open suitcase on the dresser.

"I haven't unpacked yet from my last trip," he says.

She has entered another country, a space of intimacy, crossed a border. She pulls off her boots, sweater, pants, and he's shedding his clothing, folding it neatly and setting it in the suitcase, as if he is ready to leave on another trip. She looks around the room. There isn't a place for her to put her clothing, so she lays it on top of a pile of magazines, on the journal, *The Lancet*.

She turns around and sees that he is in bed, waiting. A condom sits on the night table next to him now. She takes off her necklace, her earrings, puts them in her pants pocket. The room feels cold, and she's eager for the warmth of his body. She thinks for a moment: what am I doing? And then she doesn't think. She presses her hands against her breasts, hiding them, but then drops her hands to her sides, hurries to the bed, slides next to him.

"Finally," he whispers, "a real kiss."

"Yes," she murmurs.

This is what she has missed, this pleasure. She remembers a student she counseled a few years ago who talked about hookups. The girl liked to hook up with a friend, and called him a fuck buddy. Nina talked to her about commitment and dignity, and thought then: that's the generation gap. But maybe she's wrong. There is no gap. Maybe that's what Rick will become.

She glides her hand down his chest, to his belly, which has extra mounds, mounds of dough, she thinks, but this is what she has to offer, too, an aging, no-longer-firm body that wiggles like Jell-O. His arms have some muscles; he must work out. She moves a hand to his legs; his penis is long and firm—impervious to the insults of age. He kisses her shoulder, her waist, and their bodies entangle. Her breath is quickening and she wonders if she will come, as if she has a choice, but there is a choice—if she will allow herself to be this free with this man. Then he lies on top of her, slides into her, and it is over before it really starts. He comes with a wild groan.

"God, I'm sorry it was so quick," he mumbles, and shuts his eyes. "Damn. I really am."

He is heavy on her, heavier than she imagined he would be. "Rick." She jostles him, and he climbs off her.

"That was so good, Nina. I'm sorry about the speed. It won't be like that next time. How was it for you?"

"It was really nice," she says diplomatically, and it was, though she's a little disappointed. She leans her head on his shoulder.

And then he smiles, kisses her forehead, pulls the quilt over himself, and falls asleep.

She remembers her marriage, when things were rocky, the end in sight. If her husband hadn't left, she would have left him. Nights when they made love wordlessly, and he fell asleep just as they finished, and she lay in bed beside him, but felt utterly alone. It was an odd juxtaposition, maybe not so unusual, she thinks. How many people can you be intimate with? How many people can really assuage a sense of loneliness? Even if that person is your spouse.

She feels this now in Rick's room, in his bed, an essential aloneness, and it is not an unpleasant feeling. She is content, a free agent. She knows she will never again have what people who've been together for a long time, for decades, have. That continuity. The comfort. Or entrenched dissension. She is still getting used to this. But she can have companionship. Is that the most she can hope for? If she's lucky, maybe new love.

Sounds of occasional traffic from Riverside Drive push into the room. The shriek of a siren. The winter wind is whipping against the window, seeping into the room, too. Nina lies on her back beneath the sheet for a long time and then realizes the window is open wide. Rick sleeps with the windows open. She likes the windows closed. She didn't notice before, and she feels chilled.

The white down quilt is wrapped around Rick, and he's clutching the fabric. It would be impolite to wake him, she thinks, or to yank the quilt so she can cover herself, too. There is always something to negotiate in a relationship, even at the beginning, even now. If they knew each other longer, for months, she would wake him.

She moves closer to him and tries to soak in the warmth from his body, from the quilt. After a while, she realizes she won't be able to sleep. She envies him, his ability to tumble into sleep, an intensity as he sleeps. She gets out of bed. If she doesn't sleep, she will be useless the next day.

Faint light floats in from the window, and she gathers her clothing and boots, tiptoes to the living room, and finds her purse on the couch. She traipses to the bathroom in the hallway, next to the closet of artifacts, using the flashlight on her cell phone to guide the way. A navy blue towel hangs on a chrome bar there, folded neatly. She lifts it from the bar, holds part of the towel under the faucet, then quickly washes herself, washes him off her, breaking the code of order here. Then she dries herself with another corner of the towel and gets dressed.

She rinses the corners of the towel and hangs it back on the bar. The towel should dry by the morning; she wants to preserve the order of his apartment. She turns around, catching a glimpse of herself in the mirror. Mascara is smeared beneath her eyes, and her face has a flushed softness to it. She takes a piece of toilet paper, dabs away the rogue mascara.

She finds paper and a pen in her purse, and writes a note:

Dear Rick,
Couldn't sleep. It was really nice. Have to see my daughter early tomorrow. Thank you for tonight, everything. We'll be in touch.
—Nina

She leaves the note on the dining room table. She hopes he will understand. She glances down his hallway again at the closet of artifacts, thinking about the unexpected beauty of the objects hidden there. Then she grabs her coat and shuts the front door behind her.

She has never left a date like this. She has never been in this position before. She has to babysit her granddaughter in the morning. But that's an excuse. It is easier, she thinks, to slip away now, into the night, and be in her bed in her own home rather than lie awake and wonder what she is doing here. Here, meaning not just his bed and his apartment, but here, in her life.

She makes her way past the rows of paint and the ladders, the sheets of drywall leaning against the walls of the lobby. The doorman's head droops onto his chest, and he's snoring.

Some experiences make her feel fully alive, she thinks. When she and her ex were still in love. Walking outside in the cold or in a snowstorm. Painting. Talking to her daughter or son. Holding her granddaughter. Maybe lying in bed, next to Rick.

Riverside Drive is dark and silent, except for the wind blowing fiercely, pushing so hard against her, as if it is trying to push her back to his building, to his apartment. Her down coat feels as thin as paper. She searches her pockets for her hat. It must have dropped somewhere, maybe in Rick's apartment. She pulls up the collar of her coat. She isn't going to retrace her steps to look for the hat now. She will get it another time. Or not. There will be another time, she hopes. But she can't stay tonight. It feels too intimate, waking up next to each other—if she finally fell asleep—or lying awake all night next to him, still almost strangers. Maybe in time, if things develop. She will see. And so will he.

She thinks about something she once read by Isaac Bashevis Singer. She doesn't remember the exact words: there's always a kinship between souls; souls are either close to one another or far from each other. How do you gauge that kinship? she wonders. She had hopes for Rick. She doesn't know if he and she are that close, their souls. How long will it take to find out?

She soldiers on, turning on Seventy-Eighth Street, and at West End, she sees a taxi in the distance and flags it.

She's been left by men and she's left them, gone on dates; things have fizzled and there has been no resolution, no contact, as if one or the other has fallen off the earth, disappeared. Ghosted. She will call Rick in the morning.

The taxi driver interrupts her thoughts. He's a middle-aged man, balding. "It's late," he says, eyeing her in the rearview mirror, "for you to be wandering around in this cold, a person your age. No offense intended. Good for you. Where are you going?"

"It's a good question," she says, giving him her address. "New York. The city that never sleeps."

"Well, happy New Year. I guess you can still say it, even though the year changed a few days ago. There's no rule. You know, I've made my resolutions. Life is so short. But if you ask me, money is nothing. I work to pay the bills. No more, no less. See everything you can. Do whatever good you can do, whatever it is. That's how I want to live my life."

"That's what I'm doing," Nina says. "Trying to do."

Or is she? She understands the psychology of children, development, of adults, but after all this time, even though she feels more like herself, she still doesn't quite understand every aspect of herself. She almost asks the man to turn around and drop her at Rick's apartment.

Her heart is hammering in her chest. She realizes she's woozy from the wine. Manischewitz goes down so easily, like water, more potent than she remembered. The only way to see what happens in the labyrinth of a relationship, she thinks, is to move through it. She will step into the labyrinth with Rick, if he's willing.

She leans her head against the seat. She and the driver sit in silence. The man maneuvers the taxi on the transverse through Central Park, and she stares out the front window, straight ahead.

Thanks

Thank you to those who have encouraged my work. My gratitude to the New York Foundation for the Arts for awarding me a fellowship in fiction. Thank you to the Bread Loaf Writers' Conference and The Ragdale Foundation.

My great thanks to my literary friends and colleagues for their camaraderie and suggestions. I'm deeply grateful to David Milofsky for his steady support and insights about the stories in this book.

Gratitude to Donna Baier Stein, Anne Korkeakivi, Louise Farmer Smith, Eva Mekler, Mina Samuels, and the late Susan Malus. Much appreciation to Jules Hucke and Steven Bauer for invaluable editing advice. Thank you to Lauren Cerand, Dallas Hudgens, Margot Livesey, John Benditt, Kevin Burke, and Danielle Ofri. I'm grateful to Betsy Werthan, Bart Schwartz, Melissa Bloch, Robert Roth, David Flitter, Charles E. Gerber, Leah Latta, Monica Glickman, Diane Pincus, the Uslans, Nancy Kaufman, and Jack David Marcus for friendship and encouragement.

Immense gratitude to my wonderful family, particularly Nancy Levine, Connie Rubin, and Lisa Rubin, and to all my cousins, especially Barbara Keer, Gloria Henllan-Jones, and Rachel Wineberg.

Thank you to the editors of literary journals who first gave my stories a home, to Relegation Books, and New Rivers Press. My thanks to the Denver Woman's Press Club for giving early, much appreciated recognition of my writing, and for honoring a story in this collection.

I am indebted to Serving House Books and especially to Walter Cummins—for his belief in my work, his great kindness, and his help shaping the individual stories into a book.

A special thank-you to my children, Daniel, Genia, and Simone. You were patient as I sat at my desk in the study at home, day after day, year after year, trying to become a writer. Then and now, I'm grateful for the moments of my days I spend with each of you.

About the Author

Ronna Wineberg is the author of *Nine Facts That Can Change Your Life*, a collection of short stories, which received Honorable Mention for the Eric Hoffer Book Award; *On Bittersweet Place*, a novel, winner of the Shelf Unbound Best Indie Book Competition; and a debut collection of stories, *Second Language*, winner of the New Rivers Press Many Voices Project Literary Competition, and the runner-up for the Reform Judaism Prize for Jewish Fiction. Her stories have appeared in *Michigan Quarterly Review*, *North Dakota Quarterly*, *Colorado Review*, *American Way*, and other literary journals, and have been broadcast on NPR. She was awarded a fellowship in fiction from the New York Foundation for the Arts, a scholarship in fiction to the Bread Loaf Writers' Conference, and residencies to The Ragdale Foundation and the Virginia Center for the Creative Arts. She is the founding fiction editor of the *Bellevue Literary Review* and lives in New York.

Visit Ronna online at www.ronnawineberg.com.

0

CPSIA information can be obtained
at www.ICGtesting.com
Printed in the USA
BVHW081410280922
648209BV00001B/24

9 781947 175563